3 9158 0

D0734341

ALONG THE SHORE

L. M. Montgomery

Along the Shore

TALES BY THE SEA

edited by Rea Wilmshurst

M&S

Canadian Cataloguing in Publication Data

Montgomery, L.M. (Lucy Maud), 1874–1942.
Along the shore

ISBN 0-7710-6158-7

I. Wilmshurst, Rea, 1941–   . II. Title.

PS8526.045A83 1989   C813'.52   C88-095318-7
PR9199.2.M6A83 1989

The interior illustrations have been reproduced from
the original publications.

Printed and bound in Canada by
John Deyell Company

McClelland & Stewart Inc.
The Canadian Publishers
481 University Avenue
Toronto, Ontario
M5G 2E9

Contents

Introduction

WHEN L. M. MONTGOMERY married the Reverend Ewan Macdonald in 1911 and went to Ontario from Prince Edward Island, she left the place that furnished the background for her immense body of work, nearly all of which is set in the Maritimes, and most of it in P.E.I. After her marriage she returned to the Island many times, and the letters she wrote after these visits, especially the letters to G. B. MacMillan, her Scottish pen-friend, demonstrate the strong love she retained for her home province. A very important part of the appeal of P.E.I. was the sea: "Leaskdale is a very pretty country place – would be almost as pretty as Cavendish if it had the sea – which by the way, I miss heart-breakingly at times" (20 January 1912).

Between 1895 and 1909, while Montgomery was still in Cavendish, she published well over 300 stories, in nineteen of which the sea plays a major role; after she left the Island she wrote only one more sea story, "A House Divided Against Itself" (1930). The sixteen tales reprinted here are eloquent statements of Montgomery's love for the sea. In them are all the elements that appear in her other tales: vivid descriptions, living characters, humour, romance. There are some children's adventure stories; several romances, both light-hearted and sober; one humorous tale about two unromantic old fishermen; and one story with a darker outcome than one might expect.

A mistress of the art of word-painting, Montgomery gives us pictures of the sea and of the shore, shows us different effects of weather and light, and vividly describes places and people. A born story-teller, she gives us tales of adventure and romance, with tide and weather always at hand to increase the possibility of danger or even death; out of her personal longing for the sea she tells us of people with a passionate desire to go to sea or to remain by its shores.

Montgomery's sea stories contain many passages of description that evoke the love she felt for the shore and for the sea in all its moods. Like the artist in "The Waking of Helen," Montgomery can "revel in those transcendent sunsets and sunrises, those marvellous moonlights, those wonderful purple shores and sweeps of shimmering blue water." In her earlier stories the descriptions take perhaps too large a role, yet they are obviously thoughtful and purposeful. In 1897 she gave readers this lengthy sunset: "The sun, red as a smouldering ember, was half buried in the silken violet rim of the sea; the west was a vast lake of saffron and rose and ethereal green, through which floated the curved shallop of a thin new moon, slowly deepening from lustreless white, through gleaming silver, into burnished gold, and attended by one solitary, pearl-white star. The vast concave of sky above was of violet, infinite and flawless. Far out dusky amethystine islets clustered like gems on the shining breast of the bay. The little pools of water along the low shores glowed like mirrors of polished jacinth. The small, pine-fringed headlands ran out into the water, cutting its lustrous blue expanse like purple wedges" ("A Strayed Allegiance"). Later, she seems to have taken to heart Mr. Harrison's advice to Anne in *Anne of the Island*, to "let the sun rise and set in the usual quiet way without much fuss over the fact"; the descriptions are still there, but somewhat abbreviated. In "The Life-Book of Uncle Jesse" (1909) Mary and her mother look out over the harbour entrance and see "a splendid golden sunrise flooding it, coming out of the wonderful sea and sky beyond and billowing through that narrow passage in waves of light."

In these stories men are still using sailboats for fishing, and Montgomery pictures their masts "coming out in slender silhouette against the sky," "nodding against the gracious horizon," or "bowing landward on the swell." But in the letter of 3 September 1924 to MacMillan, she lamented their passing: "But one poetry has vanished from the gulf forever. It is never now dotted with hundreds of white sails. The fishermen now have motor boats which chug-chug out in the morning and chug-chug back at night and are not on speaking terms with romance."

The fishermen's boats are picturesque, and their houses are no less so. They "seemed like nothing so much as larger shells washed up by the sea, so grey and bleached were they from long exposure to sea winds and spray" ("A Strayed Allegiance"). Some may be "small, uncouth," "with children playing noisily on the paths between them" ("The Magical Bond of the Sea"), but others present a more pleasing aspect: "The dooryard was scrupulously clean and unlittered; the little footpath through it was neatly bordered by white clam shells; several thrifty geraniums in bloom looked out from the muslin-curtained windows" ("A Strayed Allegiance").

The people from these homes are as varied as their homes. We meet fishermen both uncultured and unusually refined, their quietly long-suffering wives, and a few uncommon and breathtakingly beautiful women like Magdalen in "A Strayed Allegiance" and Nora Shelley in "The Magical Bond of the Sea": "Very slim and straight was

Nora, with a skin as white as the foam-flakes crisping over the sands, and eyes of the tremulous, haunting blue that deepens on the water after a fair sunset."

A placid note is struck in three of the romances. "A Sandshore Wooing," "Fair Exchange and No Robbery" and "The Unhappiness of Miss Farquhar" are light and happy tales that take place beside a sea which may know rain but never storm; its violence is not in evidence. The sea itself stays calm in "A Strayed Allegiance" too, but the characters' lives and passions are tempest-tossed. Magdalen Crawford's "marvellous beauty" catches the attention of Esterbrook Elliott and awakens his dormant capacity for love. Realizing that her fiancé has fallen in love with Magdalen, Marian Lesley pretends that she no longer cares for him, breaks her engagement, gives up her dreams of happiness, and leaves him free to marry Magdalen.

A less placid note is contained in the tales involving tides and sea-side weather. There may be people unaware of what the tide can do or how dangerous it can be, but anyone who lives by the sea respects its power and is constantly aware of its ebb and flow.

Although predictable, tide times may be forgotten, and danger threaten. Panic sweeps through an adolescent boy, a non-swimmer, when he discovers that his boat has drifted away: "Then a thought flashed into my mind that made me dizzy with fear. The tide would be high that night. If I could not escape from Island Rock I would inevitably be drowned" ("An Adventure on Island Rock"). The happy outcome of this story is in complete contrast to "The Waking of Helen," which also involves the tide. Helen learns to love Robert Reeves, a visiting artist, and rescues him when he is caught by the tide in the Kelpy's Cave. The reader may expect a very romantic ending, but here Montgomery gives us the unexpected.

The sea can be dangerous, but danger offers the chance

for bravery, and two of these tales show children's capacity for bravery in dangerous situations. In "The Light on the Big Dipper" twelve-year-old Mary Margaret has to row through a snowstorm to the lighthouse on a neighbouring island, and in "Natty of Blue Point" young Nat rows out in a night fog to rescue two men whose boat has overturned. Dogs can be brave too. One helped with the rescue in "An Adventure on Island Rock"; another, in "How Don Was Saved," saves the crew of a wrecked ship.

In the "adventure" tales for older readers, the situations are more romantic, although the endings are not always happy. In "Young Si" Ethel Lennox's estranged fiancé saves her in a storm at sea, and they are reconciled; but in "Mackereling out in the Gulf" Benjamin Selby has to force himself to rescue Frank Braithwaite, the man who has stolen the girl he loves. Alan Douglas, in "Four Winds," has no trouble summoning up the courage to rescue a ship-wrecked sailor; but when he discovers that the man he has saved is the long-absent, blackguard husband of Lynde, the girl he has fallen in love with, he might be forgiven if he regretted his bravery. However, the rescue clears up the mystery of her vanished husband.

The sea shows its dangerous strength in these stories. It has another strength, that of holding fast those born by its shores, so that whether they live near it or not, they long for it. On 13 September 1913, after one of her visits to the Island, Montgomery wrote to MacMillan about the pull that the sea exerted on her: "I shall never forget my first glimpse of the sea again. . . . I was not prepared for the flood of emotion which swept over me when I saw it. I was stirred to the very deeps of my being – tears filled my eyes – I trembled! For a moment it seemed passionately to me that I could *never* leave it again." In her novels, Montgomery voiced this fervent feeling most strongly in *Anne's House of Dreams*: "The ways of Four Winds were less staid and settled and grooved than those of Avonlea; winds of change blew over them; the sea called ever to the dwellers on shore, and even those who might not answer its call felt the thrill and unrest and mystery and possibilities of it." One of the characters in that novel is Captain Jim, a retired sailor and lighthouse keeper; the thread of his tale, woven into the book, is adapted from an earlier story, "The Life-Book of Uncle Jesse," reprinted here. The tragedy of Captain Jim's/Uncle Jesse's life was the loss of his sweet-heart, Margaret, who "had fallen asleep one day in her father's dory, and drifted . . . across the harbour and out of the Gate, to perish in the black thundersquall that had come up so suddenly that long ago afternoon." His loss does not drive him from the shore; on the contrary, he refuses to visit Mary and her mother in town during the winter because "If lost Margaret called me I mightn't hear her there. I must be here when my time comes."

But even those who wish to leave the sea often find that they are tied to it more strongly than they think. Nora Shelley desperately wants a chance at another life than that offered by her fishing village, and willingly goes away with a rich family for a year. But at the end of that time she returns, never to leave again: "Then I knew – it came to me all at once, like a flood of understanding. I knew I could never go away again – that I must stay here forever where I could hear that call of wind and waves" ("The Magical Bond of the Sea"). In Nora's case her love for a young man combines with her love for the sea to keep her by the shore. Love pulls young Paul too, in "A Soul That Was Not at Home": love for the sea, for his adoptive father, and for his fancied companions on the shore. Paul is very much like Paul Irving of *Anne of Avonlea* in his fancies, but his life is quite different. This Paul's mother "couldn't live away from the shore. She fretted and pined and broke her heart for it." After her death, Paul is taken in by Stephen, a fisherman who loved her. His serene and imaginative life is interrupted by the advent of a city woman who offers to adopt him, take him to town, and give him all the advantages of books and travel that Stephen cannot. But Paul does not last even one night away from the sea: "what were books and strange countries? – what was even Miss Trevor, the friend of a month? – to the call of the sea and Stephen's kind, deep eyes and his dear rock people? He could not stay away from them – never – never." He leaves a note and walks through the night back to his home.

Montgomery spent half her life away from her beloved Island, but when she died her body was returned to the Cavendish cemetery, to lie within sight and sound of the sea she loved so well. The poem "Anne" wrote for Mr. Mitchell's obituary (in *Anne of Ingleside*), and which Montgomery had published as "An Old Man's Grave" in 1906, could be adapted, by altering the pronouns, for Montgomery's epitaph:

Make it where the winds may sweep
Through the pine boughs soft and deep,
And the murmur of the sea
Come across the orient lea,
And the falling raindrops sing
Gently to her slumbering
. . . .

Since these things to her were dear
Through full many a well-spent year,
It is surely meet their grace
Should be on her resting-place,
And the murmur of the sea
Be her dirge eternally.

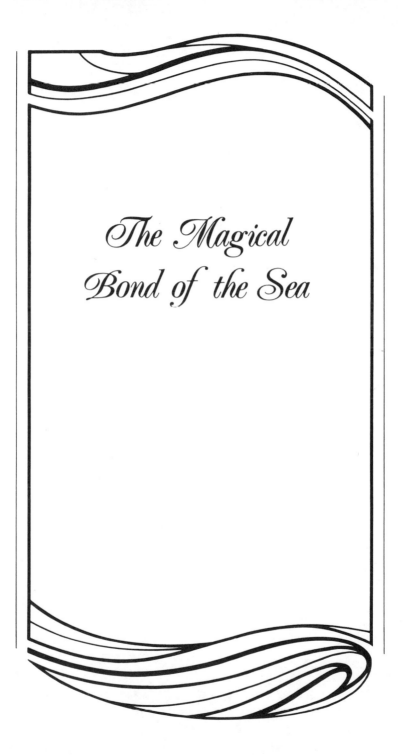

The Magical
Bond of the Sea

LATE SEPTEMBER wind from the northwest was sweeping over the waters of Racicot Harbour. It blew in, strong with the tang of the salt seas, past the grim lighthouse rock on the one hand and the sandbars on the other, up the long, narrow funnel of darkly blue water, until it whistled among the masts of the boats at anchor and among the stovepipe chimneys of the fishing village. It was a wind that sang and piped and keened of many things – but what it sang to each listener was only what was in that listener's heart. And Nora Shelley, standing at the door of her father's bleached cottage on the grey sands, heard a new strain in it. The wind had sung often to her of the outer world she longed for, but there had never been the note of fulfilment in it before.

There's a new life beyond, Nora, whistled the wind. A good life – and it's yours for the taking. You have but to put out your hand and all you've wished for will be in your grasp.

Nora leaned out from the door to meet the wind. She loved that northwest gale; it was a staunch old friend of hers. Very slim and straight was Nora, with a skin as white as the foam flakes crisping over the sands, and eyes of the tremulous, haunting blue that deepens on the water after a fair sunset. But her hair was as black as midnight, and her lips blossomed out with a ripe redness against the uncoloured purity of her face. She was far and away the most beautiful of the harbour girls, but hardly the most popular. Men and women alike thought her proud. Even her friends felt themselves called upon to make excuses for her unlikeness to themselves.

Nora had closed the door behind her to shut in the voices. She wanted to be alone with the wind while she made her decision. Before her the sandy shingle, made

17

firm by a straggling growth of some pale sea-ivy, sloped down to the sapphire cup of the harbour. Around her were the small, uncouth houses of the village – no smaller or more uncouth than the one which was her home – with children playing noisily on the paths between them. The mackerel boats curtsied and nodded outside; beyond them the sharp tip of Sandy Point was curdled white with seagulls. Down at the curve of the cove a group of men were laughing and talking loudly in front of French Joe's fish-house. This was the life that she had always known.

Across the harbour, on a fir-fringed headland, stood Dalveigh. John Cameron, childless millionaire, had built a summer cottage on that point two years ago, and given it the name of the old ancestral estate in Scotland. To the Racicot fishing folk the house and grounds were as a dream of enchantment made real. Few of them had ever seen anything like it.

Nora Shelley knew Dalveigh well. She had been the Camerons' guest many times that summer, finding in the luxury and beauty of their surroundings something that entered with a strange aptness into her own nature. It was as if it were hers by right of fitness. And this was the life that might be hers, did she so choose.

In reality, her choice was already made, and she knew it. But it pleased her to pretend for a little time that it was not, and to dally tenderly with the old loves and emotions that tugged at her heart and clamoured to be remembered.

Within, in the low-ceilinged living-room, with its worn, uneven floor and its blackened walls hung with fish nets and oilskins, four people were sitting. John Cameron and his wife were given the seats of honour in the middle of the room. Mrs. Cameron was a handsome, well-dressed woman, with an expression that was discontented and, at times, petulant. Yet her face had a good deal of plain common sense in it, and not even the most critical of the Racicot folks could say that she "put on airs." Her husband was a small, white-haired man, with a fresh, young-looking face. He was popular in Racicot, for he mingled freely with the sailors and fishermen. Moreover, Dalveigh was an excellent market for fresh mackerel.

Nathan Shelley, in his favourite corner behind the stove, sat lurching forward with his hands on his knees. He had laid aside his pipe out of deference to Mrs. Cameron, and it was hard for him to think without it. He wished his wife would go to work; it seemed uncanny to see her idle. She had sat idle only once that he remembered – the day they had brought Ned Shelley in, dank and dripping, after the August storm ten years before. Mrs. Shelley sat by the crooked, small-paned window and looked out down the harbour. The coat she had been patching for her husband when the Camerons came still lay in her lap, and she had folded her hands upon it. She was a big woman, slow of speech and manner, with a placid, handsome face – a face that had not visibly stirred even when she had heard the Camerons' proposition.

They wanted Nora – these rich people who had so much in life wanted the blossom of girlhood that had never bloomed for them. John Cameron pleaded his cause well.

"We will look on her as our own," he said at last. "We have grown to love her this summer. She is beautiful and clever – she has a right to more than Racicot can give her. You have other children – we are childless. And we do not take her from you utterly. You will see her every summer when we come to Dalveigh."

"It won't be the same thing quite," said Nathan Shelley drily. "She'll belong to your life then – not ours. And no matter how many young ones folks has, they don't want to lose none of 'em. But I dunno as we ought to let our feelings stand in Nora's light. She's clever, and she's been hankering for more'n we can ever give her. I was the same way once. Lord, how I raged at Racicot! I broke away finally – went to a city and got work. But it wasn't no use. I'd left it too long. The sea had got into my blood. I toughed it out for two years, and then I had to come back. I didn't want to, mark you, but I had to come. Been here ever since. But maybe 'twill be different with the girl. She's younger than I was; if the hankering for the sea and the life of the shore hasn't got into her too deep, maybe she'll be able to cut loose for good. But you don't know how the sea calls to one of its own."

Cameron smiled. He thought that this dry old salt was a bit of a poet in his own way. Very likely Nora got her ability and originality from him. There did not seem to be a great deal in the phlegmatic, good-looking mother.

"What say, wife?" asked Shelley at last.

His wife had said in her slow way, "Leave it to Nora," and to Nora it was left.

When she came in at last, her face stung to radiant beauty by the northwest wind, she found it hard to tell them after all. She looked at her mother appealingly.

"Is it go or stay, girl," demanded her father brusquely.

"I think I'll go," said Nora slowly. Then, catching sight of her mother's face, she ran to her and flung her arms about her. "But I'll never forget you, Mother," she cried. "I'll love you always – you and Father."

Her mother loosened the clinging arms and pushed her gently toward the Camerons.

"Go to them," she said calmly. "You belong to them now."

The news spread quickly over Racicot. Before night everyone on the harbour shore knew that the Camerons were going to adopt Nora Shelley and take her away with them. There was much surprise and more envy. The shore women tossed their heads.

"Reckon Nora is in great feather," they said. "She always did think herself better than anyone else. Nate Shelley and his wife spoiled her ridiculous. Wonder what Rob Fletcher thinks of it?"

Nora asked her brother to tell the news to Rob Fletcher himself, but Merran Andrews was before him. She was at Rob before he had fairly landed, when the fishing boats came in at sunset.

"Have you heard the news, Rob? Nora's going away to be a fine lady. The Camerons have been daft about her all summer, and now they are going to adopt her."

Merran wanted Rob herself. He was a big, handsome fellow, and well-off – the pick of the harbour men in every way. He had slighted her for Nora, and it pleased her to stab him now, though she meant to be nice to him later on.

He turned white under his tan, but he did not choose to make a book of his heart for Merran's bold black eyes to read. "It's a great thing for her," he answered calmly. "She was meant for better things than can be found at Racicot."

"She was always too good for common folks, if that is what you mean," said Merran spitefully.

Nora and Rob did not meet until the next evening, when she rowed herself home from Dalveigh. He was at the shore to tie up her boat and help her out. They walked up the sands together in the heart of the autumn sunset, with the northwest wind whistling in their ears and the great star of the lighthouse gleaming wanly out against the golden sky. Nora felt uncomfortable, and resented it. Rob Fletcher was nothing to her; he never had been anything but the good friend to whom she told her strange thoughts and longings. Why should her heart ache over him? She wished he would talk, but he strode along in silence, with his fine head drooping a little.

"I suppose you have heard that I am going away, Rob?" she said at last.

He nodded. "Yes, I've heard it from a hundred mouths, more or less," he answered, not looking at her.

"It's a splendid thing for me, isn't it?" dared Nora.

"Well, I don't know," he said slowly. "Looking at it from the outside, it seems so. But from the inside it mayn't look the same. Do you think you'll be able to cut twenty years of a life out of your heart without any pain?"

"Oh, I'll be homesick, if that is what you mean," said Nora petulantly. "Of course I'll be that at first. I expect it – but people get over that. And it is not as if I were going away for good. I'll be back next summer – every summer."

"It'll be different," said Rob stubbornly, thinking as old Nathan Shelley had thought. "You'll be a fine lady – oh, all the better for that perhaps – but you'll not be the same. No, no, the new life will change you; not all at once, maybe, but in the end. You'll be one of them, not one of us. But will you be happy? That's the question I'm asking."

In anyone else Nora would have resented this. But she never felt angry with Rob.

"I think I shall be," she said thoughtfully. "And, anyway, I must go. It doesn't seem as if I could help myself if I wanted to. Something – out beyond there – is calling me, always has been calling me ever since I was a tiny girl and found out there was a big world far away from Racicot. And it always seemed to me that I would find a way to it some day. That was why I kept going to school long after the other girls stopped. Mother thought I'd better stop home; she said too much book learning would make me discontented and too different from the people I had to live along. But Father let me go; he understood; he said I was like him when he was young. I learned everything and read everything I could. It seems to me as if I had been walking along a narrow pathway all my life. And now it seems as if a gate were opened before me and I can pass through into a wider world. It isn't the luxury and the pleasure or the fine house and dresses that tempt me, though the people here think so – even Mother thinks so. But it is not. It's just that something seems to be in my grasp that I've always longed for, and I must go – Rob, I must go."

"Yes, if you feel like that you must go," he answered, looking down at her troubled face gently. "And it's best for you to go, Nora. I believe that, and I'm not so selfish as not to be able to hope that you'll find all you long for. But it will change you all the more if it is so. Nora! Nora! Whatever am I going to do without you!"

The sudden passion bursting out in his tone frightened her.

"Don't, Rob, don't! And you won't miss me long. There's many another."

"No, there isn't. Don't fling me that dry bone of comfort. There's no other, and never has been any other – none but you, Nora, and well you know it."

"I'm sorry," she said faintly.

"You needn't be," said Rob grimly. "After all, I'd rather love you than not, hurt as it will. I never had much hope of getting you to listen to me, so there's no great disappointment there. You're too good for me – I've always known that. A girl that is fit to mate with the Camerons is far above Rob Fletcher, fisherman."

"I never had such a thought," protested Nora.

"I know it," he said, casing himself up in his quietness again. "But it's so – and now I've got to lose you. But there'll never be any other for me, Nora."

He left her at her father's door. She watched his stalwart figure out of sight around the point, and raged to find tears in her eyes and a bitter yearning in her heart. For a moment she repented – she would stay – she could not go.

Then over the harbour flashed out the lights of Dalveigh. The life behind them glittered, allured, beckoned. Nay, she must go on – she had made her choice. There was no turning back now.

NORA SHELLEY went away with the Camerons, and Dalveigh was deserted. Winter came down on Racicot Harbour, and the colony of fisher folk at its head gave themselves over to the idleness of the season – a time for lounging and gossiping and long hours of lazy contentment smoking in the neighbours' chimney corners, when tales were told of the sea and the fishing. The Harbour laid itself out to be sociable in winter. There was no time for that in summer. People had to work eighteen hours out of the twenty-four then. In the winter there was spare time to laugh and quarrel, woo and wed and – were a man so minded – dream, as did Rob Fletcher in his loneliness.

In a Racicot winter much was made of small things. The arrival of Nora Shelley's weekly letter to her father and mother was an event in the village. The post-mistress in the Cove store spread the news that it had come, and that night the Shelley kitchen would be crowded. Isobel Shelley, Nora's younger sister, read the letter aloud by virtue of having gone to school long enough to be able to pronounce the words and tell where the places named were situated.

The Camerons had spent the autumn in New York and had then gone south for the winter. Nora wrote freely of her new life. In the beginning she admitted great homesickness, but after the first few letters she made no further mention of that. She wrote little of herself, but she described fully the places she had visited, the people she had met, the wonderful things she had seen. She sent affectionate messages to all her old friends and asked after all her old interests. But the letters came to be more and more like those of a stranger and one apart from the Racicot life, and the father and mother felt it.

"She's changing," muttered old Nathan. "It had to be so – it's well for her that it is so – but it hurts. She ain't ours any more. We've lost the girl, wife, lost her forever."

Rob Fletcher always came and listened to the letters in silence while the others buzzed and commented. Rob, so the Harbour folk said, was much changed. He had grown unsociable and preferred to stay home and read books rather than go a-visiting as did others. The Harbour folk shook their heads over this. There was something wrong with a man who read books when there was a plenty of other amusements. Jacob Radnor had read books all one winter and had drowned himself in the spring – jumped overboard from his dory at the herring nets. And that was what came of books, mark you.

The Camerons came later to Dalveigh the next summer, on account of John Cameron's health, which was not good. It was the first of August before a host of servants came to put Dalveigh in habitable order, and a week later the family came. They brought a houseful of guests with them.

At sunset on the day of her arrival Nora Shelley looked out cross the harbour to the fishing village. She was tired after her journey, and she had not meant to go over until the morning, but now she knew she must go at once. Her mother was over there; the old life called to her; the northwest wind swept up the channel and whistled alluringly to her at the window of her luxurious room. It brought to her the tang of the salt wastes and filled her heart with a great, bitter-sweet yearning.

She was more beautiful than ever. In the year that had passed she had blossomed out to a gracious fulfilment of womanhood. Even the Camerons had wondered at her swift adaptation to her new surroundings. She seemed to have put Racicot behind her as one puts by an old garment. In everything she had held her own royally. Her adopted parents were proud of her beauty and her nameless, untamed charm. They had lavished every indulgence upon her. In those few short months she had lived more keenly and fully than in all her life before. The Nora Shelley who went away was not, so it would seem, the Nora Shelley who came back.

But when she looked from her window to the waves and saw the star of the lighthouse and the blaze of the sunset in the window of the fishing-houses and heard the summons of the wind, something broke loose in her soul and overwhelmed her, like a wave of the sea. She must go at once – at once – at once. Not a moment could she wait.

She was dressed for dinner, but with tingling fingers she threw off her costly gown and put on her dark travelling suit again. She left her hair as it was and knotted a crimson scarf about her head. She would slip away quietly to the boathouse, get Davy to launch the little sailboat for her – and then for a fleet skim over the harbour before that glorious wind! She hoped not to be seen, but Mrs. Cameron met her in the hall.

"Nora!" she said in astonishment.

"Oh, I must go, Aunty! I must go!" the girl cried feverishly. She was afraid Mrs. Cameron would try to prevent her going, and all at once she knew that she could not bear that.

"Must go? Where? Dinner is almost ready, and – "

"Oh, I don't want any dinner. I'm going home – I will sail over."

"My dear child, don't be foolish. It's too late to go over the harbour tonight. They won't be expecting you. Wait until the morning."

"No – oh, you don't understand. I must go – I must! My mother is over there."

Something in the girl's last sentence or the tone in which it was uttered brought a look of pain to Mrs. Cameron's face. But she made no further attempt to dissuade her.

"Well, if you must. But you cannot go alone – no, Nora, I cannot allow it. The wind is too high and it is too late for you to go over by yourself. Clark Bryant will take you."

Nora would have protested but she knew it would be in vain. She submitted somewhat sullenly and walked down to the shore in silence. Clark Bryant strode beside her, humouring her mood. He was a tall, stout man, with an ugly, clever, sarcastic face. He was as clever as he looked, and was one of the younger millionaires whom John Cameron drew around him in the development of his huge financial schemes. Bryant was in love with Nora. This was why the Camerons had asked him to join their August house party at Dalveigh, and why he had accepted. It had occurred to Nora that this was the case, but as yet she had never troubled to think the situation over seriously.

She liked Clark Bryant well enough, but just at the moment he was in the way. She did not want to take him over to Racicot – just why she could not have explained. There was in her no snobbish shame of her humble home. But he did not belong there; he was an alien, and she wished to go back to it for the first time alone.

At the boathouse Davy launched the small sailboat and Nora took the tiller. She knew every inch of the harbour. As the sail filled before the wind and the boat sprang across the upcurling waves, her brief sullenness fell away from her. She no longer resented Clark Bryant's presence – she forgot it. He was no more to her than the mast by which he stood. The spell of the sea and the wind surged into her heart and filled it with wild happiness and measureless content. Over yonder, where the lights gleamed on the darkening shore under the high-sprung arch of pale golden sky, was home. How the wind whistled to welcome her back! The lash of it against her face – the flick of salt spray on her lips – the swing of the boat as it cut through the racing crests – how glorious it all was!

Clark Bryant watched her, understanding all at once that he was nothing to her, that he had no part or lot in her heart. He was as one forgotten and left behind. And how lovely, how desirable she was! He had never seen her look so beautiful. The shawl had slipped down to her shoulders and her head rose out of it like some magnificent flower out of a crimson calyx. The masses of her black hair lifted from her face in the rush of the wind and swayed back again like rich shadows. Her lips were stung scarlet with the sea's sharp caresses, and her eyes, large and splendid, looked past him unseeing to the harbour lights of Racicot.

When they swung in by the wharf Nora sprang from the boat before Bryant had time to moor it. Pausing for an instant, she called down to him, carelessly, "Don't wait for me. I shall not go back tonight."

Then she caught her shawl around her head and almost ran up the wharf and along the shore. No one was abroad, for it was supper hour in Racicot. In the Shelley kitchen the family was gathered around the table, when the door was flung open and Nora stood on the threshold. For a moment they gazed at her as at an apparition. They had not known the precise day of her coming and were not aware of the Camerons' arrival at Dalveigh.

"It's the girl herself. It's Nora," said old Nathan, rising from his bench.

"Mother!" cried Nora. She ran across the room and buried her face in her mother's breast, sobbing.

When the news spread, the Racicot people crowded in to see Nora until the house was full. They spent a noisy, merry, whole-hearted evening of the old sort. The men smoked and most of the women knitted while they talked. They were pleased to find that Nora did not put on any airs. Old Jonas Myers bluntly told her that he didn't see as her year among rich folks had done her much good, after all.

"You're just the same as when you went away," he said. "They haven't made a fine lady of you. Folks here thought you'd be something wonderful."

Nora laughed. She was glad that they did not find her changed. Old Nathan chuckled in his dry way. There was a difference in the girl, and he saw it, though the neighbours did not, but it was not the difference he had feared. His daughter was not utterly taken from him yet.

Nora sat by her mother and was happy. But as the evening wore away she grew very quiet, and watched the door with something piteous in her eyes. Old Nathan noticed it and thought she was tired. He gave the curious neighbours a good-natured hint, and they presently withdrew. When they had all gone Nora went out to the door alone.

The wind had died down and the shore, gemmed with its twinkling lights, was very still, for it was too late an hour for Racicot folk to be abroad in the mackerel season. The moon was rising and the harbour was a tossing expanse of silver waves. The mellow light fell on a tall figure lurking at the angle of the road that led past the Shelley cottage. Nora saw and recognized it. She flew down the sandy slope with outstretched hands.

"Rob – Rob!"

"Nora!" he said huskily, holding out his hand. But she flung herself on his breast and clung to him, half laughing, half crying.

"Oh, Rob! I've been looking for you all the evening. Every time there was a step I said to myself, 'That is Rob, now.'

And when the door opened to let in another, my heart died within me. I dared not even ask after you for fear of what they might tell me. Why didn't you come?"

"I didn't know that I'd be welcome," he whispered, holding her closer to him. "I've been hanging about thinking to get a glimpse of you unbeknown. I thought maybe you wouldn't want to see me tonight."

"Not want to see you! Oh, Rob, this evening at Dalveigh, when I looked across to Racicot, it was you I thought of before all – even before Mother."

She drew back and looked at him with her soul in her eyes.

"What a splendid fellow you are – how handsome you are, Rob!" she cried. All the reserve of womanhood fell away from her in the inrush of emotions. For the moment she was a child again, telling out her thoughts with all a child's frankness. "I've been in a dream this past year – a lovely dream – a fair dream, but only a dream, after all. And now I've wakened. And you are part of the wakening – the best part! Oh, to think I never knew before!"

"Knew what, my girl?"

He had her close against his heart now; the breath of her lips mingled with his, but he would not kiss her yet.

"That I loved you," she whispered back. "Oh, Rob, you are all the world to me. I belong to you and the sea. But I never knew it until I crossed the harbour tonight. Then I knew – it came to me all at once, like a flood of understanding. I knew I could never go away again – that I must stay here forever where I could hear that call of wind and waves. The new life was good – good – but it could not go deep enough. And when you did not come I knew what was in my heart for you as well."

THAT NIGHT Nora lay beside her sisters in the tiny room that looked out on the harbour. The younger girls slept soundly, but Nora kept awake to listen to the laughter of the wind outside, and con over what she and Rob had said to each other. There was no blot on her happiness save a sorry wonder what the Camerons would say when they knew.

"They will think me ungrateful and fickle," she sighed. "They don't know that I can't help it even if I would. They will never understand."

Nor did they. When Nora told them that she was going back to Racicot, they laughed at her kindly at first, treating it as the passing whim of a homesick girl. Later, when they came to understand that she meant it, they were grieved and angry. There were scenes of pleading and tears and reproaches. Nora cried bitterly in Mrs. Cameron's arms, but stood rock-firm. She could never go back to them – never.

They appealed to Nathan Shelley finally, but he refused to say anything.

"It can't be altered," he told them. "The sea has called her and she'll listen to naught else. I'm sorry enough for the girl's own sake. It would have been better for her if she could have cut loose from it all and lived your life, I dare say. But you've made a fair trial and it's of no use. I know what's in her heart – it was in mine once – and I'll say no word of rebuke to her. She's free to go or stay as she chooses – just as free as she was last year."

Mrs. Cameron made one more appeal to Nora. She told the girl bitterly that she was ungrateful.

"I'm not that," said Nora with quivering lips. "I love you, and I'm grateful to you. But your life isn't for me, after all. I thought it was – I longed so for it. And I loved it, too – I love it yet. But there's something stronger in me that holds me here."

"I don't think you realize what you are doing, Nora. You have been a little homesick and you are glad to be back.

31

But after we have gone and you must settle into the old Racicot life again, you will not be contented. You will find that your life with us will have unfitted you for this. There will be no real place for you here – nothing for you to do. You will be as a stranger here."

"Oh, no. I am going to marry Rob Fletcher," said Nora proudly.

"Marry Rob Fletcher! And you might have married Clark Bryant, Nora!"

Nora shook her head. "That could never have been. I thought it might once – but I know better now. You see, I love Rob."

There did not seem to be anything more to say after that. Mrs. Cameron did not try to say anything. She went away in sorrow.

Nora cried bitterly after she had gone. But there were no tears in her eyes that night when she walked on the shore with Rob Fletcher. The wind whistled around them, and the stars came out in the great ebon dome of the sky over the harbour. Laughter and song of the fishing folk were behind them, and the deep, solemn call of the sea before. Over the harbour gleamed the score of lights at Dalveigh. Rob looked from them to Nora.

"Do you think you'll ever regret yon life, my girl?"

"Never, Rob. It seems to me now like a beautiful garment put on for a holiday and worn easily and pleasantly for a time. But I've put it off now, and put on workaday clothes again. It is only a week since I left Dalveigh, but it seems long ago. Listen to the wind, Rob! It is singing of the good days to be for you and me."

He bent over and kissed her.

"My own dear lass!" he said softly.

The Life-Book of Uncle Jesse

"I THINK, MARY, I'D FIND LOST MARGARET THERE."

NCLE JESSE! The name calls up the vision of him as I saw him so often in those two enchanted summers at Golden Gate; as I saw him the first time, when he stood in the open doorway of the little low-eaved cottage on the harbour shore, welcoming us to our new domicile with the gentle, unconscious courtesy that became him so well. A tall, ungainly figure, somewhat stooped, yet suggestive of great strength and endurance; a clean-shaven old face deeply lined and bronzed; a thick mane of iron-grey hair falling quite to his shoulders; and a pair of remarkably blue, deep-set eyes, which sometimes twinkled and sometimes dreamed, but oftener looked out seaward with a wistful question in them, as of one seeking something precious and lost. I was to learn one day what it was for which Uncle Jesse looked.

It cannot be denied that Uncle Jesse was a homely man. His spare jaws, rugged mouth, and square brow were not fashioned on the lines of beauty, but though at first sight you thought him plain you never thought anything more about it – the spirit shining through that rugged tenement beautified it so wholly.

Uncle Jesse was quite keenly aware of his lack of outward comeliness and lamented it, for he was a passionate worshipper of beauty in everything. He told Mother once that he'd rather like to be made over again and made handsome.

"Folks say I'm good," he remarked whimsically, "but I sometimes wish the Lord had made me only half as good and put the rest of it into looks. But I reckon He knew what He was about, as a good Captain should. Some of us have to be homely or the purty ones – like Miss Mary there – wouldn't show up so well."

I was not in the least pretty but Uncle Jesse was always telling me I was – and I loved him for it. He told the fib so prettily and sincerely that he almost made me believe it for the time being, and I really think he believed it himself. All women were lovely and of good report in his eyes, because of one he had loved. The only time I ever saw Uncle Jesse really angered was when someone in his hearing cast an aspersion on the character of a shore girl. The wretched man who did it fairly cringed when Uncle Jesse turned on him with lightning of eye and thundercloud of brow. At that moment I no longer found it hard to reconcile Uncle Jesse's simple, kindly personality with the wild, adventurous life he had lived.

We went to Golden Gate in the spring. Mother's health had not been good and her doctor recommended sea air and quiet. Uncle James, when he heard it, proposed that we take possession of a small cottage at Golden Gate, to which he had recently fallen heir by the death of an old aunt who had lived in it.

"I haven't been up to see it," he said, "but it is just as Aunt Elizabeth left it and she was the pink of neatness. The key is in the possession of an old sailor living nearby – Jesse Boyd is the name, I think. I imagine you can be very comfortable in it. It is built right on the harbour shore, inside the bar, and it is within five minutes' walk of the outside shore."

Uncle James' offer fitted in very opportunely with our limp family purse, and we straightway betook ourselves to Golden Gate. We telegraphed to Jesse Boyd to have the house opened for us and, one crisp spring day, when a rollicking wind was scudding over the harbour and the dunes, whipping the water into white caps and washing the sandshore with long lines of silvery breakers, we alighted at the little station and walked the half mile to our new home, leaving our goods and chattels to be carted over in the evening by an obliging station agent's boy.

OUR FIRST GLIMPSE of Aunt Elizabeth's cottage was a delight to soul and sense; it looked so like a big grey seashell stranded on the shore. Between it and the harbour was only a narrow strip of shingle, and behind it was a gnarled and battered fir wood where the winds were in the habit of harping all sorts of weird and haunting music. Inside, it was to prove even yet more quaint and delightful, with its low, dark-beamed ceilings and square, deep-set windows by which, whether open or shut, sea breezes entered at their own sweet will. The view from our door was magnificent, taking in the big harbour and sweeps of purple hills beyond. The entrance of the harbour gave it its name – a deep, narrow channel between the bar of sand dunes on the one side and a steep, high, frowning red sandstone cliff on the other. We appreciated its significance the first time we saw a splendid golden sunrise flooding it, coming out of the wonderful sea and sky beyond and billowing through that narrow passage in waves of light. Truly, it was a golden gate through which one might sail to "faerie lands forlorn."

As we went along the path to our little house we were agreeably surprised to see a blue spiral of smoke curling up from its big, square chimney, and the next moment Uncle Jesse (we were calling him Uncle Jesse half an hour after we met him, so it seems scarcely worthwhile to begin with anything else) came to the door.

"Welcome, ladies," he said, holding out a big, hard, but scrupulously clean hand. "I thought you'd be feeling a bit tired and hungry, maybe, so when I came over to open up I put on a fire and brewed you up a cup of tea. I just delight in being neighbourly and 'tain't often I have the chance."

We found that Uncle Jesse's "cup of tea" meant a veritable spread. He had aired the little dining room, set out the table daintily with Aunt Elizabeth's china and linen – "knowed jest where to put my hands on 'em – often and often helped old Miss Kennedy wash 'em. We were cronies, her and me. I miss her terrible" – and adorned it with mayflowers which, as we afterwards discovered, he had tramped several miles to gather. There was good bread and butter, "store" biscuits, a dish of tea fit for the gods on high Olympus, and a platter of the most delicious sea trout, done to a turn.

"Thought they'd be tasty after travelling," said Uncle Jesse. "They're fresh as trout can be, ma'am. Two hours ago they was swimming in Johnson's pond yander. I caught 'em – yes, ma'am. It's about all I'm good for now, catching trout and cod occasional. But 'tweren't always so – not by no manner of means. I used to do other things, as you'd admit if you saw my life-book."

I was so hungry and tired that I did not then "rise to the bait" of Uncle Jesse's "life-book." I simply wanted to begin on those trout. Mother insisted that Uncle Jesse sit down and help us eat the repast he had prepared, and he assented without undue coaxing.

"Thank ye kindly. 'Twill be a real treat. I mostly has to eat my meals alone, with the reflection of my ugly old phiz in a looking glass opposite for company. 'Tisn't often I have the chance to sit down with two such sweet purty ladies."

Uncle Jesse's compliments look bald enough on paper, but he paid them with such gracious, gentle deference of tone and look that the woman who received them felt that she was being offered a queen's gift in kingly fashion.

He broke bread with us and from that moment we were all friends together and forever. After we had eaten all we could, we sat at our table for an hour and listened to Uncle Jesse telling us stories of his life.

"If I talk too much you must jest check me," he said seriously, but with a twinkle in his eyes. "When I do get a chance to talk to anyone I'm apt to run on terrible."

He had been a sailor from the time he was ten years old, and some of his adventures had such a marvellous edge that I secretly wondered if Uncle Jesse were not drawing a rather long bow at our credulous expense. But in this, as I found later, I did him injustice. His tales were all literally true, and Uncle Jesse had the gift of the born story-teller, whereby "unhappy, far-off things" can be brought vividly before the hearer and made to live again in all their pristine poignancy.

Mother and I laughed and shivered over Uncle Jesse's tales, and once we found ourselves crying. Uncle Jesse surveyed our tears with pleasure shining out through his face like an illuminating lamp.

"I like to make folks cry that way," he remarked. "It's a compliment. But I can't do justice to the things I've seen and helped do. I've got 'em all jotted down in my life-book but I haven't got the knack of writing them out properly. If I had, I could make a great book, if I had the knack of hitting on just the right words and stringing everything together proper on paper. But I can't. It's in this poor human critter," Uncle Jesse patted his breast sorrowfully, "but he can't get it out."

When Uncle Jesse went home that evening Mother asked him to come often to see us.

"I wonder if you'd give that invitation if you knew how likely I'd be to accept it," he remarked whimsically.

"Which is another way of saying you wonder if I meant it," smiled Mother. "I do, most heartily and sincerely."

"Then I'll come. You'll likely be pestered with me at any hour. And I'd be proud to have you drop over to visit me now and then too. I live on that point yander. Neither me nor my house is worth coming to see. It's only got one room and a loft and a stovepipe sticking out of the roof for a chimney. But I've got a few little things lying around that I picked up in the queer corners I used to be poking my nose into. Mebbe they'd interest you."

Uncle Jesse's "few little things" turned out to be the most interesting collection of curios I had ever seen. His one neat little living room was full of them – beautiful, hideous or quaint as the case might be, and almost all having some weird or exciting story attached.

Mother and I had a beautiful summer at Golden Gate. We lived the life of two children with Uncle Jesse as a playmate. Our housekeeping was of the simplest description and we spent our hours rambling along the shores, reading on the rocks or sailing over the harbour in Uncle Jesse's trim little boat. Every day we loved the simple-souled, true, manly old sailor more and more. He was as refreshing as a sea breeze, as interesting as some ancient chronicle. We never tired of listening to his stories, and his quaint remarks and comments were a continual delight to us. Uncle Jesse was one of those interesting and rare people who, in the picturesque phraseology of the shore folks, "never speak but they say something." The milk of human kindness and the wisdom of the serpent were mingled in Uncle Jesse's composition in delightful proportions.

One day he was absent all day and returned at nightfall.

"Took a tramp back yander." "Back yander" with Uncle Jesse might mean the station hamlet or the city a hundred miles away or any place between – "to carry Mr. Kimball a mess of trout. He likes one occasional and it's all I can do for a kindness he did me once. I stayed all day to talk to him. He likes to talk to me, though he's an eddicated man, because he's one of the folks that's *got* to talk or they're miserable, and he finds listeners scarce round here. The folks fight shy of him because they think he's an infidel.

He ain't *that* far gone exactly – few men is, I reckon – but he's what you might call a heretic. Heretics are wicked but they're mighty interesting. It's just that they've got sorter lost looking for God, being under the impression that He's hard to find – which He ain't, never. Most of 'em blunder to Him after a while I guess. I don't think listening to Mr. Kimball's arguments is likely to do *me* much harm. Mind you, I believe what I was brought up to believe. It saves a vast of trouble – and back of it all, God is good. The trouble with Mr. Kimball is, he's a leetle *too* clever. He thinks he's bound to live up to his cleverness and that it's smarter to thrash out some new way of getting to heaven than to go by the old track the common, ignorant folks is travelling. But he'll get there sometime all right and then he'll laugh at himself."

NOTHING EVER seemed to put Uncle Jesse out or depress him in any way.

"I've kind of contracted a habit of enjoying things," he remarked once, when Mother had commented on his invariable cheerfulness. "It's got so chronic that I believe I even enjoy the disagreeable things. It's great fun thinking they can't last. 'Old rheumatiz,' I says, when it grips me hard, 'you've *got* to stop aching sometime. The worse you are the sooner you'll stop, perhaps. I'm bound to get the better of you in the long run, whether in the body or out of the body.' "

Uncle Jesse seldom came to our house without bringing us something, even if it were only a bunch of sweet grass.

"I favour the smell of sweet grass," he said. "It always makes me think of my mother."

"She was fond of it?"

"Not that I knows on. Dunno's she ever saw any sweet grass. No, it's because it has a kind of motherly perfume – not too young, you understand – something kind of seasoned and wholesome and dependable – just like a mother."

Uncle Jesse was a very early riser. He seldom missed a sunrise.

"I've seen all kinds of sunrises come in through that there Gate," he said dreamily one morning when I myself had made a heroic effort at early rising and joined him on the rocks halfway between his house and ours. "I've been all over the world and, take it all in all, I've never seen a finer sight than a summer sunrise out there beyant the Gate. A man can't pick his time for dying, Mary – jest got to go when the Captain gives his sailing orders. But if I could I'd go out when the morning comes in there at the Gate. I've watched it a many times and thought what a thing it would be to pass out through that great white glory to whatever was waiting beyant, on a sea that ain't mapped out on any airthly chart. I think, Mary, I'd find lost Margaret there."

He had already told me the story of "lost Margaret," as he always called her. He rarely spoke of her, but when he did his love for her trembled in every tone – a love that had never grown faint or forgetful. Uncle Jesse was seventy; it was fifty years since lost Margaret had fallen asleep one day in her father's dory and drifted – as was supposed, for nothing was ever known certainly of her fate – across the harbour and out of the Gate, to perish in the black thunder squall that had come up suddenly that long-ago afternoon. But to Uncle Jesse those fifty years were but as yesterday when it is past.

"I walked the shore for months after that," he said sadly, "looking to find her dear, sweet little body, but the sea never gave her back to me. But I'll find her sometime. I wisht I could tell you just how she looked but I can't. I've seen a fine silvery mist hanging over the Gate at sunrise that seemed like her – and then again I've seen a white birch in the woods back yander that made me think of her. She had pale brown hair and a little white face, and long slender fingers like yours, Mary, only browner, for she was a shore girl. Sometimes I wake up in the night and hear the sea calling to me in the old way and it seems as if lost Margaret called in it. And when there's a storm and the waves are sobbing and moaning I hear her lamenting among them. And when they laugh on a gay day it's *her* laugh – lost Margaret's sweet little laugh. The sea took her from me but some day I'll find her, Mary. It can't keep us apart forever."

I had not been long at Golden Gate before I saw Uncle Jesse's "life-book," as he quaintly called it. He needed no coaxing to show it and he proudly gave it to me to read. It was an old leather-bound book filled with the record of his voyages and adventures. I thought what a veritable treasure trove it would be to a writer. Every sentence was a nugget. In itself the book had no literary merit; Uncle Jesse's charm of story-telling failed him when he came to pen and ink; he could only jot down roughly the outlines of his famous tales, and both spelling and grammar were sadly askew. But I felt that if anyone possessing the gift could take that simple record of a brave, adventurous life, reading between the bald lines the tale of dangers staunchly faced and duties manfully done, a wonderful story might be made from it. Pure comedy and thrilling tragedy were both lying hidden in Uncle Jesse's "life-book," waiting for the touch of the magician's hand to waken the laughter and grief and horror of thousands. I thought of my cousin, Robert Kennedy, who juggled with words in a masterly fashion, but complained that he found it hard to create incidents or characters. Here were both ready to his hand, but Robert was in Japan in the interests of his paper.

In the fall, when the harbour lay black and sullen under

November skies, Mother and I went back to town, parting with Uncle Jesse regretfully. We wanted him to visit us in town during the winter but he shook his head.

"It's too far away, Mary. If lost Margaret called me I mightn't hear her there. I must be here when my time comes. It can't be very far off now."

I wrote often to Uncle Jesse through the winter and sent him books and magazines. He enjoyed them but he thought – and truly enough – that none of them came up to his life-book for real interest.

"If my life-book could be took and writ by someone that knowed how, it would beat them holler," he wrote in one of his few letters to me.

In the spring we returned joyfully to Golden Gate. It was as golden as ever and the harbour as blue; the winds still rollicked as gaily and sweetly and the breakers boomed outside the bar as of yore. All was unchanged save Uncle Jesse. He had aged greatly and seemed frail and bent. After he had gone home from his first call on us, Mother cried.

"Uncle Jesse will soon be going to seek lost Margaret," she said.

In June Robert came. I took him promptly over to see Uncle Jesse, who was very much excited when he found that Robert was a "real writing man."

"Robert wants to hear some of your stories, Uncle Jesse," I said. "Tell him the one about the captain who went crazy and imagined he was the Flying Dutchman."

This was Uncle Jesse's best story. It was a compound of humour and horror, and though I had heard it several times, I laughed as heartily and shivered as fearsomely over it as Robert did. Other tales followed; Uncle Jesse told how his vessel had been run down by a steamer, how he had been boarded by Malay pirates, how his ship had caught fire, how he had helped a political prisoner escape

44

from a South American republic. He never said a boastful word, but it was impossible to help seeing what a hero the man had been – brave, true, resourceful, unselfish, skilful. He sat there in his poor little room and made those things live again for us. By a lift of the eyebrow, a twist of the lip, a gesture, a word, he painted some whole scene or character so that we saw it as it was.

Finally, he lent Robert his life-book. Robert sat up all night reading it and came to the breakfast table in great excitement.

"Mary, this is a wonderful book. If I could take it and garb it properly – work it up into a systematic whole and string it on the thread of Uncle Jesse's romance of lost Margaret, it would be the novel of the year. Do you suppose he would let me do it?"

"Let you! I think he would be delighted," I answered.

And he was. He was as excited as a schoolboy over it. At last his cherished dream was to be realized and his life-book given to the world.

"We'll collaborate," said Robert. "You will give the soul and I the body. Oh, we'll write a famous book between us, Uncle Jesse. And we'll get right to work."

Uncle Jesse was a happy man that summer. He looked upon the little back room we gave up to Robert for a study as a sacred shrine. Robert talked everything over with Uncle Jesse but would not let him see the manuscript. "You must wait till it is published," he said. "Then you'll get it all at once in its best shape."

Robert delved into the treasures of the life-book and used them freely. He dreamed and brooded over lost Margaret until she became a vivid reality to him and lived in his pages. As the book progressed it took possession of him and he worked at it with feverish eagerness. He let me read the manuscript and criticize it; and the concluding chapter of the book, which the critics later on were pleased to call idyllic, was modelled after my suggestions, so that I felt as if I had a share in it too.

It was autumn when the book was finished. Robert went back to town, but Mother and I decided to stay at Golden Gate all winter. We loved the spot and, besides, I wished to remain for Uncle Jesse's sake. He was failing all the time, and after Robert went and the excitement of the book-making was past, he failed still more rapidly. His tramping expeditions were over and he seldom went out in his boat. Neither did he talk a great deal. He liked to come over and sit silently for hours at our seaward window, looking out wistfully toward the Gate with his swiftly whitening head leaning on his hand. The only keen interest he still had was in Robert's book. He waited and watched impatiently for its publication.

"I want to live till I see it," he said, "just that long – then I'll be ready to go. He said it would be out in the spring – I must hang on till it comes, Mary."

There were times when I doubted sadly if he would "hang on." As the winter wore away he grew frailer and frailer. But ever he looked forward to the coming of spring and "the book," his book, transformed and glorified.

One day in young April the book came at last. Uncle Jesse had gone to the post office faithfully every day for a month, expecting it, but this day he was too feeble to go and I went for him. The book was there. It was called simply, *The Life-Book of Jesse Boyd*, and on the title page the names of Robert Kennedy and Jesse Boyd were printed as collaborators.

I shall never forget Uncle Jesse's face as I handed it to him. I came away and left him reading it, oblivious to all else. All night the light burned in his window, and I looked out across the sands to it and pictured the delight of the old man poring over the printed pages whereon his own life was portrayed. I wondered how he would like the

46

ending – the ending I had suggested. I was never to know.

After breakfast I went over to Uncle Jesse's house, taking some little delicacy Mother had cooked for him. It was an exquisite morning, full of delicate spring tints and sounds. The harbour was sparkling and dimpling like a girl, the winds were playing hide and seek roguishly among the stunted firs, and the silver-flashing gulls were soaring over the bar. Beyond the Gate was a shining, wonderful sea.

When I reached the little house on the point I saw the lamp still burning wanly in the window. A quick alarm struck at my heart. Without waiting to knock, I lifted the latch and entered.

Uncle Jesse was lying on the old sofa by the window, with the book clasped to his heart. His eyes were closed and on his face was a look of the most perfect peace and happiness – the look of one who has long sought and found at last.

We could not know at what hour he had died, but somehow I think he had his wish and went out when the morning came in through the Golden Gate. Out on that shining tide his spirit drifted, over the sunrise sea of pearl and silver, to the haven where lost Margaret waited beyond the storms and calms.

*Mackereling
out in the Gulf*

HE MACKEREL BOATS were all at anchor on the fishing grounds; the sea was glassy calm – a pallid blue, save for a chance streak of deeper azure where some stray sea breeze ruffled it.

It was about the middle of the afternoon, and intensely warm and breathless. The headlands and coves were blurred by a purple heat haze. The long sweep of the sand shore was so glaringly brilliant that the pained eye sought relief among the rough rocks, where shadows were cast by the big red sandstone boulders. The little cluster of fishing houses nearby were bleached to a silvery grey by long exposure to wind and rain. Far off were several "Yankee" fishing schooners, their sails dimly visible against the white horizon.

Two boats were hauled upon the "skids" that ran from the rocks out into the water. A couple of dories floated below them. Now and then a white gull, flashing silver where its plumage caught the sun, soared landward.

A young man was standing by the skids, watching the fishing boats through a spyglass. He was tall, with a straight, muscular figure clad in a rough fishing suit. His face was deeply browned by the gulf breezes and was attractive rather than handsome, while his eyes, as blue and clear as the gulf waters, were peculiarly honest and frank.

Two wiry, dark-faced French-Canadian boys were perched on one of the boats, watching the fishing fleet with lazy interest in their inky-black eyes, and wondering if the "Yanks" had seined many mackerel that day.

Presently three people came down the steep path from the fish-houses. One of them, a girl, ran lightly forward and touched Benjamin Selby's arm. He lowered his glass with a start and looked around. A flash of undisguised delight transfigured his face.

"Why, Mary Stella! I didn't expect you'd be down this

hot day. You haven't been much at the shore lately," he added reproachfully.

"I really haven't had time, Benjamin," she answered carelessly, as she took the glass from his hand and tried to focus it on the fishing fleet. Benjamin steadied it for her; the flush of pleasure was still glowing on his bronzed cheek. "Are the mackerel biting now?"

"Not just now. Who is that stranger with your father, Mary Stella?"

"That is a cousin of ours – a Mr. Braithwaite. Are you very busy, Benjamin?"

"Not busy at all – idle as you see me. Why?"

"Will you take me out for a little row in the dory? I haven't been out for so long."

"Of course. Come – here's the dory – your namesake, you know. I had her fresh painted last week. She's as clean as an eggshell."

The girl stepped daintily off the rocks into the little cream-coloured skiff, and Benjamin untied the rope and pushed off.

"Where would you like to go, Mary Stella?"

"Oh, just upshore a little way – not far. And don't go out into very deep water, please, it makes me feel frightened and dizzy."

Benjamin smiled and promised. He was rowing along with the easy grace of one used to the oar. He had been born and brought up in sound of the gulf's waves; its never-ceasing murmur had been his first lullaby. He knew it and loved it in every mood, in every varying tint and smile, in every change of wind and tide. There was no better skipper alongshore than Benjamin Selby.

Mary Stella waved her hand gaily to the two men on the rocks. Benjamin looked back darkly.

"Who is that young fellow?" he asked again. "Where does he belong?"

"He is the son of Father's sister – his favourite sister, although he has never seen her since she married an American years ago and went to live in the States. She made Frank come down here this summer and hunt us up. He is splendid, I think. He is a New York lawyer and very clever."

Benjamin made no response. He pulled in his oars and let the dory float amid the ripples. The bottom of white sand, patterned over with coloured pebbles, was clear and distinct through the dark-green water. Mary Stella leaned over to watch the distorted reflection of her face by the dory's side.

"Have you had pretty good luck this week, Benjamin? Father couldn't go out much – he has been so busy with his hay, and Leon is such a poor fisherman."

"We've had some of the best hauls of the summer this week. Some of the Rustler boats caught six hundred to a line yesterday. We had four hundred to the line in our boat."

Mary Stella began absently to dabble her slender brown hand in the water. A silence fell between them, with which Benjamin was well content, since it gave him a chance to feast his eyes on the beautiful face before him.

He could not recall the time when he had not loved Mary Stella. It seemed to him that she had always been a part of his inmost life. He loved her with the whole strength and fidelity of a naturally intense nature. He hoped that she loved him, and he had no rival that he feared. In secret he exalted and deified her as something almost too holy for him to aspire to. She was his ideal of all that was beautiful and good; he was jealously careful over all his words and thoughts and actions that not one might make him more unworthy of her. In all the hardship and toil of his life his love was as his guardian angel, turning his feet from every dim and crooked byway; he trod in no path where he would not have the girl he loved to follow. The roughest labour was glorified if it lifted him a step nearer the altar of his worship.

But today he felt faintly disturbed. In some strange, indefinable way it seemed to him that Mary Stella was different from her usual self. The impression was vague and evanescent – gone before he could decide wherein the difference lay. He told himself that he was foolish, yet the vexing, transient feeling continued to come and go.

Presently Mary Stella said it was time to go back. Benjamin was in no hurry, but he never disputed her lightest inclination. He turned the dory about and rowed shoreward.

Back on the rocks, Mosey Louis and Xavier, the French Canadians, were looking through the spyglass by turns and making characteristic comments on the fleet. Mr. Murray and Braithwaite were standing by the skids, watching the dory.

"Who is that young fellow?" asked the latter. "What a splendid physique he has! It's a pleasure to watch him rowing."

"That," said the older man, with a certain proprietary pride in his tone, "is Benjamin Selby – the best mackerel fisherman on the island. He's been high line all along the gulf shore for years. I don't know a finer man every way you take him. Maybe you'll think I'm partial," he continued with a smile. "You see, he and Mary Stella think a good deal of each other. I expect to have Benjamin for a son-in-law some day if all goes well."

Braithwaite's expression changed slightly. He walked over to the dory and helped Mary Stella out of it while Benjamin made the painter fast. When the latter turned, Mary Stella was walking across the rocks with her cousin. Benjamin's blue eyes darkened, and he strode moodily over to the boats.

"You weren't out this morning, Mr. Murray?"

"No, that hay had to be took in. Reckon I missed it – pretty good catch, they tell me. Are they getting any now?"

"No. It's not likely the fish will begin to bite again for another hour."

"I see someone standing up in that off boat, don't I?" said Mr. Murray, reaching for the spyglass.

"No, that's only Rob Leslie's crew trying to fool us. They've tried it before this afternoon. They think it would be a joke to coax us out there to broil like themselves."

"Frank," shouted Mr. Murray, "come here, I want you."

Aside to Benjamin he said, "He's my nephew – a fine young chap. You'll like him, I know."

Braithwaite came over, and Mr. Murray put one hand on his shoulder and one on Benjamin's.

"Boys, I want you to know each other. Benjamin, this is Frank Braithwaite. Frank, this is Benjamin Selby, the high line of the gulf shore, as I told you."

While Mr. Murray was speaking, the two men looked steadily at each other. The few seconds seemed very long; when they had passed, Benjamin knew that the other man was his rival.

Braithwaite was the first to speak. He put out his hand with easy cordiality.

"I am glad to meet you, Mr. Selby," he said heartily, "although I am afraid I should feel very green in the presence of such a veteran fisherman as yourself."

His frank courtesy compelled some return. Benjamin took the proffered hand with restraint.

"I'm sorry there's no mackerel going this afternoon," continued the American. "I wanted to have a chance at them. I never saw mackerel caught before. I suppose I'll be very awkward at first."

"It's not a very hard thing to do," said Benjamin stiffly, speaking for the first time since their meeting. "Most

anybody could catch mackerel for a while – it's the sticking to it that counts."

He turned abruptly and went back to his boat. He could
not force himself to talk civilly to the stranger, with that
newly born demon of distrust gnawing at his heart.

"I think I'll go out," he said. "It's freshening up. I
shouldn't wonder if the mackerel schooled soon."

"I'll go, too, then," said Mr. Murray. "Hi, up there! Leon
and Pete! Hi, I say!"

Two more French Canadians came running down from
the Murray fish-house, where they had been enjoying a
siesta. They fished in the Murray boat. A good deal of
friendly rivalry as to catch went on between the two boats,
while Leon and Mosey Louis were bitter enemies on their
own personal account.

"Think you'll try it, Frank?" shouted Mr. Murray.

"Well, not this afternoon," was the answer. "It's rather
hot. I'll see what it is like tomorrow."

The boats were quickly launched and glided out from
the shadow of the cliffs. Benjamin stood at his mast. Mary
Stella came down to the water's edge and waved her hand
gaily.

"Good luck to you and the best catch of the season," she
called out.

Benjamin waved his hat in response. His jealousy was
forgotten for the moment and he felt that he had been
churlish to Braithwaite.

"You'll wish you'd come," he shouted to him. "It's going
to be a great evening for fish."

When the boats reached the fishing grounds, they came
to and anchored, their masts coming out in slender silhouette against the sky. A row of dark figures was standing
up in every boat; the gulf's shining expanse was darkened
by odd black streaks – the mackerel had begun to school.

Frank Braithwaite went out fishing the next day and

caught 30 mackerel. He was boyishly proud of it. He visited the shore daily after that and soon became very popular. He developed into quite an expert fisherman; nor, when the boats came in, did he shirk work, but manfully rolled up his trousers and helped carry water and "gib" mackerel as if he enjoyed it. He never put on any "airs," and he stoutly took Leon's part against the aggressive Mosey Louis. Even the French Canadians, those merciless critics, admitted that the "Yankee" was a good fellow. Benjamin Selby alone held stubbornly aloof.

One evening the loaded boats came in at sunset. Benjamin sprang from his as it bumped against the skids, and ran up the path. At the corner of his fish-house he stopped and stood quite still, looking at Braithwaite and Mary Stella, who were standing by the rough picket fence of the pasture land. Braithwaite's back was to Benjamin; he held the girl's hand in his and was talking earnestly. Mary Stella was looking up at him, her delicate face thrown back a little. There was a look in her eyes that Benjamin had never seen there before – but he knew what it meant.

His face grew pale and rigid; he clenched his hands and a whirlpool of agony and bitterness surged up in his heart. All the great blossoms of the hope that had shed beauty and fragrance over his rough life seemed suddenly to shrivel up into black unsightliness.

He turned and went swiftly and noiselessly down the road to his boat. The murmur of the sea sounded very far off. Mosey Louis was busy counting out the mackerel, Xavier was dipping up buckets of water and pouring it over the silvery fish. The sun was setting in a bank of purple cloud, and the long black headland to the west cut the golden seas like a wedge of ebony. It was all real and yet unreal. Benjamin went to work mechanically.

Presently Mary Stella came down to her father's boat.

Braithwaite followed slowly, pausing a moment to exchange some banter with saucy Mosey Louis. Benjamin
bent lower over his table; now and then he caught the
clear tones of Mary Stella's voice or her laughter at some
sally of Pete or Leon. He knew when she went up the road
with Braithwaite; he caught the last glimpse of her light
dress as she passed out of sight on the cliffs above, but he
worked steadily on and gave no sign.

It was late when they finished. The tired French Canadians went quickly off to their beds in the fish-house loft.
Benjamin stood by the skids until all was quiet, then he
walked down the cove to a rocky point that jutted out into
the water. He leaned against a huge boulder and laid his
head on his arm, looking up into the dark sky. The stars
shone calmly down on his misery; the throbbing sea
stretched out before him; its low, murmuring moan
seemed to be the inarticulate voice of his pain.

The air was close and oppressive; fitful flashes of heat
lightning shimmered here and there over the heavy banks
of cloud on the horizon; little wavelets sobbed at the base
of the rocks.

When Benjamin lifted his head he saw Frank Braithwaite standing between him and the luminous water. He
took a step forward, and they came face to face as Braithwaite turned with a start.

Benjamin clenched his hands and fought down a
hideous temptation to thrust his rival off the rock.

"I saw you today," he said in a low, intense tone. "What
do you think of yourself, coming down here to steal the
girl I loved from me? Weren't there enough girls where you
came from to choose among? I hate you. I'd kill you – "

"Selby, stop! You don't know what you are saying. If I
have wronged you, I swear I did it unintentionally. I loved
Stella from the first – who could help it? But I thought she
was virtually bound to you, and I did not try to win her

away. You don't know what it cost me to remain passive. I know that you have always distrusted me, but hitherto you have had no reason to. But today I found that she was free – that she did not care for you! And I found – or thought I found – that there was a chance for me. I took it. I forgot everything else then."

"So she loves you?" said Benjamin dully.

"Yes," said Braithwaite softly.

Benjamin turned on him with sudden passion.

"I hate you – and I am the most miserable wretch alive, but if she is happy, it is no matter about me. You've won easily what I've slaved and toiled all my life for. You won't value it as I'd have done – but if you make her happy, nothing else matters. I've only one favour to ask of you. Don't let her come to the shore after this. I can't stand it."

August throbbed and burned itself out. Affairs along shore continued as usual. Benjamin shut his sorrow up in himself and gave no outward sign of suffering. As if to mock him, the season was one of phenomenal prosperity; it was a "mackerel year" to be dated from. He worked hard and unceasingly, sparing himself in no way.

Braithwaite seldom came to the shore now. Mary Stella never. Mr. Murray had tried to speak of the matter, but Benjamin would not let him.

"It's best that nothing be said," he told him with simple dignity. He was so calm that Mr. Murray thought he did not care greatly, and was glad of it. The older man regretted the turn of affairs. Braithwaite would take his daughter far away from him, as his sister had been taken, and he loved Benjamin as his own son.

One afternoon Benjamin stood by his boat and looked anxiously at sea and sky. The French Canadians were eager to go out, for the other boats were catching.

"I don't know about it," said Benjamin doubtfully. "I don't half like the look of things. I believe we're in for a squall before long. It was just such a day three years ago when that terrible squall came up that Joe Otway got drowned in."

The sky was dun and smoky, the glassy water was copper-hued, the air was heavy and breathless. The sea purred upon on the shore, lapping it caressingly like some huge feline creature biding its time to seize and crunch its victim.

"I reckon I'll try it," said Benjamin after a final scrutiny. "If a squall does come up, we'll have to run for the shore mighty quick, that's all."

They launched the boat speedily; as there was no wind, they had to row. As they pulled out, Braithwaite and Leon came down the road and began to launch the Murray boat.

"If dem two gits caught in a squall dey'll hav a tam," grinned Mosey Louis. "Dat Leon, he don't know de fust ting 'bout a boat, no more dan a cat!"

Benjamin came to anchor close in, but Braithwaite and Leon kept on until they were further out than any other boat.

"Reckon dey's after cod," suggested Xavier.

The mackerel bit well, but Benjamin kept a close watch on the sky. Suddenly he saw a dark streak advancing over the water from the northwest. He wheeled around.

"Boys, the squall's coming! Up with the anchor – quick!"

"Dere's plenty tam," grumbled Mosey Louis, who hated to leave the fish. "None of de oder boats is goin' in yit."

The squall struck the boat as he spoke. She lurched and staggered. The water was tossing choppily. There was a sudden commotion all through the fleet and sails went rapidly up. Mosey Louis turned pale and scrambled about without delay. Benjamin was halfway to the shore before the sail went up in the Murray boat.

"Don' know what dey're tinkin' of," growled Mosey Louis. "Dey'll be drown fust ting!"

Benjamin looked back anxiously. Every boat was making for the shore. The gale was steadily increasing. He had his doubts about making a landing himself, and Braithwaite would be twenty minutes later.

"But it isn't my lookout," he muttered.

Benjamin had landed and was hauling up his boat when Mr. Murray came running down the road.

"Frank?" he gasped. "Him and Leon went out, the foolish boys! They neither of them know anything about a time like this."

"I guess they'll be all right," said Benjamin reassuringly. "They were late starting. They may find it rather hard to land."

The other boats had all got in with more or less difficulty. The Murray boat alone was out. Men came scurrying along the shore in frightened groups of two and three.

The boat came swiftly in before the wind. Mr. Murray was half beside himself.

"It'll be all right, sir," said one of the men. "If they can't land here, they can beach her on the sandshore."

"If they only knew enough to do that," wailed the old man. "But they don't – they'll come right on to the rocks."

"Why don't they lower their sail?" said another. "They will upset if they don't."

"They're lowering it now," said Benjamin.

The boat was now about 300 yards from the shore. The sail did not go all the way down – it seemed to be stuck.

"Good God, what's wrong?" exclaimed Mr. Murray.

As he spoke, the boat capsized. A yell of horror rose from the beach. Mr. Murray sprang toward Benjamin's boat, but one of the men held him back.

"You can't do it, sir. I don't know that anybody can."

Braithwaite and Leon were clinging to the boat. Benjamin Selby, standing in the background, his lips set, his hands clenched, was fighting the hardest battle of his life. He knew that he alone, out of all the men there, possessed the necessary skill and nerve to reach the boat if she could be reached at all. There was a bare chance and a great risk. This man whom he hated was drowning before his eyes. Let him drown, then! Why should he risk – ay, and perchance lose – his life for his enemy? No one could blame him for refusing – and if Braithwaite were out of the way, Mary Stella might yet be his!

The temptation and victory passed in a few brief seconds. He stepped forward, cool and self-possessed.

"I'm going out. I want one man with me. No one with child or wife. Who'll go?"

"I will," shouted Mosey Louis. "I haf some spat wid dat Leon, but I not lak to see him drown for all dat!"

Benjamin offered no objection. The French Canadian's arm was strong and he possessed skill and experience. Mr. Murray caught Benjamin's arm.

"No, no, Benjamin – not you – I can't see both my boys drowned."

Benjamin gently loosed the old man's hold.

"It's for Mary Stella's sake," he said hoarsely. "If I don't come back, tell her that."

They launched the large dory with difficulty and pulled out into the surf. Benjamin did not lose his nerve. His quick arm, his steady eye did not fail. A dozen times the wild-eyed watchers thought the boat was doomed, but as often she righted triumphantly.

At last the drowning men were reached and somehow or other hauled on board Benjamin's craft. It was easier to come back, for they beached the boat on the sand. With a wild cheer the men on the shore rushed into the surf and helped to carry the half-unconscious Braithwaite and

Leon ashore and up to the Murray fish-house. Benjamin went home before anyone knew he had gone. Mosey Louis was left behind to reap the honours; he sat in a circle of admiring lads and gave all the details of the rescue.

"Dat Leon, he not tink he know so much now!" he said.

Braithwaite came to the shore next day somewhat pale and shaky. He went straight to Benjamin and held out his hand.

"Thank you," he said simply.

Benjamin bent lower over his work.

"You needn't thank me," he said gruffly. "I wanted to let you drown. But I went out for Mary Stella's sake. Tell me one thing – I couldn't bring myself to ask it of anyone else. When are you to be – married?"

"The 12th of September."

Benjamin did not wince. He turned away and looked out across the sea for a few moments. The last agony of his great renunciation was upon him. Then he turned and held out his hand.

"For her sake," he said earnestly.

Frank Braithwaite put his slender white hand into the fisherman's hard brown palm. There were tears in both men's eyes. They parted in silence.

On the morning of the 12th of September Benjamin Selby went out to the fishing grounds as usual. The catch was good, although the season was almost over. In the afternoon the French Canadians went to sleep. Benjamin intended to row down the shore for salt. He stood by his dory, ready to start, but he seemed to be waiting for something. At last it came: a faint train whistle blew, a puff of white smoke floated across a distant gap in the sand-hills.

Mary Stella was gone at last – gone forever from his life. The honest blue eyes looking out over the sea did not falter; bravely he faced his desolate future.

The white gulls soared over the water, little swishing ripples lapped on the sand, and through all the gentle, dreamy noises of the shore came the soft, unceasing murmur of the gulf.

Fair Exchange
and No Robbery

ATHERINE RANGELY was packing up. Her chum and roommate, Edith Wilmer, was sitting on the bed watching her in that calm disinterested fashion peculiarly maddening to a bewildered packer.

"It does seem too provoking," said Katherine, as she tugged at an obstinate shawl strap, "that Ned should be transferred here now, just when I'm going away. The powers that be might have waited until vacation was over. Ned won't know a soul here and he'll be horribly lonesome."

"I'll do my best to befriend him, with your permission," said Edith consolingly.

"Oh, I know. You're a special Providence, Ede. Ned will be up tonight first thing, of course, and I'll introduce him. Try to keep the poor fellow amused until I get back. Two months! Just fancy! And Aunt Elizabeth won't abate one jot or tittle of the time I promised to stay with her. Harbour Hill is so frightfully dull, too."

Then the talk drifted around to Edith's affairs. She was engaged to a certain Sidney Keith, who was a professor in some college.

"I don't expect to see much of Sidney this summer," said Edith. "He's writing another book. He is so terribly addicted to literature."

"How lovely," sighed Katherine, who had aspirations in that line herself. "If only Ned were like him I should be perfectly happy. But Ned is so prosaic. He doesn't care a rap for poetry, and he laughs when I enthuse. It makes him quite furious when I talk of taking up writing seriously. He says women writers are an abomination on the face of the earth. Did you ever hear anything so ridiculous?"

"He is very handsome, though," said Edith, with a

glance at his photograph on Katherine's dressing table. "And that is what Sid is not. He is rather distinguished looking, but as plain as he can possibly be."

Edith sighed. She had a weakness for handsome men and thought it rather hard that fate should have allotted her so plain a lover.

"He has lovely eyes," said Katherine comfortingly, "and handsome men are always vain. Even Ned is. I have to snub him regularly. But I think you'll like him."

Edith thought so too when Ned Ellison appeared that night. He was a handsome off-handed young fellow, who seemed to admire Katherine immensely, and be a little afraid of her into the bargain.

"Edith will try to make Riverton pleasant for you while I am away," she told him in their good-bye chat. "She is a dear girl – you'll like her, I know. It's really too bad I have to go away now, but it can't be helped."

"I shall be awfully lonesome," grumbled Ned. "Don't you forget to write regularly, Kitty."

"Of course I'll write, but for pity's sake, Ned, don't call me Kitty. It sounds so childish. Well, bye-bye, dear boy. I'll be back in two months and then we'll have a lovely time."

WHEN KATHERINE had been at Harbour Hill for a week she wondered how upon earth she was going to put in the remaining seven. Harbour Hill was noted for its beauty, but not every woman can live by scenery alone.

"Aunt Elizabeth," said Katherine one day, "does anybody ever die in Harbour Hill? Because it doesn't seem to me it would be any change for them if they did."

Aunt Elizabeth's only reply to this was a shocked look.

To pass the time Katherine took to collecting seaweeds, and this involved long tramps along the shore. On one of these occasions she met with an adventure. The place was a remote spot far up the shore. Katherine had taken off

68

her shoes and stockings, tucked up her skirt, rolled her sleeves high above her dimpled elbows, and was deep in the absorbing process of fishing up seaweeds off a craggy headland. She looked anything but dignified while so employed, but under the circumstances dignity did not matter.

Presently she heard a shout from the shore and, turning around in dismay, she beheld a man on the rocks behind her. He was evidently shouting at her. What on earth could the creature want?

"Come in," he called, gesticulating wildly. "You'll be in the bottomless pit in another moment if you don't look out."

"He certainly must be a lunatic," said Katherine to herself, "or else he's drunk. What am I to do?"

"Come in, I tell you," insisted the stranger. "What in the world do you mean by wading out to such a place? Why, it's madness."

Katherine's indignation got the better of her fear.

"I do not think I am trespassing," she called back as icily as possible.

The stranger did not seem to be snubbed at all. He came down to the very edge of the rocks where Katherine could see him plainly. He was dressed in a somewhat well-worn grey suit and wore spectacles. He did not look like a lunatic, and he did not seem to be drunk.

"I implore you to come in," he said earnestly. "You must be standing on the very brink of the bottomless pit."

He is certainly off his balance, thought Katherine. He must be some revivalist who has gone insane on one point. I suppose I'd better go in. He looks quite capable of wading out here after me if I don't.

She picked her steps carefully back with her precious specimens. The stranger eyed her severely as she stepped on the rocks.

"I should think you would have more sense than to risk your life in that fashion for a handful of seaweeds," he said.

"I haven't the faintest idea what you mean," said Miss Rangely. "You don't look crazy, but you talk as if you were."

"Do you mean to say you don't know that what the people hereabouts call the Bottomless Pit is situated right off that point – the most dangerous spot along the whole coast?"

"No, I didn't," said Katherine, horrified. She remembered now that Aunt Elizabeth had warned her to be careful of some bad hole along shore, but she had not been paying much attention and had supposed it to be in quite another direction. "I am a stranger here."

"Well, I hardly thought you'd be foolish enough to be out there if you knew," said the other in mollified accents. "The place ought not to be left without warning, anyhow. It is the most careless thing I ever heard of. There is a big hole right off that point and nobody has ever been able to find the bottom of it. A person who got into it would never be heard of again. The rocks there form an eddy that sucks everything right down."

"I am very grateful to you for calling me in," said Katherine humbly. "I had no idea I was in such danger."

"You have a very fine bunch of seaweeds, I see," said the unknown.

But Katherine was in no mood to converse on seaweeds. She suddenly realized what she must look like – bare feet, draggled skirts, dripping arms. And this creature whom she had taken for a lunatic was undoubtedly a gentleman. Oh, if he would only go and give her a chance to put on her shoes and stockings!

Nothing seemed further from his intentions. When Katherine had picked up the aforesaid articles and turned homeward, he walked beside her, still discoursing on seaweeds as eloquently as if he were commonly accustomed to walking with barefooted young women. In spite of herself, Katherine couldn't help listening to him, for he managed to invest seaweeds with an absorbing interest. She finally decided that as he didn't seem to mind her bare feet, she wouldn't either.

He knew so much about seaweeds that Katherine felt decidedly amateurish beside him. He looked over her specimens and pointed out the valuable ones. He explained the best method of preserving and mounting them, and told her of other and less dangerous places along the shore where she might get some new varieties.

When they came in sight of Harbour Hill, Katherine began to wonder what on earth she would do with him. It wasn't exactly permissible to snub a man who had practically saved your life, but, on the other hand, the prospect of walking through the principal street of Harbour Hill barefooted and escorted by a scholarly looking gentleman discoursing on seaweeds was not to be calmly contemplated.

The unknown cut the Gordian knot himself. He said that he must really go back or he would be late for dinner, lifted his hat politely, and departed. Katherine waited until he was out of sight, then sat down on the sand and put on her shoes and stockings.

"Who on earth can he be?" she said to herself. "And where have I seen him before? There was certainly something familiar about his appearance. He is very nice, but he must have thought me crazy. I wonder if he belongs to Harbour Hill."

The mystery was solved when she got home and found a letter from Edith awaiting her.

"I see Ned quite often," wrote the latter, "and I think he is perfectly splendid. You are a lucky girl, Kate. But oh, do you know that Sidney is actually at Harbour Hill, too, or at least quite near it? I had a letter from him yesterday. He has gone down there to spend his vacation, because it is so quiet, and to finish up some horrid scientific book he is working at. He's boarding at some little farmhouse up the shore. I've written to him today to hunt you up and consider himself introduced to you. I think you'll like him, for he's just your style."

Katherine smiled when Sidney Keith's card was brought up to her that evening and went down to meet him. Her companion of the morning rose to meet her.

"You!" he said.

"Yes, me," said Miss Rangely cheerfully and ungrammatically. "You didn't expect it, did you? I was sure I had seen you before – only it wasn't you but your photograph."

When Professor Keith went away it was with a cordial invitation to call again. He did not fail to avail himself of it – in fact, he became a constant visitor at Sycamore Villa. Katherine wrote all about it to Edith and cultivated Professor Keith with a clear conscience.

They got on capitally together. They went on long expeditions up shore after seaweeds, and when seaweeds were exhausted they began to make a collection of the Harbour Hill flora. This involved more long, companionable expeditions. Katherine sometimes wondered when Professor Keith found time to work on his book, but as he made no reference to the subject, neither did she.

Once in a while, when she had time to think of them, she wondered how Ned and Edith were getting on. At first Edith's letters had been full of Ned, but in her last two or three she had said little about him. Katherine wrote and jokingly asked Edith if she and Ned had quarreled. Edith wrote back and said, "What nonsense." She and Ned were as good friends as ever, but he was getting acquainted in Riverton now and wasn't so dependent on her society, etc.

Katherine sighed and went on a fern hunt with Professor Keith. It was getting near the end of her vacation and she had only two weeks more. They were sitting down to rest on the side of the road when she mentioned this fact inconsequently. The professor prodded the harmless dust with his cane. Well, he supposed she would find a return to work pleasant and would doubtless be glad to see her Riverton friends again.

"I'm dying to see Edith," said Katherine.

"And Ned?" suggested Professor Keith.

"Oh yes. Ned, of course," assented Katherine without enthusiasm. There didn't seem to be anything more to say. One cannot talk everlastingly about ferns, so they got up and went home.

Katherine wrote a particularly affectionate letter to Ned that night. Then she went to bed and cried.

When Professor Keith came up to bid Miss Rangely good-bye on the eve of her departure from Harbour Hill, he looked like a man who was being led to execution without benefit of clergy. But he kept himself well in hand and talked calmly on impersonal subjects. After all, it was Katherine who made the first break when she got up to say good-bye. She was in the middle of some conventional sentence when she suddenly stopped short, and her voice trailed off in a babyish quiver.

The professor put out his arm and drew her close to him. His hat dropped under their feet and was trampled on, but I doubt if Professor Keith knows the difference to this day, for he was fully absorbed in kissing Katherine's hair. When she became cognizant of this fact, she drew herself away.

"Oh, Sidney, don't! – think of Edith! I feel like a traitor."

"Do you think she would care very much if I – if you – if we – " hesitated the professor.

"Oh, it would break her heart," cried Katherine with convincing earnestness. "I know it would – and Ned's too. They must never know."

The professor stooped and began hunting for his mal-treated hat. He was a long time finding it, and when he did he went softly to the door. With his hand on the knob, he paused and looked back.

"Good-bye, Miss Rangely," he said softly.

But Katherine, whose face was buried in the cushions of the lounge, did not hear him and when she looked up he was gone.

KATHERINE FELT that life was stale, flat and unprofitable when she alighted at Riverton station in the dusk of the next evening. She was not expected until a later train and there was no one to meet her. She walked drearily through the streets to her boarding house and entered her room unannounced. Edith, who was lying on the bed, sprang up with a surprised greeting. It was too dark to be sure, but Katherine had an uncomfortable suspicion that her friend had been crying, and her heart quaked guiltily. Could Edith have suspected anything?

"Why, we didn't think you'd be up till the 8:30 train, and Ned and I were going to meet you."

"I found I could catch an earlier train, so I took it," said Katherine, as she dropped listlessly into a chair. "I am tired to death and I have such a headache. I can't see anyone tonight, not even Ned."

"You poor dear," said Edith sympathetically, beginning a search for the cologne. "Lie down on the bed and I'll bathe your poor head. Did you have a good time at Harbour Hill? And how did you leave Sid? Did he say anything about coming up?"

"Oh, he was quite well," said Katherine wearily. "I didn't

hear him say if he intended to come up or not. There, thanks – that will do nicely."

After Edith had gone down, Katherine tossed about restlessly. She knew Ned had come and she did not want to see him. But, after all, it was only putting off the evil day, and it was treating him rather shabbily. She would go down for a minute.

There were two doors to the parlour, and Katherine went by way of the library one, over which a portiere was hanging. Her hand was lifted to draw it back when she heard something that arrested the movement.

A woman was crying in the room beyond. It was Edith – and what was she saying?

"Oh, Ned, it is all perfectly dreadful! I couldn't look Katherine in the face when she came home. I'm so ashamed of myself and I never meant to be so false. We must never let her suspect for a minute."

"It's pretty rough on a fellow," said another voice – Ned's voice – in a choked sort of a way. "Upon my word, Edith, I don't see how I'm going to keep it up."

"You must," sobbed Edith. "It would break her heart – and Sidney's too. We must just make up our minds to forget each other, Ned, and you must marry Katherine."

Just at this point Katherine became aware that she was eavesdropping and she went away noiselessly. She did not look in the least like a person who has received a mortal blow, and she had forgotten her headache altogether.

When Edith came up half an hour later, she found the worn-out invalid sitting up and reading a novel.

"How is your headache, dear?" she asked, carefully keeping her face turned away from Katherine.

"Oh, it's all gone," said Miss Rangely cheerfully.

"Why didn't you come down then? Ned was here."

"Well, Ede, I did go down, but I thought I wasn't particularly wanted, so I came back."

Edith faced her friend in dismay, forgetful of swollen lids and tear-stained cheeks.

"Katherine!"

"Don't look so conscience stricken, my dear child. There is no harm done."

"You heard – "

"Some surprising speeches. So you and Ned have gone and fallen in love with one another?"

"Oh, Katherine," sobbed Edith, "we – we – couldn't help it – but it's all over. Oh, don't be angry with me!"

"Angry? My dear, I'm delighted."

"Delighted?"

"Yes, you dear goose. Can't you guess, or must I tell you? Sidney and I did the very same, and had just such a melancholy parting last night as I suspect you and Ned had tonight."

"Katherine!"

"Yes, it's quite true. And of course we made up our minds to sacrifice ourselves on the altar of duty and all that. But now, thank goodness, there is no need of such wholesale immolation. So just let's forgive each other."

"Oh," sighed Edith happily, "it is almost too good to be true."

"It is really providentially ordered, isn't it?" said Katherine. "Ned and I would never have got on together in the world, and you and Sidney would have bored each other to death. As it is, there will be four perfectly happy people instead of four miserable ones. I'll tell Ned so tomorrow."

Natty
of Blue Point

ATTY MILLER strolled down to the wharf where Bliss Ford was tying up the *Cockawee*. Bliss was scowling darkly at the boat, a trim new one, painted white, whose furled sails seemed unaccountably wet and whose glistening interior likewise dripped with moisture. A group of fishermen on the wharf were shaking their heads sagely as Natty drew near.

"Might as well split her up for kindlings, Bliss," said Jake McLaren. "You'll never get men to sail in her. It passed the first time, seeing as only young Johnson was skipper, but when a boat turns turtle with Captain Frank in command, there's something serious wrong with her."

"What's up?" asked Natty.

"The *Cockawee* upset out in the bay again this morning," answered Will Scott. "That's the second time. The *Grey Gull* picked up the men and towed her in. It's no use trying to sail her. Lobstermen ain't going to risk their lives in a boat like that. How's things over at Blue Point, Natty?"

"Pretty well," responded Natty laconically. Natty never wasted words. He had not talked a great deal in his fourteen years of life, but he was much given to thinking. He was rather undersized and insignificant looking, but there were a few boys of his own age on the mainland who knew that Natty had muscles.

"Has Everett heard anything from Ottawa about the lighthouse business yet?" asked Will.

Natty shook his head.

"Think he's any chance of getting the app'intment?" queried Adam Lewis.

"Not the ghost of a chance," said Cooper Creasy decidedly. "He's on the wrong side of politics, that's what. Er rather his father was. A Tory's son ain't going to get an app'intment from a Lib'ral government, that's what."

"Mr. Barr says that Everett is too young to be trusted in such a responsible position," quoted Natty gravely.

Cooper shrugged his shoulders.

"Mebbe – mebbe. Eighteen is kind of green, but everybody knows that Ev's been the real lighthouse keeper for two years, since your father took sick. Irving Elliott wants that light – has wanted it for years – and he's a pretty strong pull at headquarters, that's what. Barr owes him something for years of hard work at elections. I ain't saying anything against Elliott, either. He's a good man, but your father's son ought to have that light as sure as he won't get it, that's what."

"Any of you going to take in the sports tomorrow down at Summerside?" asked Will Scott, in order to switch Cooper away from politics, which were apt to excite him.

"I'm going, for one," said Adam. "There's to be a yacht race atween the Summerside and Charlottetown boat clubs. Yes, I am going. Give you a chance down to the station, Natty, if you want one."

Natty shook his head.

"Not going," he said briefly.

"You should celebrate Victoria Day," said Adam, patriotically. " 'Twenty-fourth o' May's the Queen's birthday, Ef we don't get a holiday we'll all run away,' as we used to say at school. The good old Queen is dead, but the day's been app'inted a national holiday in honour of her memory and you should celebrate it becoming, Natty-boy."

"Ev and I can't both go, and he's going," explained Natty. "Prue and I'll stay home to light up. Must be getting back now. Looks squally."

"I misdoubt if we'll have Queen's weather tomorrow," said Cooper, squinting critically at the sky. "Looks like a northeast blow, that's what. There goes Bliss, striding off and looking pretty mad. The *Cockawee*'s a dead loss to him, that's what. Nat's off – he knows how to handle a boat

80

middling well, too. Pity he's such a puny youngster. Not much to him, I reckon."

Natty had cast loose in his boat, the *Merry Maid*, and hoisted his sail. In a few minutes he was skimming gaily down the bay. The wind was fair and piping and the *Merry Maid* went like a bird. Natty, at the rudder, steered for Blue Point Island, a reflective frown on his face. He was feeling in no mood for Victoria Day sports. In a very short time he and Ev and Prue must leave Blue Point lighthouse, where they had lived all their lives. To Natty it seemed as if the end of all things would come then. Where would life be worth living away from lonely, windy Blue Point Island?

David Miller had died the preceding winter after a long illness. He had been lighthouse keeper at Blue Point for thirty years. His three children had been born and brought up there, and there, four years ago, the mother had died. But womanly little Prue had taken her place well, and the boys were devoted to their sister. When their father died, Everett had applied for the position of lighthouse keeper. The matter was not yet publicly decided, but old Cooper Creasy had sized the situation up accurately. The Millers had no real hope that Everett would be appointed.

Victoria Day, while not absolutely stormy, proved to be rather unpleasant. A choppy northeast wind blew up the bay, and the water was rough enough. The sky was overcast with clouds, and the May air was raw and chilly. At Blue Point the Millers were early astir, for if Everett wanted to sail over to the mainland in time to catch the excursion train, no morning naps were permissible. He was going alone. Since only one of the boys could go, Natty had insisted that it should be Everett, and Prue had elected to stay home with Natty. Prue had small heart for Victoria Day that year. She did not feel even a thrill of enthusiasm when Natty hoisted a flag and wreathed the Queen's picture with creeping spruce. Prue felt as badly about leaving Blue Point Island as the boys did.

The day passed slowly. In the afternoon the wind fell away to a dead calm, but there was still a heavy swell on, and shortly before sunset a fog came creeping up from the east and spread over the bay and islands, so thick and white that Prue and Natty could not even see Little Bear Island on the right.

"I'm glad Everett isn't coming back tonight," said Prue. "He could never find his way cross the harbour in that fog."

"Isn't it thick, though," said Natty. "The light won't show far tonight."

At sunset they lighted the great lamps and then settled down to an evening of reading. But it was not long before Natty looked up from his book to say, "Hello, Prue, what was that? Thought I heard a noise."

"So did I," said Prue. "It sounded like someone calling."

They hurried to the door, which looked out on the harbour. The night, owing to the fog, was dark with a darkness that seemed almost tangible. From somewhere out of that darkness came a muffled shouting, like that of a person in distress.

"Prue, there's somebody in trouble out there!" exclaimed Natty.

"Oh, it's surely never Ev!" cried Prue.

Natty shook his head.

"Don't think so. Ev had no intention of coming back tonight. Get that lantern, Prue. I must go and see what and who it is."

"Oh, Natty, you mustn't," cried Prue in distress. "There's a heavy swell on yet – and the fog – oh, if you get lost – "

"I'll not get lost, and I must go, Prue. Maybe somebody is drowning out there. It's not Ev, of course, but suppose it were! That's a good girl."

Prue, with set face, had brought the lantern, resolutely choking back the words of fear and protest that rushed to her lips. They hurried down to the shore and Natty sprang into the little skiff he used for rowing. He hastily lashed the lantern in the stern, cast loose the painter, and lifted the oars.

"I'll be back as soon as possible," he called to Prue. "Wait here for me."

In a minute the shore was out of sight, and Natty found himself alone in the black fog, with no guide but the cries for help, which already were becoming fainter. They seemed to come from the direction of Little Bear, and thither Natty rowed. It was a tough pull, and the water was rough enough for the little dory. But Natty had been at home with the oars from babyhood, and his long training and tough sinews stood him in good stead now. Steadily and intrepidly he rowed along. The water grew rougher as he passed out from the shelter of Blue Point into the channel between the latter and Little Bear. The cries were becoming very faint. What if he should be too late? He bent to the oars with all his energy. Presently, by the smoother water, he knew he must be in the lea of Little Bear. The cries sounded nearer. He must already have rowed nearly a mile. The next minute he shot around a small headland and right before him, dimly visible in the faint light cast by the lantern through the fog, was an upturned boat with two men clinging to it, one on each side, evidently almost exhausted. Natty rowed cautiously up to the one nearest him, knowing that he must be wary lest the grip of the drowning man overturn his own light skiff.

"Let go when I say," he shouted, "and don't – grab – anything, do you hear? Don't – grab. Now, let go."

The next minute the man lay in the dory, dragged over the stern by Natty's grip on his collar.

"Lie still," ordered Natty, clutching the oars. To row

around the overturned boat, amid the swirl of water about her, was a task that taxed Natty's skill and strength to the utmost. The other man was dragged in over the bow, and with a gasp of relief Natty pulled away from the sinking boat. Once clear of her he could not row for a few minutes; he was shaking from head to foot with the reaction from tremendous effort and strain.

"This'll never do," he muttered. "I'm not going to be a baby now. But will I ever be able to row back?"

Presently, however, he was able to grip his oars again and pull for the lighthouse, whose beacon loomed dimly through the fog like a great blur of whiter mist. The men, obedient to his orders, lay quietly where he had placed them, and before long Natty was back again at the lighthouse landing, where Prue was waiting, wild with anxiety. The men were helped out and assisted up to the lighthouse, where Natty went to hunt up dry clothes for them, and Prue flew about to prepare hot drinks.

"To think that that child saved us!" exclaimed one of the men. "Why, I didn't think a grown man had the strength to do what he did. He is your brother, I suppose, Miss Miller. You have another brother, I think?"

"Oh, yes – Everett – but he is away," explained Prue. "We heard your shouts and Natty insisted on going at once to your rescue."

"Well, he came just in time. I couldn't have held on another minute – was so done up I couldn't have moved or spoken all the way here even if he hadn't commanded me to keep perfectly still."

Natty returned at this moment and exclaimed, "Why, it is Mr. Barr. I didn't recognize you before."

"Barr it is, young man. This gentleman is my friend, Mr. Blackmore. We have been celebrating Victoria Day by a shooting tramp over Little Bear. We hired a boat from Ford at the harbour head this morning – the *Cockawee*, he called her – and sailed over. I don't know much about running a boat, but Blackmore here thinks he does. We were at the other side of the island when the fog came up. We hurried across it, but it was almost dark when we reached our boat. We sailed around the point and then the boat just simply upset – don't know why – "

"But I know why," interrupted Natty indignantly. "That *Cockawee* does nothing but upset. She has turned turtle twice out in the harbour in fine weather. Ford was a rascal to let her to you. He might have known what would happen. Why – why – it was almost murder to let you go!"

"I thought there must be something queer about her," declared Mr. Blackmore. "I do know how to handle a boat despite my friend's gibe, and there was no reason why she should have upset like that. That Ford ought to be horse-whipped."

Thanks to Prue's stinging hot decoctions of black currant drink, the two gentlemen were no worse for their drenching and exposure, and the next morning Natty took them to the mainland in the *Merry Maid*. When he parted with them, Mr. Barr shook his hand heartily and said: "Thank you, my boy. You're a plucky youngster and a skilful one, too. Tell your brother that if I can get the Blue Point lighthouse berth for him I will, and as for yourself, you will always find a friend in me, and if I can ever do anything for you I will."

Two weeks later Everett received an official document formally appointing him keeper of Blue Point Island light. Natty carried the news to the mainland, where it was joyfully received among the fishermen.

"Only right and fair," said Cooper Creasy. "Blue Point without a Miller to light up wouldn't seem the thing at all, that's what. And it's nothing but Ev's doo."

"Guess Natty had more to do with it than Ev," said Adam, perpetrating a very poor pun and being immensely applauded therefor. It keyed Will Scott up to rival Adam.

"You said that Irving had a pull and the Millers hadn't," he said jocularly. "But it looks as if 'twas Natty's pull did the business after all – his pull over to Bear Island and back."

"It was about a miracle that a boy could do what he did on such a night," said Charles Macey.

"Where's Ford?" asked Natty uncomfortably. He hated to have his exploit talked about.

"Ford has cleared out," said Cooper, "gone down to Summerside to go into Tobe Meekins' factory there. Best thing he could do, that's what. Folks here hadn't no use for him after letting that death trap to them two men – even if they was Lib'rals. The *Cockawee* druv ashore on Little Bear, and there she's going to remain, I guess. D'ye want a berth in my mackerel boat this summer, Natty?"

"I do," said Natty, "but I thought you said you were full."

"I guess I can make room for you," said Cooper. "A boy with such grit and muscle ain't to be allowed to go to seed on Blue Point, that's what. Yesser, we'll make room for you."

And Natty's cup of happiness was full.

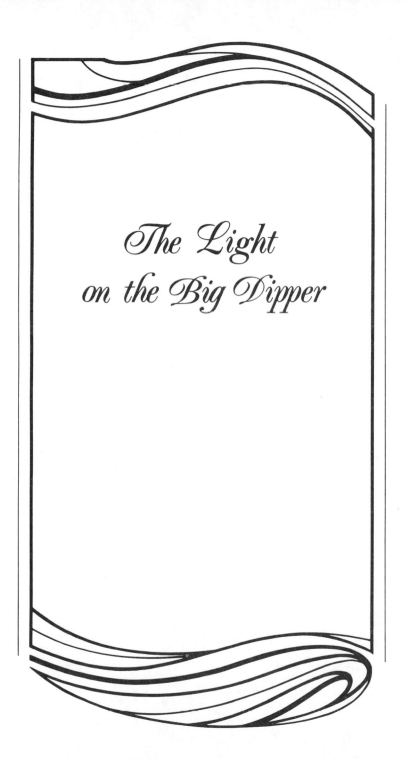

The Light
on the Big Dipper

"**D**ON'T LET NELLIE run out of doors, Mary Margaret, and be careful of the fire, Mary Margaret. I expect we'll be back pretty soon after dark, so don't be lonesome, Mary Margaret."

Mary Margaret laughed and switched her long, thick braid of black hair from one shoulder to the other.

"No fear of my being lonesome, Mother Campbell. I'll be just as careful as can be and there are so many things to be done that I'll be as busy and happy as a bee all day long. Nellie and I will have just the nicest kind of a time. I won't get lonesome, but if I should feel just tempted to, I'll think, 'Father is on his way home. He will soon be here.' And that would drive the lonesomeness away before it dared to show its face. Don't you worry, Mother Campbell."

Mother Campbell smiled. She knew she could trust Mary Margaret – careful, steady, prudent little Mary Margaret. Little! Ah, that was just the trouble. Careful and steady and prudent as Mary Margaret might be, she was only twelve years old, after all, and there would not be another soul besides her and Nellie on the Little Dipper that whole day. Mrs. Campbell felt that she hardly dared to go away under such circumstances. And yet she *must* dare it. Oscar Bryan had sailed over from the mainland the evening before with word that her sister Nan – her only sister, who lived in Cartonville – was ill and about to undergo a serious operation. She must go to see her, and Uncle Martin was waiting with his boat to take her over to the mainland to catch the morning train for Cartonville.

If five-year-old Nellie had been quite well Mrs. Campbell would have taken both her and Mary Margaret and locked up the house. But Nellie had a very bad cold and was quite unfit to go sailing across the harbour on a raw, chilly November day. So there was nothing to do but leave Mary

Margaret in charge, and Mary Margaret was quite pleased at the prospect.

"You know, Mother Campbell, I'm not afraid of anything except tramps. And no tramps ever come to the Dippers. You see what an advantage it is to live on an island! There, Uncle Martin is waving. Run along, little mother."

Mary Margaret watched the boat out of sight from the window and then betook herself to the doing of her tasks, singing blithely all the while. It was rather nice to be left in sole charge like this – it made you feel so important and grown-up. She would do everything very nicely and Mother would see when she came back what a good housekeeper her daughter was.

Mary Margaret and Nellie and Mrs. Campbell had been living on the Little Dipper ever since the preceding April. Before that they had always lived in their own cosy home at the Harbour Head. But in April Captain Campbell had sailed in the *Two Sisters* for a long voyage and, before he went, Mrs. Campbell's brother, Martin Clowe, had come to them with a proposition. He ran a lobster cannery on the Little Dipper, and he wanted his sister to go and keep house for him while her husband was away. After some discussion it was so arranged, and Mrs. Campbell and her two girls moved to the Little Dipper. It was not a lonesome place then, for the lobstermen and their families lived on it, and boats were constantly sailing to and fro between it and the mainland. Mary Margaret enjoyed her summer greatly; she bathed and sailed and roamed over the rocks, and on fine days her Uncle George, who kept the light-house on the Big Dipper, and lived there all alone, often came over and took her across to the Big Dipper. Mary Margaret thought the lighthouse was a wonderful place. Uncle George taught her how to light the lamps and manage the light.

When the lobster season closed, the men took up cod-fishing and carried this on till October, when they all moved back to the mainland. But Uncle Martin was building a house for himself at Harbour Head and did not wish to move until the ice formed over the bay because it would then be so much easier to transport his goods and chattels; so the Campbells stayed with him until the Captain should return.

Mary Margaret found plenty to do that day and wasn't a bit lonesome. But when evening came she didn't feel quite so cheerful. Nellie had fallen asleep, and there wasn't another living creature except the cat on the Little Dipper. Besides, it looked like a storm. The harbour was glassy calm, but the sky was very black and dour in the northeast – like snow, thought weather-wise Mary Margaret. She hoped her mother would get home before it began, and she wished the lighthouse star would gleam out on the Big Dipper. It would seem like the bright eye of a steady old friend. Mary Margaret always watched for it every night; just as soon as the sun went down the big lighthouse star would flash goldenly out in the northeastern sky.

"I'll sit down by the window and watch for it," said Mary Margaret to herself. "Then, when it is lighted, I'll get up a nice warm supper for Mother and Uncle Martin."

Mary Margaret sat down by the kitchen window to watch. Minute after minute passed, but no light flashed out on the Big Dipper. What was the matter? Mary Margaret began to feel uneasy. It was too cloudy to tell just when the sun had set, but she was sure it must be down, for it was quite dark in the house. She lighted a lamp, got the almanac, and hunted out the exact time of sunsetting. The sun had been down fifteen minutes!

And there was no light on the Big Dipper!

Mary Margaret felt alarmed and anxious. What was

wrong at the Big Dipper? Was Uncle George away? Or had something happened to him? Mary Margaret was sure he had never forgotten!

Fifteen minutes longer did Mary Margaret watch restlessly at the window. Then she concluded that something was desperately wrong somewhere. It was half an hour after sunset and the Big Dipper light, the most important one along the whole coast, was not lighted. What would she do? What *could* she do?

The answer came swift and clear into Mary Margaret's steady, sensible little mind. She must go to the Big Dipper and light the lamps!

But could she? Difficulties came crowding thick and fast into her thoughts. It was going to snow; the soft broad flakes were falling already. Could she row the two miles to the Big Dipper in the darkness and the snow? If she could, dare she leave Nellie all alone in the house? Oh, she couldn't! Somebody at the Harbour Head would surely notice that the Big Dipper light was unlighted and would go over to investigate the cause. But suppose they shouldn't? If the snow came thicker they might never notice the absence of the light. And suppose there was a ship away out there, as there nearly always was, with the dangerous rocks and shoals of the outer harbour to pass, with precious lives on board and no guiding beacon on the Big Dipper.

Mary Margaret hesitated no longer. She must go.

Bravely, briskly and thoughtfully she made her preparations. First, the fire was banked and the draughts closed; then she wrote a little note for her mother and laid it on the table. Finally she wakened Nellie.

"Nellie," said Mary Margaret, speaking very kindly and determinedly, "there is no light on the Big Dipper and I've got to row over and see about it. I'll be back as quickly as I can, and Mother and Uncle Martin will soon be here. You won't be afraid to stay alone, will you, dearie? You mustn't be afraid, because I have to go. And, Nellie, I'm going to tie you in your chair; it's necessary, because I can't lock the door, so you mustn't cry; nothing will hurt you, and I want you to be a brave little girl and help sister all you can."

Nellie, too sleepy and dazed to understand very clearly what Mary Margaret was about, submitted to be wrapped up in quilts and bound securely in her chair. Then Mary Margaret tied the chair fast to the wall so that Nellie couldn't upset it. That's safe, she thought. Nellie can't run out now or fall on the stove or set herself afire.

Mary Margaret put on her jacket, hood and mittens, and took Uncle Martin's lantern. As she went out and closed the door, a little wail from Nellie sounded on her ear. For a moment she hesitated, then the blackness of the Big Dipper confirmed her resolution. She must go. Nellie was really quite safe and comfortable. It would not hurt her to cry a little, and it might hurt somebody a great deal if the Big Dipper light failed. Setting her lips firmly, Mary Margaret ran down to the shore.

Like all the Harbour girls, Mary Margaret could row a boat from the time she was nine years old. Nevertheless, her heart almost failed her as she got into the little dory and rowed out. The snow was getting thick. Could she pull across those black two miles between the Dippers before it got so much thicker that she would lose her way? Well, she must risk it. She had set the light in the kitchen window; she must keep it fair behind her and then she would land on the lighthouse beach. With a murmured prayer for help and guidance she pulled staunchly away.

It was a long, hard row for the little twelve-year-old arms. Fortunately there was no wind. But thicker and thicker came the snow; finally the kitchen light was hidden in it. For a moment Mary Margaret's heart sank in despair; the next it gave a joyful bound, for, turning, she saw the dark tower of the lighthouse directly behind her. By the aid of her lantern she rowed to the landing, sprang out and made her boat fast. A minute later she was in the lighthouse kitchen.

The door leading to the tower stairs was open and at the foot of the stairs lay Uncle George, limp and white.

"Oh, Uncle George," gasped Mary Margaret, "what is the matter? What has happened?"

"Mary Margaret! Thank God! I was just praying to Him to send somebody to 'tend the light. Who's with you?"

"Nobody. . . . I got frightened because there was no light and I rowed over. Mother and Uncle Martin are away."

"You don't mean to say you rowed yourself over here alone in the dark and snow! Well, you are the pluckiest little girl about this harbour! It's a mercy I've showed you how to manage the light. Run up and start it at once. Don't mind about me. I tumbled down those pesky stairs like the awkward old fool I am and I've broke my leg and hurt my back so bad I can't crawl an inch. I've been lying here for three mortal hours and they've seemed like three years. Hurry with the light, Mary Margaret."

Mary Margaret hurried. Soon the Big Dipper light was once more gleaming cheerfully athwart the stormy harbour. Then she ran back to her uncle. There was not much she could do for him beyond covering him warmly with quilts, placing a pillow under his head, and brewing him a hot drink of tea.

"I left a note for Mother telling her where I'd gone, Uncle George, so I'm sure Uncle Martin will come right over as soon as they get home."

"He'll have to hurry. It's blowing up now . . . hear it . . . and snowing thick. If your mother and Martin haven't left the Harbour Head before this, they won't leave it tonight. But, anyhow, the light is lit. I don't mind my getting smashed up compared to that. I thought I'd go crazy lying here picturing to myself a vessel out on the reefs."

That night was a very long and anxious one. The storm grew rapidly worse, and snow and wind howled around the lighthouse. Uncle George soon grew feverish and delirious, and Mary Margaret, between her anxiety for him and her dismal thoughts of poor Nellie tied in her chair over at the Little Dipper, and the dark possibility of her mother and Uncle Martin being out in the storm, felt almost distracted. But the morning came at last, as mornings blessedly will, be the nights never so long and anxious, and it dawned fine and clear over a white world. Mary Margaret ran to the shore and gazed eagerly across at the Little Dipper. No smoke was visible from Uncle Martin's house!

She could not leave Uncle George, who was raving wildly, and yet it was necessary to obtain assistance somehow. Suddenly she remembered the distress signal. She must hoist it. How fortunate that Uncle George had once shown her how!

Ten minutes later there was a commotion over at Harbour Head where the signal was promptly observed, and very soon – although it seemed long enough to Mary Margaret – a boat came sailing over to the Big Dipper. When the men landed they were met by a very white-faced little girl who gasped out a rather disjointed story of a light that hadn't been lighted and an uncle with a broken leg and a sister tied in her chair, and would they please see to Uncle George at once, for she must go straight over to the other Dipper?

One of the men rowed her over, but before they were halfway there another boat went sailing across the harbour, and Mary Margaret saw a woman and two men land from it and hurry up to the house.

That is Mother and Uncle Martin, but who can the other man be? wondered Mary Margaret.

When she reached the cottage her mother and Uncle Martin were reading her note, and Nellie, just untied from the chair where she had been found fast asleep, was in the arms of a great, big, brown, bewhiskered man. Mary Margaret just gave one look at the man. Then she flew across the room with a cry of delight.

"Father!"

For ten minutes not one intelligible word was said, what with laughing and crying and kissing. Mary Margaret was the first to recover herself and say briskly, "Now, *do* explain, somebody. Tell me how it all happened."

"Martin and I got back to Harbour Head too late last night to cross over," said her mother. "It would have been madness to try to cross in the storm, although I was nearly wild thinking of you two children. It's well I didn't know the whole truth or I'd have been simply frantic. We stayed at the Head all night, and first thing this morning came your father."

"We came in last night," said Captain Campbell, "and it was pitch dark, not a light to be seen and beginning to snow. We didn't know where we were and I was terribly worried, when all at once the Big Dipper light I'd been looking for so vainly flashed out, and everything was all right in a moment. But, Mary Margaret, if that light hadn't appeared, we'd never have got in past the reefs. You've saved your father's ship and all the lives in her, my brave little girl."

"Oh!" Mary Margaret drew a long breath and her eyes were starry with tears of happiness. "Oh, I'm so thankful I went over. And I *had* to tie Nellie in her chair, Mother, there was no other way. Uncle George broke his leg and is very sick this morning, and there's no breakfast ready for anyone and the fire black out . . . but that doesn't matter when Father is safe . . . and oh, I'm so tired!"

And then Mary Margaret sat down just for a moment, intending to get right up and help her mother light the fire, laid her head on her father's shoulder, and fell sound asleep before she ever suspected it.

An Adventure
on Island Rock,

"HO WAS THE MAN I saw talking to you in the hayfield?" asked Aunt Kate, as Uncle Richard came in to dinner.

"Bob Marks," said Uncle Richard briefly. "I've sold Laddie to him."

Ernest Hughes, the twelve-year-old orphan boy whom Uncle "boarded and kept" for the chores he did, suddenly stopped eating.

"Oh, Mr. Lawson, you're not going to sell Laddie?" he cried chokily.

Uncle Richard stared at him. Never before, in the five years that Ernest had lived with him, had the quiet little fellow spoken without being spoken to, much less ventured to protest against anything Uncle Richard might do.

"Certainly I am," answered the latter curtly. "Bob offered me twenty dollars for the dog, and he's coming after him next week."

"Oh, Mr. Lawson," said Ernest, rising to his feet, his small, freckled face crimson. "Oh, don't sell Laddie! *Please*, Mr. Lawson, don't sell him!"

"What nonsense is this?" said Uncle Richard sharply. He was a man who brooked no opposition from anybody, and who never changed his mind when it was once made up.

"Don't sell Laddie!" pleaded Ernest miserably. "He is the only friend I've got. I can't live if Laddie goes away. Oh, don't sell him, Mr. Lawson!"

"Sit down and hold your tongue," said Uncle Richard sternly. "The dog is mine, and I shall do with him as I think fit. He is sold, and that is all there is about it. Go on with your dinner."

But Ernest for the first time did not obey. He snatched his cap from the back of his chair, dashed it down over his eyes, and ran from the kitchen with a sob choking his breath. Uncle Richard looked angry, but Aunt Kate hastened to soothe him.

"Don't be vexed with the boy, Richard," she said. "You know he is very fond of Laddie. He's had to do with him ever since he was a pup, and no doubt he feels badly at the thought of losing him. I'm rather sorry myself that you have sold the dog."

"Well, he *is* sold and there's an end of it. I don't say but that the dog is a good dog. But he is of no use to us, and twenty dollars will come in mighty handy just now. He's worth that to Bob, for he is a good watch dog, so we've both made a fair bargain."

Nothing more was said about Ernest or Laddie. I had taken no part in the discussion, for I felt no great interest in the matter. Laddie was a nice dog; Ernest was a quiet, inoffensive little fellow, five years younger than myself; that was all I thought about either of them.

I was spending my vacation at Uncle Richard's farm on the Nova Scotian Bay of Fundy shore. I was a great favourite with Uncle Richard, partly because he had been much attached to my mother, his only sister, partly because of my strong resemblance to his only son, who had died several years before. Uncle Richard was a stern, undemonstrative man, but I knew that he entertained a deep and real affection for me, and I always enjoyed my vacation sojourns at his place.

"What are you going to do this afternoon, Ned?" he asked, after the disturbance caused by Ernest's outbreak had quieted down.

"I think I'll row out to Island Rock," I replied. "I want to take some views of the shore from it."

Uncle Richard nodded. He was much interested in my new camera.

"If you're on it about four o'clock, you'll get a fine view of the 'Hole in the Wall' when the sun begins to shine on the water through it," he said. "I've often thought it would make a handsome picture."

"After I've finished taking the pictures, I think I'll go down shore to Uncle Adam's and stay all night," I said. "Jim's dark room is more convenient than mine, and he has some pictures he is going to develop tonight, too."

I started for the shore about two o'clock. Ernest was sitting on the woodpile as I passed through the yard, with his arms about Laddie's neck and his face buried in Laddie's curly hair. Laddie was a handsome and intelligent black-and-white Newfoundland, with a magnificent coat. He and Ernest were great chums. I felt sorry for the boy who was to lose his pet.

"Don't take it so hard, Ern," I said, trying to comfort him. "Uncle will likely get another pup."

"I don't want any other pup!" Ernest blurted out. "Oh, Ned, won't you try and coax your uncle not to sell him? Perhaps he'd listen to you."

I shook my head. I knew Uncle Richard too well to hope that.

"Not in this case, Ern," I said. "He would say it did not concern me, and you know nothing moves him when he determines on a thing. You'll have to reconcile yourself to losing Laddie, I'm afraid."

Ernest's tow-coloured head went down on Laddie's neck again, and I, deciding that there was no use in saying anything more, proceeded towards the shore, which was about a mile from Uncle Richard's house. The beach along his farm and for several farms along shore was a lonely, untenanted one, for the fisher-folk all lived two miles further down, at Rowley's Cove. About three hundred yards from the shore was the peculiar formation known as Island Rock. This was a large rock that stood abruptly up out of the water. Below, about the usual water-line, it was seamed and fissured, but its summit rose up in a narrow, flat-topped peak. At low tide twenty feet of it was above water, but at high tide it was six feet and often more under water.

I pushed Uncle Richard's small flat down the rough path and rowed out to Island Rock. Arriving there, I thrust the painter deep into a narrow cleft. This was the usual way of mooring it, and no doubt of its safety occurred to me.

I scrambled up the rock and around to the eastern end, where there was a broader space for standing and from which some capital views could be obtained. The sea about the rock was calm, but there was quite a swell on and an off-shore breeze was blowing. There were no boats visible. The tide was low, leaving bare the curious caves and headlands along shore, and I secured a number of excellent snapshots. It was now three o'clock. I must wait another hour yet before I could get the best view of the "Hole in the Wall" – a huge, arch-like opening through a jutting headland to the west of me. I went around to look at it, when I saw a sight that made me stop short in dismay. This was nothing less than the flat, drifting outward around the point. The swell and suction of the water around the rock must have pulled her loose – and I was a prisoner! At first my only feeling was one of annoyance. Then a thought flashed into my mind that made me dizzy with fear. The tide would be high that night. If I could not escape from Island Rock I would inevitably be drowned.

I sat down limply on a ledge and tried to look matters fairly in the face. I could not swim; calls for help could not reach anybody; my only hope lay in the chance of somebody passing down the shore or of some boat appearing.

I looked at my watch. It was a quarter past three. The tide would begin to turn about five, but it would be at least ten before the rock would be covered. I had, then, little more than six hours to live unless rescued.

The flat was by this time out of sight around the point. I hoped that the sight of an empty flat drifting down shore might attract someone's attention and lead to investigation. That seemed to be my only hope. No alarm would be felt at Uncle Richard's because of my non-appearance. They would suppose I had gone to Uncle Adam's.

I have heard of time seeming long to a person in my predicament, but to me it seemed fairly to fly, for every moment decreased my chance of rescue. I determined I would not give way to cowardly fear, so, with a murmured prayer for help, I set myself to the task of waiting for death as bravely as possible. At intervals I shouted as loudly as I could and, when the sun came to the proper angle for the best view of the "Hole in the Wall," I took the picture. It afterwards turned out to be a great success, but I have never been able to look at it without a shudder.

At five the tide began to come in. Very, very slowly the water rose around Island Rock. Up, up, up it came, while I watched it with fascinated eyes, feeling like a rat in a trap. The sun fell lower and lower; at eight o'clock the moon rose large and bright; at nine it was a lovely night, clear, calm, bright as day, and the water was swishing over the highest ledge of the rock. With some difficulty I climbed to the top and sat there to await the end. I had no longer any hope of rescue but, by a great effort, I preserved self-control. If I had to die, I would at least face death staunchly. But when I thought of my mother at home, it tasked all my energies to keep from breaking down utterly.

Suddenly I heard a whistle. Never was sound so sweet. I stood up and peered eagerly shoreward. Coming around the "Hole in the Wall" headland, on top of the cliffs, I saw a boy and a dog. I sent a wild halloo ringing shoreward.

The boy started, stopped and looked out towards Island Rock. The next moment he hailed me. It was Ernest's voice, and it was Laddie who was barking beside him.

"Ernest," I shouted wildly, "run for help – quick! quick! The tide will be over the rock in half an hour! Hurry, or you will be too late!"

Instead of starting off at full speed, as I expected him to do, Ernest stood still for a moment, and then began to pick his steps down a narrow path over the cliff, followed by Laddie.

"Ernest," I shouted frantically, "what are you doing? Why don't you go for help?"

Ernest had by this time reached a narrow ledge of rock just above the water-line. I noticed that he was carrying something over his arm.

"It would take too long," he shouted. "By the time I got to the Cove and a boat could row back here, you'd be drowned. Laddie and I will save you. Is there anything there you can tie a rope to? I've a coil of rope here that I think will be long enough to reach you. I've been down to the Cove and Alec Martin sent it up to your uncle."

I looked about me; a smooth, round hole had been worn clean through a thin part of the apex of the rock.

"I could fasten the rope if I had it!" I called. "But how can you get it to me?"

For answer Ernest tied a bit of driftwood to the rope and put it into Laddie's mouth. The next minute the dog was swimming out to me. As soon as he came close I caught the rope. It was just long enough to stretch from shore to rock, allowing for a couple of hitches which Ernest gave around a small boulder on the ledge. I tied my camera case on my head by means of some string I found in my pocket, then I slipped into the water and, holding to the rope, went hand over hand to the shore with Laddie swimming beside me. Ernest held on to the shoreward end of the rope like grim death, a task that was no light one for his small arms. When I finally scrambled up beside him, his face was dripping with perspiration and he trembled like a leaf.

"Ern, you are a brick!" I exclaimed. "You've saved my life!"

"No, it was Laddie," said Ernest, refusing to take any credit at all.

We hurried home and arrived at Uncle Richard's about ten, just as they were going to bed. When Uncle Richard heard what had happened, he turned very pale, and murmured, "Thank God!" Aunt Kate got me out of my wet clothes as quickly as possible, put me away to bed in hot blankets and dosed me with ginger tea. I slept like a top and felt none the worse for my experience the next morning.

At the breakfast table Uncle Richard scarcely spoke. But, just as we finished, he said abruptly to Ernest, "I'm not going to sell Laddie. You and the dog saved Ned's life between you, and no dog who helped do that is ever going to be sold by me. Henceforth he belongs to you. I give him to you for your very own."

"Oh, Mr. Lawson!" said Ernest, with shining eyes.

I never saw a boy look so happy. As for Laddie, who was sitting beside him with his shaggy head on Ernest's knee, I really believe the dog understood, too. The look in his eyes was almost human. Uncle Richard leaned over and patted him.

"Good dog!" he said. "Good dog!"

How
Don Was Saved

ILL BARRIE went whistling down the lane of the Locksley farm, took a short cut over a field of clover aftermath and through a sloping orchard where the trees were laden with apples, and emerged into the farmhouse yard where Curtis Locksley was sitting on a pile of logs, idly whittling at a stick.

"You look as if you had a corner in time, Curt," said Will. "I call that luck, for I want you to go chestnutting up to Grier's Hill with me. I met old Tom Grier on the road yesterday, and he told me I might go any day. Nice old man, Tom Grier."

"Good!" said Curtis heartily, as he sprang up. "If I haven't exactly a corner in time, I have a day off, at least. Uncle doesn't need me today. Wait till I whistle for Don. May as well take him with us."

Curtis whistled accordingly, but Don, his handsome Newfoundland dog, did not appear. After calling and whistling about the yard and barns for several minutes, Curtis turned away disappointedly.

"He can't be anywhere around. It is very strange. Don never used to go away from home without me, but lately he has been missing several times, and twice last week he wasn't here in the morning and didn't turn up until mid-day."

"I'd keep him shut up until I broke him of the habit of playing truant, if I were you," said Will, as they turned into the lane.

"Don hates to be shut up, howls all the time so mournfully that I can't stand it," responded Curtis.

"Well," said Will, hesitatingly, "maybe that would be better after all than letting him stray away with other dogs who may teach him bad habits. I saw Don myself one evening last week ambling down the harbour road with that big brown dog of Sam Ventnor's. Ventnor's dog is beginning to have a bad reputation, you know. There have been several sheep worried lately, and – "

"Don wouldn't touch a sheep!" interrupted Curtis hotly.

"I daresay not, not yet. But Ventnor's dog is under suspicion, and if Don runs with him he'll learn the trick sure as preaching. The farmers are growling a good bit already, and if they hear of Don and Ventnor's dog going about in company, they'll put it on them both. Better keep Don shut up awhile, let him howl as he likes."

"I believe I will," said Curtis soberly. "I don't want Don to fall under suspicion of sheep-worrying, though I'm sure he would never do it. Anyhow, I don't want him to run with Ventnor's dog. I'll chain him up in the barn when I go home. I couldn't stand it if anything happened to Don. After you, he's the only chum I've got – and he's a good one."

Will agreed. He was almost as fond of Don as Curtis was. But he did not feel so sure that the dog would not worry a sheep. Will knew that Don was suspected already, but he did not like to tell Curtis so. And of course there was as yet no positive proof – merely mutterings and suggestions among the Bayside farmers who had lost sheep and were anxious to locate their slayer. There were many other dogs in Bayside and the surrounding districts who were just as likely to be the guilty animals, and Will hoped that if Don were shut up for a time, suspicion might be averted from him, especially if the worryings still went on.

He had felt a little doubtful about hinting the truth to Curtis, who was a high-spirited lad and always resented any slur cast upon Don much more bitterly than if it were meant for himself. But he knew that Curtis would take it better from him than from the other Bayside boys, one or the other of whom would be sure soon to cast something up to Curtis about his dog. Will felt decidedly relieved to find that Curtis took his advice in the spirit in which it was offered.

"Who have lost sheep lately?" queried Curtis, as they left the main road and struck into a wood path through the ranks of beeches on Tom Grier's land.

"Nearly everybody on the Hollow farms," answered Will. "Until last week nobody on the Hill farms had lost any. But Tuesday night old Paul Stockton had six fine sheep killed in his upland pasture behind the fir woods. He is furious about it, I believe, and vows he'll find out what dog did it and have him shot."

Curtis looked grave. Paul Stockton's farm was only about a quarter of a mile from the Locksley homestead, and he knew that Paul had an old family grudge against his Uncle Arnold, which included his nephew and all belonging to him. Moreover, Curtis remembered with a sinking heart that Wednesday morning had been one of the mornings upon which Don was missing.

"But I don't care!" he thought miserably. "I know Don didn't kill those sheep."

"Talking of old Paul," said Will, who thought it advisable to turn the conversation, "reminds me that they are getting anxious at the Harbour about George Finley's schooner, the *Amy Reade*. She was due three days ago and there's no sign of her yet. And there have been two bad gales since she left Morro. Oscar Stockton is on board of her, you know, and his father is worried about him. There are five other men on her, all from the Harbour, and their folks down there are pretty wild about the schooner."

Nothing more was said about the sheep, and soon, in the pleasures of chestnutting, Curtis forgot his anxiety. Old Tom Grier had called to the boys as they passed his house to come back and have dinner there when the time came. This they did, and it was late in the afternoon when

Curtis, with his bag of chestnuts over his shoulder, walked into the Locksley yard.

His uncle was standing before the open barn doors, talking to an elderly, grizzled man with a thin, shrewd face.

Curtis' heart sank as he recognized old Paul Stockton. What could have brought him over?

"Curtis," called his uncle, "come here."

As Curtis crossed the yard, Don came bounding down the slope from the house to meet him. He put his hand on the dog's big head and the two of them walked slowly to the barn. Old Paul included them both in a vindictive scowl.

"Curtis," said his uncle gravely, "here's a bad business. Mr. Stockton tells me that your dog has been worrying his sheep."

"It's a – " began Curtis angrily. Then he checked himself and went on more calmly.

"That can't be so, Mr. Stockton. My dog would not harm anything."

"He killed or helped to kill six of the finest sheep in my flock!" retorted old Paul.

"What proof have you of it?" demanded Curtis, trying to keep his anger within bounds.

"Abner Peck saw your dog and Ventnor's running together through my sheep pasture at sundown on Tuesday evening," answered old Paul. "Wednesday morning I found this in the corner of the pasture where the sheep were worried. Your uncle admits that it was tied around your dog's neck on Tuesday."

And old Paul held out triumphantly a faded red ribbon. Curtis recognized it at a glance. It was the ribbon his little cousin, Lena, had tied around Don's neck Tuesday afternoon. He remembered how they had laughed at the effect of that frivolous red collar and bow on Don's massive body.

"I'm sure Don isn't guilty!" he cried passionately.

Mr. Locksley shook his head.

"I'm afraid he is, Curtis. The case looks very black against him, and sheep-stealing is a serious offence."

"The dog must be shot," said old Paul decidedly. "I leave the matter in your hands, Mr. Locksley. I've got enough proof to convict the dog and, if you don't have him killed, I'll make you pay for the sheep he worried."

As old Paul strode away, Curtis looked beseechingly at his uncle.

"Don mustn't be shot, Uncle!" he said desperately. "I'll chain him up all the time."

"And have him howling night and day as if we had a brood of banshees about the place?" said Mr. Locksley sarcastically. He was a stern man with little sentiment in his nature and no understanding whatever of Curtis' affection for Don. The Bayside people said that Arnold Locksley had always been very severe with his nephew. "No, no, Curtis, you must look at the matter sensibly. The dog is a nuisance and must be shot. You can't keep him shut up forever, and, if he has once learned the trick of sheep-worrying, he will never forget it. You can get another dog if you must have one. I'll get Charles Pippey to come and shoot Don tomorrow. No sulking now, Curtis. You are too big a boy for that. Tie the dog up for the night and then go and put the calves in. There is a storm coming. The wind is blowing hard from the northeast now."

His uncle walked away, leaving the boy white and miserable in the yard. He looked at Don, who sat on his haunches and returned his gaze frankly and open-heartedly. He did not look like a guilty dog. Could it be possible that he had really worried those sheep?

"I'll never believe it of you, old fellow!" Curtis said, as he led the dog into a corner of the carriage house and tied him up there. Then he flung himself down on a pile of sacks beside him and buried his face in Don's curly black fur. The boy felt sullen, rebellious and wretched.

He lay there until dark, thinking his own bitter thoughts and listening to the rapidly increasing gale. Finally he got up and flung off after the calves, with Don's melancholy howls at finding himself deserted ringing in his ears.

He'll be quiet enough tomorrow night, thought Curtis wretchedly, as he went upstairs to bed after housing the calves. For a long while he lay awake, but finally dropped into a heavy slumber which lasted until his aunt called him for milking.

The wind was blowing more furiously than ever. Up over the fields came the roar and crash of the surges on the outside shore. The Harbour to the east of Bayside was rough and stormy.

They were just rising from breakfast when Will Barrie burst into the kitchen.

"The *Amy Reade* is ashore on Gleeson's rocks!" he shouted. "Struck there at daylight this morning! Come on, Curt!"

Curtis sprang for his cap, his uncle following suit more deliberately. As the two boys ran through the yard, Curtis heard Don howling.

"I'll take him with me!" he muttered. "Wait a minute, Will."

The Harbour road was thronged with people hurrying to the outside shore, for the news of the *Amy Reade*'s disaster had spread rapidly. As the boys, with the rejoicing Don at their heels, pelted along, Sam Morrow overtook them in a cart and told them to jump in. Sam had already been down to the shore and had gone back to tell his father. As they jolted along, he screamed information at them over the shriek of the gale.

"Bad business, this! She's pounding on a reef 'bout a

quarter of a mile out. They're sure she's going to break up – old tub, you know – leaky – rotten. The sea's tremenjus high, and the surf's going clean over her. There can't be no boat launched for hours yet – they'll all be drowned. Old Paul's down there like a madman – offering everything he's got to the man who'll save Oscar, but it can't be done."

By this time they had reached the shore, which was black with excited people. Out on Gleeson's Reef the ill-fated little schooner was visible amid the flying spray. A grizzled old Harbour fisherman, to whom Sam shouted a question, shook his head.

"No, can't do nothin'! No boat c'd live in that surf f'r a moment. The schooner'll go to pieces mighty soon, I'm feared. It's turrible! turrible! to stan' by an' watch yer neighbours drown like this!"

Curtis and Will elbowed their way down to the water's edge. The relatives of the crew were all there in various stages of despair, but old Paul Stockton seemed like a man demented. He ran up and down the beach, crying and praying. His only son was on the *Amy Reade*, and he could do nothing to save him!

"What are they doing?" asked Will of Martin Clark.

"Trying to get a line ashore by throwing out a small rope with a stick tied to it," answered Martin. "It's young Stockton that's trying now. But it isn't any use. The cross-currents on that reef are too powerful."

"Why, Don will bring that line ashore!" exclaimed Curtis. "Here, Don! Don, I say!"

The dog bounded back along the shore with a quick bark. Curtis grasped him by the collar and pointed to the stick which young Stockton had just hurled again into the water. Don, with another bark of comprehension, dashed into the sea. The onlookers, grasping the situation, gave a cheer and then relapsed into silence. Only the shriek of the gale and the crash of the waves could be heard as they watched the magnificent dog swimming out through the breakers, his big black head now rising on the crest of a wave and now disappearing in the hollow behind it. When Don finally reached the tossing stick, grasped it in his mouth and turned shoreward, another great shout went up from the beach. A woman behind Curtis, whose husband was on the schooner, dropped on her knees on the pebbles, sobbing and thanking God. Curtis himself felt the stinging tears start to his eyes.

When Don reached the shore he dropped the stick at Curtis' feet and gave himself a tremendous shake. Curtis caught at the stick, while a dozen men and women threw themselves bodily on Don, hugging him and kissing his wet fur like distracted creatures. Old Paul Stockton was among them. Over his shoulder Don's big black head looked up, his eyes asking as plainly as speech what all this fuss was about.

Meanwhile some of the men had already pulled a big hawser ashore and made it fast. In half an hour the crew of the *Amy Reade* were safe on shore, chilled and dripping. Before they were hurried away to warmth and shelter, old Paul Stockton caught Curtis' hand. The tears were running freely down his hard, old face.

"Tell your uncle he is not to lay a finger on that dog!" he said. "He never killed a sheep of mine – he couldn't! And if he did I don't care! He's welcome to kill them all, if nothing but mutton'll serve his turn."

Curtis walked home with a glad heart. Mr. Locksley heard old Paul's message with a smile. He, too, had been touched by Don's splendid feat.

"Well, Curtis, I'm very glad that it has turned old Paul in his favour. But we must shut Don up for a week or so, no matter how hard he takes it. You can see that for yourself. After all, he might have worried the sheep. And, anyway, he must be broken of his intimacy with Ventnor's dog."

Curtis acknowledged the justice of this and poor Don was tied up again. His captivity was not long, however, for Ventnor's dog was soon shot. When Don was released, Curtis had an anxious time for a week or two. But no more sheep were worried, and Don's innocence was triumphantly established. As for old Paul Stockton, it seemed as if he could not do enough for Curtis and Don. His ancient grudge against the Locksleys was completely forgotten, and from that date he was a firm friend of Curtis. In regard to Don, old Paul would say:

"Why, there never was such a dog before, sir, never! He just talks with his eyes, that dog does. And if you'd just 'a' seen him swimming out to that schooner! Bones? Yes, sir! Every time that dog comes here he's to get the best bones we've got for him – and more'n bones, too. That dog's a hero, sir, that's what he is!"

A Soul That
Was Not at Home

HERE WAS a very fine sunset on the night Paul and Miss Trevor first met, and she had lingered on the headland beyond Noel's Cove to delight in it. The west was splendid in daffodil and rose; away to the north there was a mackerel sky of little fiery golden clouds; and across the water straight from Miss Trevor's feet ran a sparkling path of light to the sun, whose rim had just touched the throbbing edge of the purple sea. Off to the left were softly swelling violet hills and beyond the sandshore, where little waves were crisping and silvering, there was a harbour where scores of slender masts were nodding against the gracious horizon.

Miss Trevor sighed with sheer happiness in all the wonderful, fleeting, elusive loveliness of sky and sea. Then she turned to look back at Noel's Cove, dim and shadowy in the gloom of the tall headlands, and she saw Paul.

It did not occur to her that he could be a shore boy – she knew the shore type too well. She thought his coming mysterious, for she was sure he had not come along the sand, and the tide was too high for him to have come past the other headland. Yet there he was, sitting on a red sandstone boulder, with his bare, bronzed, shapely little legs crossed in front of him and his hands clasped around his knee. He was not looking at Miss Trevor but at the sunset – or, rather, it seemed as if he were looking through the sunset to still grander and more radiant splendours beyond, of which the things seen were only the pale reflections, not worthy of attention from those who had the gift of further sight.

Miss Trevor looked him over carefully with eyes that had seen a good many people in many parts of the world for more years than she found it altogether pleasant to acknowledge, and she concluded that he was quite the handsomest lad she had ever seen. He had a lithe, supple body, with sloping shoulders and a brown, satin throat. His hair was thick and wavy, of a fine reddish chestnut; his brows were very straight and much darker than his hair; and his eyes were large and grey and meditative. The modelling of chin and jaw was perfect and his mouth was delicious, being full without pouting, the crimson lips just softly touching, and curving into finely finished little corners that narrowly escaped being dimpled.

His attire was a blue cotton shirt and a pair of scanty corduroy knickerbockers, but he wore it with such an unconscious air of purple and fine linen that Miss Trevor was tricked into believing him much better dressed than he really was.

Presently he smiled dreamily, and the smile completed her subjugation. It was not merely an affair of lip and eye, as are most smiles; it seemed an illumination of his whole body, as if some lamp had suddenly burst into flame inside of him, irradiating him from his chestnut crown to the tips of his unspoiled toes. Best of all, it was involuntary, born of no external effort or motive, but simply the outflashing of some wild, delicious thought that was as untrammelled and freakish as the wind of the sea.

Miss Trevor made up her mind that she must find out all about him, and she stepped out from the shadows of the rocks into the vivid, eerie light that was glowing all along the shore. The boy turned his head and looked at her, first with surprise, then with inquiry, then with admiration. Miss Trevor, in a white dress with a lace scarf on her dark, stately head, was well worth admiring. She smiled at him and Paul smiled back. It was not quite up to his first smile, having more of the effect of being put on from the outside, but at least it conveyed the subtly flattering impression that it had been put on solely for her, and they were as good friends from that moment as if they had known each other for a hundred years. Miss Trevor had enough discrimination to realize this and know that she need not waste time in becoming acquainted.

"I want to know your name and where you live and what you were looking at beyond the sunset," she said.

"My name is Paul Hubert. I live over there. And I can't tell just what I saw in the sunset, but when I go home I'm going to write it all in my foolscap book."

In her surprise over the second clause of his answer, Miss Trevor forgot, at first, to appreciate the last. "Over there," according to his gesture, was up at the head of Noel's Cove, where there was a little grey house perched on the rocks and looking like a large seashell cast up by the tide. The house had a stovepipe coming out of its roof in lieu of a chimney, and two of its window panes were replaced by shingles. Could this boy, who looked as young princes should – and seldom do – live there? Then he was a shore boy after all.

"Who lives there with you?" she asked. "You see" – plaintively – "I must ask questions about you. I know we like each other, and that is all that really matters. But there are some tiresome items which it would be convenient to know. For example, have you a father – a mother? Are there any more of you? How long have you been yourself?"

Paul did not reply immediately. He clasped his hands behind him and looked at her affectionately.

"I like the way you talk," he said. "I never knew anybody did talk like that except folks in books and my rock people."

"Your rock people?"

"I'm eleven years old. I haven't any father or mother, they're dead. I live over there with Stephen Kane. Stephen is splendid. He plays the violin and takes me fishing in his boat. When I get bigger he's going shares with me. I love him, and I love my rock people too."

"What do you mean by your rock people?" asked Miss

Trevor, enjoying herself hugely. This was the only child she had ever met who talked as she wanted children to talk and who understood her remarks without having to have them translated.

"Nora is one of them," said Paul, "the best one of them. I love her better than all the others because she came first. She lives around that point and she has black eyes and black hair and she knows all about the mermaids and water kelpies. You ought to hear the stories she can tell. Then there are the Twin Sailors. They don't live anywhere – they sail all the time, but they often come ashore to talk to me. They are a pair of jolly tars and they have seen everything in the world – and more than what's in the world, if you only knew it. Do you know what happened to the Youngest Twin Sailor once? He was sailing and he sailed right into a moonglade. A moonglade is the track the full moon makes on the water when it is rising from the sea, you know. Well, the Youngest Twin Sailor sailed along the moonglade till he came right up to the moon, and there was a little golden door in the moon and he opened it and sailed right through. He had some wonderful adventures inside the moon – I've got them all written down in my foolscap book. Then there is the Golden Lady of the Cave. One day I found a big cave down the shore and I went in and in and in – and after a while I found the Golden Lady. She has golden hair right down to her feet, and her dress is all glittering and glistening like gold that is alive. And she has a golden harp and she plays all day long on it – you might hear the music if you'd listen carefully, but prob'bly you'd think it was only the wind among the rocks. I've never told Nora about the Golden Lady, because I think it would hurt her feelings. It even hurts her feelings when I talk too long with the Twin Sailors. And I hate to hurt Nora's feelings, because I do love her best of all my rock people."

"Paul! How much of this is true?" gasped Miss Trevor.

"Why, none of it!" said Paul, opening his eyes widely and reproachfully. "I thought you would know that. If I'd s'posed you wouldn't I'd have warned you there wasn't any of it true. I thought you were one of the kind that would know."

"I am. Oh, I am!" said Miss Trevor eagerly. "I really would have known if I had stopped to think. Well, it's getting late now. I must go back, although I don't want to. But I'm coming to see you again. Will you be here tomorrow afternoon?"

Paul nodded.

"Yes. I promised to meet the Youngest Twin Sailor down at the striped rocks tomorrow afternoon, but the day after will do just as well. That is the beauty of the rock people, you know. You can always depend on them to be there just when you want them. The Youngest Twin Sailor won't mind – he's very good-tempered. If it was the Oldest Twin I dare say he'd be cross. I have my suspicions about that Oldest Twin sometimes. I b'lieve he'd be a pirate if he dared. You don't know how fierce he can look at times. There's really something very mysterious about him."

On her way back to the hotel Miss Trevor remembered the foolscap book.

"I must get him to show it to me," she mused, smiling. "Why, the boy is a born genius – and to think he should be a shore boy! I can't understand it. And here I am loving him already. Well, a woman has to love something – and you don't have to know people for years before you can love them."

Paul was waiting on the Noel's Cove rocks for Miss Trevor the next afternoon. He was not alone; a tall man, with a lined, strong-featured face and a grey beard, was with him. The man was clad in a rough suit and looked what he was, a 'longshore fisherman. But he had deep-set,

127

kindly eyes, and Miss Trevor liked his face. He moved off to one side when she came and stood there for a little, apparently gazing out to sea, while Paul and Miss Trevor talked. Then he walked away up the cove and disappeared in his little grey house.

"Stephen came down to see if you were a suitable person for me to talk to," said Paul gravely.

"I hope he thinks I am," said Miss Trevor, amused.

"Oh, he does! He wouldn't have gone away and left us alone if he didn't. Stephen is very particular who he lets me 'sociate with. Why, even the rock people now – I had to promise I'd never let the Twin Sailors swear before he'd allow me to be friends with them. Sometimes I know by the look of the Oldest Twin that he's just dying to swear, but I never let him, because I promised Stephen. I'd do anything for Stephen. He's awful good to me. Stephen's bringing me up, you know, and he's bound to do it well. We're just perfectly happy here, only I wish I'd more books to read. We go fishing, and when we come home at night I help Stephen clean the fish and then we sit outside the door and he plays the violin for me. We sit there for hours sometimes. We never talk much – Stephen isn't much of a hand for talking – but we just sit and think. There's not many men like Stephen, I can tell you."

Miss Trevor did not get a glimpse of the foolscap book that day, nor for many days after. Paul blushed all over his beautiful face whenever she mentioned it.

"Oh, I couldn't show you that," he said uncomfortably. "Why, I've never even showed it to Stephen – or Nora. Let me tell you something else instead, something that happened to me once long ago. You'll find it more interesting than the foolscap book, only you must remember it isn't true! You won't forget that, will you?"

"I'll try to remember," Miss Trevor agreed.

"Well, I was sitting here one evening just like I was last

night, and the sun was setting. And an enchanted boat came sailing over the sea and I got into her. The boat was all pearly like the inside of the mussel shells, and her sail was like moonshine. Well, I sailed right across to the sunset. Think of that – I've been in the sunset! And what do you suppose it is? The sunset is a land all flowers, like a great garden, and the clouds are beds of flowers. We sailed into a great big harbour, a thousand times bigger than the harbour over there at your hotel, and I stepped out of the boat on a 'normous meadow all roses. I stayed there for ever so long. It seemed almost a year, but the Youngest Twin Sailor says I was only away a few hours or so. You see, in Sunset Land the time is ever so much longer than it is here. But I was glad to come back too. I'm always glad to come back to the cove and Stephen. Now, you know this never really happened."

Miss Trevor would not give up the foolscap book so easily, but for a long time Paul refused to show it to her. She came to the cove every day, and every day Paul seemed more delightful to her. He was so quaint, so clever, so spontaneous. Yet there was nothing premature or unnatural about him. He was wholly boy, fond of fun and frolic, not too good for little spurts of quick temper now and again, though, as he was careful to explain to Miss Trevor, he never showed them to a lady.

"I get real mad with the Twin Sailors sometimes, and even with Stephen, for all he's so good to me. But I couldn't be mad with you or Nora or the Golden Lady. It would never do."

Every day he had some new story to tell of a wonderful adventure on rock or sea, always taking the precaution of assuring her beforehand that it wasn't true. The boy's fancy was like a prism, separating every ray that fell upon it into rainbows. He was passionately fond of the shore and water. The only world for him beyond Noel's Cove was the world of his imagination. He had no companions except Stephen and the "rock people."

"And now you," he told Miss Trevor. "I love you too, but I know you'll be going away before long, so I don't let myself love you as much – quite – as Stephen and the rock people."

"But you could, couldn't you?" pleaded Miss Trevor. "If you and I were to go on being together every day, you could love me just as well as you love them, couldn't you?"

Paul considered in a charming way he had.

"Of course I could love you better than the Twin Sailors and the Golden Lady," he announced finally. "And I think perhaps I could love you as much as I love Stephen. But not as much as Nora – oh, no, I wouldn't love you quite as much as Nora. She was first, you see; she's always been there. I feel sure I couldn't ever love anybody as much as Nora."

One day when Stephen was out to the mackerel grounds, Paul took Miss Trevor into the little grey house and showed her his treasures. They climbed the ladder in one corner to the loft where Paul slept. The window of it, small and square-paned, looked seaward, and the moan of the sea and the pipe of the wind sounded there night and day. Paul had many rare shells and seaweeds, curious flotsam and jetsam of shore storms, and he had a small shelf full of books.

"They're splendid," he said enthusiastically. "Stephen brought me them all. Every time Stephen goes to town to ship his mackerel he brings me home a new book."

"Were you ever in town yourself?" asked Miss Trevor.

"Oh, yes, twice. Stephen took me. It was a wonderful place. I tell you, when I next met the Twin Sailors it was me did the talking then. I had to tell them about all I saw and all that had happened. And Nora was ever so interested too. The Golden Lady wasn't, though – she didn't hardly listen. Golden people are like that."

"Would you like," said Miss Trevor, watching him closely, "to live always in a town and have all the books you wanted and play with real girls and boys – and visit those strange lands your twin sailors tell you of?"

Paul looked startled.

"I – don't – know," he said doubtfully. "I don't think I'd like it very well if Stephen and Nora weren't there too."

But the new thought remained in his mind. It came back to him at intervals, seeming less new and startling every time.

"And why not?" Miss Trevor asked herself. "The boy should have a chance. I shall never have a son of my own – he shall be to me in the place of one."

The day came when Paul at last showed her the foolscap book. He brought it to her as she sat on the rocks of the headland.

"I'm going to run around and talk to Nora while you read it," he said. "I'm afraid I've been neglecting her lately – and I think she feels it."

Miss Trevor took the foolscap book. It was made of several sheets of paper sewed together and encased in an oilcloth cover. It was nearly filled with writing in a round childish hand and it was very neat, although the orthography was rather wild and the punctuation capricious. Miss Trevor read it through in no very long time. It was a curious medley of quaint thoughts and fancies. Conversations with the Twin Sailors filled many of the pages; accounts of Paul's "adventures" occupied others. Sometimes it seemed impossible that a child of eleven should have written them, then would come an expression so boyish and naive that Miss Trevor laughed delightedly over it. When she finished the book and closed it she

found Stephen Kane at her elbow. He removed his pipe
and nodded at the foolscap book.

"What do you think of it?" he said.

"I think it is wonderful. Paul is a very clever child."

"I've often thought so," said Stephen laconically. He
thrust his hands into his pockets and gazed moodily out
to sea. Miss Trevor had never before had an opportunity
to talk to him in Paul's absence and she determined to
make the most of it.

"I want to know something about Paul," she said, "all
about him. Is he any relation to you?"

"No. I expected to marry his mother once, though," said
Stephen unemotionally. His hand in his pocket was
clutching his pipe fiercely, but Miss Trevor could not
know that. "She was a shore girl and very pretty. Well, she
fell in love with a young fellow that came teaching up t'
the harbour school and he with her. They got married and
she went away with him. He was a good enough sort of
chap. I know that now, though once I wasn't disposed to
think much good of him. But 'twas a mistake all the same.
Rachel couldn't live away from the shore. She fretted and
pined and broke her heart for it away there in his world.
Finally her husband died and she came back – but it was
too late for her. She only lived a month – and there was
Paul, a baby of two. I took him. There was nobody else.
Rachel had no relatives nor her husband either. I've done
what I could for him – not that it's been much, perhaps."

"I am sure you have done a great deal for him," said
Miss Trevor rather patronizingly. "But I think he should
have more than you can give him now. He should be sent
to school."

Stephen nodded.

"Maybe. He never went to school. The harbour school
was too far away. I taught him to read and write and

bought him all the books I could afford. But I can't do any more for him."

"But I can," said Miss Trevor, "and I want to. Will you give Paul to me, Mr. Kane? I love him dearly and he shall have every advantage. I'm rich – I can do a great deal for him."

Stephen continued to gaze out to sea with an expressionless face. Finally he said: "I've been expecting to hear you say something of the sort. I don't know. If you took Paul away, he'd grow to be a cleverer man and a richer man maybe, but would he be any better – or happier? He's his mother's son – he loves the sea and its ways. There's nothing of his father in him except his hankering after books. But I won't choose for him – he can go if he likes – he can go if he likes."

In the end Paul "liked," since Stephen refused to influence him by so much as a word. Paul thought Stephen didn't seem to care much whether he went or stayed, and he was dazzled by Miss Trevor's charm and the lure of books and knowledge she held out to him.

"I'll go, I guess," he said, with a long sigh.

Miss Trevor clasped him close to her and kissed him maternally. Paul kissed her cheek shyly in return. He thought it very wonderful that he was to live with her always. He felt happy and excited – so happy and excited that the parting when it came slipped over him lightly. Miss Trevor even thought he took it too easily and had a vague wish that he had shown more sorrow. Stephen said farewell to the boy he loved better than life with no visible emotion.

"Good-bye, Paul. Be a good boy and learn all you can." He hesitated a moment and then said slowly, "If you don't like it, come back."

"Did you bid good-bye to your rock people?" Miss Trevor asked him with a smile as they drove away.

"No. I – couldn't – I – I – didn't even tell them I was going away. Nora would break her heart. I'd rather not talk of them anymore, if you please. Maybe I won't want them when I've plenty of books and lots of other boys and girls – real ones – to play with."

They drove the ten miles to the town where they were to take the train the next day. Paul enjoyed the drive and the sights of the busy streets at its end. He was all excitement and animation. After they had had tea at the house of the friend where Miss Trevor meant to spend the night, they went for a walk in the park. Paul was tired and very quiet when they came back. He was put away to sleep in a bedroom whose splendours frightened him, and left alone.

At first Paul lay very still on his luxurious perfumed pillows. It was the first night he had ever spent away from the little seaward-looking loft where he could touch the rafters with his hands. He thought of it now and a lump came into his throat and a strange, new, bitter longing came into his heart. He missed the sea plashing on the rocks below him – he could not sleep without that old lullaby. He turned his face into the pillow, and the longing and loneliness grew worse and hurt him until he moaned. Oh, he wanted to be back home! Surely he had not left it – he could never have meant to leave it. Out there the stars would be shining over the harbour. Stephen would be sitting at the door, all alone, with his violin. But he would not be playing it – all at once Paul knew he would not be playing it. He would be sitting there with his head bowed and the loneliness in his heart calling to the loneliness in Paul's heart over all the miles between them. Oh, he could never have really meant to leave Stephen.

And Nora? Nora would be down on the rocks waiting for him – for him, Paul, who would never come to her more.

He could see her elfin little face peering around the point, watching for him wistfully.

Paul sat up in bed, choking with tears. Oh, what were books and strange countries? – what was even Miss Trevor, the friend of a month? – to the call of the sea and Stephen's kind, deep eyes and his dear rock people? He could not stay away from them – never – never.

He slipped out of bed very softly and dressed in the dark. Then he lighted the lamp timidly and opened the little brown chest Stephen had given him. It held his books and his treasures, but he took out only a pencil, a bit of paper and the foolscap book. With a hand shaking in his eagerness, he wrote:

dear miss Trever
Im going back home, dont be fritened about me because I know the way. Ive got to go. something is calling me. dont be cross. I love you, but I cant stay. Im leaving my foolscap book for you, you can keep it always but I must go back to stephen and nora

Paul

He put the note on the foolscap book and laid them on the table. Then he blew out the light, took his cap and went softly out. The house was very still. Holding his breath, he tiptoed downstairs and opened the front door. Before it ran the street which went, he knew, straight out to the country road that led home. Paul closed the door and stole down the steps, his heart beating painfully, but when he reached the sidewalk he broke into a frantic run under the limes. It was late and no one was out on that quiet street. He ran until his breath gave out, then walked miserably until he recovered it, and then ran again. He dared not stop running until he was out of that horrible town, which seemed like a prison closing around him, where the houses shut out the stars and the wind could only creep in a narrow space like a fettered, cringing thing, instead of sweeping grandly over great salt wastes of sea.

At last the houses grew few and scattered, and finally he left them behind. He drew a long breath; this was better – rather smothering yet, of course, with nothing but hills and fields and dark woods all about him, but at least his own sky was above him, looking just the same as it looked out home at Noel's Cove. He recognized the stars as friends; how often Stephen had pointed them out to him as they sat at night by the door of the little house.

He was not at all frightened now. He knew the way home and the kind night was before him. Every step was bringing him nearer to Stephen and Nora and the Twin Sailors. He whistled as he walked sturdily along.

The dawn was just breaking when he reached Noel's Cove. The eastern sky was all pale rose and silver, and the sea was mottled over with dear grey ripples. In the west over the harbour the sky was a very fine ethereal blue and the wind blew from there, salt and bracing. Paul was tired, but he ran lightly down the shelving rocks to the cove. Stephen was getting ready to launch his boat. When he saw Paul he started and a strange, vivid, exultant expression flashed across his face.

Paul felt a sudden chill – the upspringing fountain of his gladness was checked in mid-leap. He had known no doubt on the way home – all that long, weary walk he had known no doubt – but now?

"Stephen," he cried. "I've come back! I had to! Stephen, are you glad – are you glad?"

Stephen's face was as emotionless as ever. The burst of feeling which had frightened Paul by its unaccustomedness had passed like a fleeting outbreak of sunshine between dull clouds.

"I reckon I am," he said. "Yes, I reckon I am. I kind of –
hoped – you would come back. You'd better go in and get
some breakfast."

Paul's eyes were as radiant as the deepening dawn. He
knew Stephen was glad and he knew there was nothing
more to be said about it. They were back just where they
were before Miss Trevor came – back in their perfect,
unmarred, sufficient comradeship.

"I must just run around and see Nora first," said Paul.

Four Winds

ALAN DOUGLAS threw down his pen with an impatient exclamation. It was high time his next Sunday's sermon was written, but he could not concentrate his thoughts on his chosen text. For one thing he did not like it and had selected it only because Elder Trewin, in his call of the evening before, had hinted that it was time for a good stiff doctrinal discourse, such as his predecessor in Rexton, the Rev. Jabez Strong, had delighted in. Alan hated doctrines – "the soul's stay-laces," he called them – but Elder Trewin was a man to be reckoned with and Alan preached an occasional sermon to please him.

"It's no use," he said wearily. "I could have written a sermon in keeping with that text in November or midwinter, but now, when the whole world is reawakening in a miracle of beauty and love, I can't do it. If a northeast rainstorm doesn't set in before next Sunday, Mr. Trewin will not have his sermon. I shall take as my text instead, 'The flowers appear on the earth, the time of the singing of birds has come.' "

He rose and went to his study window, outside of which a young vine was glowing in soft tender green tints, its small dainty leaves casting quivering shadows on the opposite wall where the portrait of Alan's mother hung. She had a fine, strong, sweet face; the same face, cast in a masculine mould, was repeated in her son, and the resemblance was striking as he stood in the searching evening sunshine. The black hair grew around his forehead in the same way; his eyes were steel blue, like hers, with a similar expression, half brooding, half tender, in their depths. He had the mobile, smiling mouth of the picture, but his chin was deeper and squarer, dented with a dimple which, combined with a certain occasional whimsicality of opinion and glance, had caused Elder Trewin some qualms of doubt regarding the fitness of this young man for his high and holy vocation. The Rev. Jabez Strong had never indulged in dimples or jokes; but then, as Elder Trewin, being a just man, had to admit, the Rev. Jabez Strong had preached many a time and oft to more empty pews than full ones, while now the church was crowded to its utmost capacity on Sundays and people came to hear Mr. Douglas who had not darkened a church door for years. All things considered, Elder Trewin decided to overlook the dimple. There was sure to be some drawback in every minister.

Alan from his study looked down on all the length of the Rexton valley, at the head of which the manse was situated, and thought that Eden might have looked so in its innocence, for all the orchards were abloom and the distant hills were tremulous and aerial in springtime gauzes of pale purple and pearl. But in any garden, despite its beauty, is an element of tameness and domesticity, and Alan's eyes, after a moment's delighted gazing, strayed wistfully off to the north where the hills broke away into a long sloping lowland of pine and fir. Beyond it stretched the wide expanse of the lake, flashing in the molten gold and crimson of evening. Its lure was irresistible. Alan had been born and bred beside a faraway sea and the love of it was strong in his heart – so strong that he knew he must go back to it sometime. Meanwhile, the great lake, mimicking the sea in its vast expanse and the storms that often swept over it, was his comfort and solace. As often as he could he stole away to its wild and lonely shore, leaving the snug bounds of cultivated home lands behind him with something like a sense of relief. Down there by the lake was a primitive wilderness where man was as naught and man-made doctrines had no place. There one might walk hand in hand with nature and so come very close to God. Many of Alan's best ser-

mons were written after he had come home, rapt-eyed,
from some long shore tramp where the wilderness had
opened its heart to him and the pines had called to him in
their soft, sibilant speech.

With a half guilty glance at the futile sermon, he took his
hat and went out. The sun of the cool spring evening was
swinging low over the lake as he turned into the unfre-
quented, deep-rutted road leading to the shore. It was two
miles to the lake, but half way there Alan came to where
another road branched off and struck down through the
pines in a northeasterly direction. He had sometimes
wondered where it led but he had never explored it. Now
he had a sudden whim to do so and turned into it. It was
even rougher and lonelier than the other; between the
ruts the grasses grew long and thickly; sometimes the
pine boughs met overhead; again, the trees broke away to
reveal wonderful glimpses of gleaming water, purple
islets, dark feathery coasts. Still, the road seemed to lead
nowhere and Alan was half repenting the impulse which
had led him to choose it when he suddenly came out from
the shadow of the pines and found himself gazing on a
sight which amazed him.

Before him was a small peninsula running out into the
lake and terminating in a long sandy point. Beyond it was
a glorious sweep of sunset water. The peninsula itself
seemed barren and sandy, covered for the most part with
scrub firs and spruces, through which the narrow road
wound on to what was the astonishing feature in the
landscape – a grey and weather-beaten house built almost
at the extremity of the point and shadowed from the
western light by a thick plantation of tall pines behind it.

It was the house which puzzled Alan. He had never
known there was any house near the lake shore – had
never heard mention made of any; yet here was one, and
one which was evidently occupied, for a slender spiral of

smoke was curling upward from it on the chilly spring air. It could not be a fisherman's dwelling, for it was large and built after a quaint tasteful design. The longer Alan looked at it the more his wonder grew. The people living here were in the bounds of his congregation. How then was it that he had never seen or heard of them?

He sauntered slowly down the road until he saw that it led directly to the house and ended in the yard. Then he turned off in a narrow path to the shore. He was not far from the house now and he scanned it observantly as he went past. The barrens swept almost up to its door in front but at the side, sheltered from the lake winds by the pines, was a garden where there was a fine show of gay tulips and golden daffodils. No living creature was visible and, in spite of the blossoming geraniums and muslin curtains at the windows and the homely spiral of smoke, the place had a lonely, almost untenanted, look.

When Alan reached the shore he found that it was of a much more open and less rocky nature than the part which he had been used to frequent. The beach was of sand and the scrub barrens dwindled down to it almost insensibly. To right and left fir-fringed points ran out into the lake, shaping a little cove with the house in its curve.

Alan walked slowly towards the left headland, intending to follow the shore around to the other road. As he passed the point he stopped short in astonishment. The second surprise and mystery of the evening confronted him.

A little distance away a girl was standing – a girl who turned a startled face at his unexpected appearance. Alan Douglas had thought he knew all the girls in Rexton, but this lithe, glorious creature was a stranger to him. She stood with her hand on the head of a huge, tawny collie dog; another dog was sitting on his haunches beside her.

She was tall, with a great braid of shining chestnut hair,

showing ruddy burnished tints where the sunlight struck it, hanging over her shoulder. The plain dark dress she wore emphasized the grace and strength of her supple form. Her face was oval and pale, with straight black brows and a finely cut crimson mouth – a face whose beauty bore the indefinable stamp of race and breeding mingled with a wild sweetness, as of a flower growing in some lonely and inaccessible place. None of the Rexton girls looked like that. Who, in the name of all that was amazing, could she be?

As the thought crossed Alan's mind the girl turned, with an air of indifference that might have seemed slightly overdone to a calmer observer than was the young minister at that moment and, with a gesture of command to her dogs, walked quickly away into the scrub spruces. She was so tall that her uncovered head was visible over them as she followed some winding footpath, and Alan stood like a man rooted to the ground until he saw her enter the grey house. Then he went homeward in a maze, all thought of sermons, doctrinal or otherwise, for the moment knocked out of his head.

She is the most beautiful woman I ever saw, he thought. How is it possible that I have lived in Rexton for six months and never heard of her or of that house? Well, I daresay there's some simple explanation of it all. The place may have been unoccupied until lately – probably it is the summer residence of people who have only recently come to it. I'll ask Mrs. Danby. She'll know if anybody will. That good woman knows everything about everybody in Rexton for three generations back.

Alan found Isabel King with his housekeeper when he got home. His greeting was tinged with a slight constraint. He was not a vain man, but he could not help knowing that Isabel looked upon him with a favour that had in it much more than professional interest. Isabel herself showed it with sufficient distinctness. Moreover, he felt a certain personal dislike of her and of her hard, insistent beauty, which seemed harder and more insistent than ever contrasted with his recollection of the girl of the lake shore.

Isabel had a trick of coming to the manse on plausible errands to Mrs. Danby and lingering until it was so dark that Alan was in courtesy bound to see her home. The ruse was a little too patent and amused Alan, although he carefully hid his amusement and treated Isabel with the fine unvarying deference which his mother had engrained into him for womanhood – a deference that flattered Isabel even while it annoyed her with the sense of a barrier which she could not break down or pass. She was the daughter of the richest man in Rexton and inclined to give herself airs on that account, but Alan's gentle indifference always brought home to her an unwelcome feeling of inferiority.

"You've been tiring yourself out again tramping that lake shore, I suppose," said Mrs. Danby, who had kept house for three bachelor ministers and consequently felt entitled to hector them in a somewhat maternal fashion.

"Not tiring myself – resting and refreshing myself rather," smiled Alan. "I was tired when I went out but now I feel like a strong man rejoicing to run a race. By the way, Mrs. Danby, who lives in that quaint old house away down at the very shore? I never knew of its existence before."

Alan's "by the way" was not quite so indifferent as he tried to make it. Isabel King, leaning back posingly among the cushions of the lounge, sat quickly up as he asked his question.

"Dear me, you don't mean to say you've never heard of Captain Anthony – Captain Anthony Oliver?" said Mrs. Danby. "He lives down there at Four Winds, as they call it – he and his daughter and an old cousin."

Isabel King bent forward, her brown eyes on Alan's face.

"Did you see Lynde Oliver?" she asked with suppressed eagerness.

Alan ignored the question – perhaps he did not hear it.

"Have they lived there long?" he asked.

"For eighteen years," said Mrs. Danby placidly. "It's funny you haven't heard them mentioned. But people don't talk much about the Captain now – he's an old story – and of course they never go anywhere, not even to church. The Captain is a rank infidel and they say his daughter is just as bad. To be sure, nobody knows much about her, but it stands to reason that a girl who's had her bringing up must be odd, to say no worse of her. It's not really her fault, I suppose – her wicked old scalawag of a father is to blame for it. She's never darkened a church or school door in her life and they say she's always been a regular tomboy – running wild outdoors with dogs, and fishing and shooting like a man. Nobody ever goes there – the Captain doesn't want visitors. He must have done something dreadful in his time, if it was only known, when he's so set on living like a hermit away down on that jumping-off place. Did you see any of them?"

"I saw Miss Oliver, I suppose," said Alan briefly. "At least I met a young lady on the shore. But where did these people come from? Surely more is known of them than this."

"Precious little. The truth is, Mr. Douglas, folks don't think the Olivers respectable and don't want to have anything to do with them. Eighteen years ago Captain Anthony came from goodness knows where, bought the Four Winds point, and built that house. He said he'd been a sailor all his life and couldn't live away from the water. He brought his wife and child and an old cousin of his with him. This Lynde wasn't more than two years old then. People went to call but they never saw any of the women and the Captain let them see they weren't wanted.

Some of the men who'd been working round the place saw
his wife and said she was sickly but real handsome and
like a lady, but she never seemed to want to see anyone or
be seen herself. There was a story that the Captain had
been a smuggler and that if he was caught he'd be sent to
prison. Oh, there were all sorts of yarns, mostly coming
from the men who worked there, for nobody else ever got
inside the house. Well, four years ago his wife disappeared – it wasn't known how or when. She just wasn't
ever seen again, that's all. Whether she died or was mur-
dered or went away nobody ever knew. There was some
talk of an investigation but nothing came of it. As for the
girl, she's always lived there with her father. She must be a
perfect heathen. He never goes anywhere, but there used
to be talk of strangers visiting him – queer sort of characters who came up the lake in vessels from the American
side. I haven't heard any reports of such these past few
years, though – not since his wife disappeared. He keeps a
yacht and goes sailing in it – sometimes he cruises about
for weeks – that's about all he ever does. And now you
know as much about the Olivers as I do, Mr. Douglas."

Alan had listened to this gossipy narrative with an interest that did not escape Isabel King's observant eyes. Much
of it he mentally dismissed as improbable surmise, but the
basic facts were probably as Mrs. Danby had reported
them. He had known that the girl of the shore could be no
commonplace, primly nurtured young woman.

"Has no effort ever been made to bring these people
into touch with the church?" he asked absently.

"Bless you, yes. Every minister that's ever been in Rexton has had a try at it. The old cousin met every one of
them at the door and told him nobody was at home. Mr.
Strong was the most persistent – he didn't like being
beaten. He went again and again and finally the Captain
sent him word that when he wanted parsons or pill-

dosers he'd send for them, and till he did he'd thank them to mind their own business. They say Mr. Strong met Lynde once along shore and wanted to know if she wouldn't come to church, and she laughed in his face and told him she knew more about God now than he did or ever would. Perhaps the story isn't true. Or if it was maybe he provoked her into saying it. Mr. Strong wasn't overly tactful. I believe in judging the poor girl as charitably as possible and making allowances for her, seeing how she's been brought up. You couldn't expect her to know how to behave."

Somehow, Alan resented Mrs. Danby's charity. Then, his sense of humour being strongly developed, he smiled to think of this commonplace old lady "making allowances" for the splendid bit of femininity he had seen on the shore. A plump barnyard fowl might as well have talked of making allowances for a seagull!

Alan walked home with Isabel King but he was very silent as they went together down the long, dark, sweet-smelling country road bordered by its white orchards. Isabel put her own construction on his absent replies to her remarks and presently she asked him, "Did you think Lynde Oliver handsome?"

The question gave Alan an annoyance out of all proportion to its significance. He felt an instinctive reluctance to discussing Lynde Oliver with Isabel King.

"I saw her only for a moment," he said coldly, "but she impressed me as being a beautiful woman."

"They tell queer stories about her – but maybe they're not all true," said Isabel, unable to keep the sneer of malice out of her voice. At that moment Alan's secret contempt for her crystallized into pronounced aversion. He made no reply and they went the rest of the way in silence. At her gate Isabel said, "You haven't been over to see us very lately, Mr. Douglas."

"My congregation is a large one and I cannot visit all my people as often as I might wish," Alan answered, all the more coldly for the personal note in her tone. "A minister's time is not his own, you know."

"Shall you be going to see the Olivers?" asked Isabel bluntly.

"I have not considered that question. Good-night, Miss King."

On his way back to the manse Alan did consider the question. Should he make any attempt to establish friendly relations with the residents of Four Winds? It surprised him to find how much he wanted to, but he finally concluded that he would not. They were not adherents of his church and he did not believe that even a minister had any right to force himself upon people who plainly wished to be let alone.

When he got home, although it was late, he went to his study and began work on a new text – for Elder Trewin's seemed utterly out of the question. Even with the new one he did not get on very well. At last in exasperation he leaned back in his chair.

Why can't I stop thinking of those Four Winds people? Here, let me put these haunting thoughts into words and see if that will lay them. That girl had a beautiful face but a cold one. Would I like to see it lighted up with the warmth of her soul set free? Yes, frankly, I would. She looked upon me with indifference. Would I like to see her welcome me as a friend? I have a conviction that I would, although no doubt everybody in my congregation would look upon her as a most unsuitable friend for me. Do I believe that she is wild, unwomanly, heathenish, as Mrs. Danby says? No, I do not, most emphatically. I believe she is a lady in the truest sense of that much abused word, though she is doubtless unconventional. Having said all this, I do not see what more there is to be said. And – I – am   going – to – write – this – sermon.

Alan wrote it, putting all thought of Lynde Oliver sternly out of his mind for the time being. He had no notion of falling in love with her. He knew nothing of love and imagined that it counted for nothing in his life. He admitted that his curiosity was aflame about the girl, but it never occurred to him that she meant or could mean anything to him but an attractive enigma which once solved would lose its attraction. The young women he knew in Rexton, whose simple, pleasant friendship he valued, had the placid, domestic charm of their own sweet-breathed, windless orchards. Lynde Oliver had the fascination of the lake shore – wild, remote, untamed – the lure of the wilderness and the primitive. There was nothing more personal in his thought of her, and yet when he recalled Isabel King's sneer he felt an almost personal resentment.

DURING THE FOLLOWING FORTNIGHT Alan made many trips to the shore – and he always went by the branch road to the Four Winds point. He did not attempt to conceal from himself that he hoped to meet Lynde Oliver again. In this he was unsuccessful. Sometimes he saw her at a distance along the shore but she always disappeared as soon as seen. Occasionally as he crossed the point he saw her working in her garden but he never went very near the house, feeling that he had no right to spy on it or her in any way. He soon became convinced that she avoided him purposely and the conviction piqued him. He felt an odd masterful desire to meet her face to face and make her look at him. Sometimes he called himself a fool and vowed he would go no more to the Four Winds shore. Yet he inevitably went. He did not find in the shore the comfort and inspiration he had formerly found. Something had come between his soul and the soul of the wilderness – something he did not recognize or formulate – a nameless, haunting longing that shaped itself about the memory of a cold sweet face and starry, indifferent eyes, grey as the lake at dawn.

Of Captain Anthony he never got even a glimpse, but he saw the old cousin several times, going and coming about the yard and its environs. Finally one day he met her, coming up a path which led to a spring down in a firry hollow. She was carrying two heavy pails of water and Alan asked permission to help her.

He half expected a repulse, for the tall, grim old woman had a rather stern and forbidding look, but after gazing at him a moment in a somewhat scrutinizing manner she said briefly, "You may, if you like."

Alan took the pails and followed her, the path not being wide enough for two. She strode on before him at a rapid, vigorous pace until they came out into the yard by the house. Alan felt his heart beating foolishly. Would he see Lynde Oliver? Would –

"You may carry the water there," the old woman said, pointing to a little outhouse near the pines. "I'm washing – the spring water is softer than the well water. Thank you" – as Alan set the pails down on a bench – "I'm not so young as I was and bringing the water so far tires me. Lynde always brings it for me when she's home."

She stood before him in the narrow doorway, blocking his exit, and looked at him with keen, deep-set dark eyes. In spite of her withered aspect and wrinkled face, she was not an uncomely old woman and there was about her a dignity of carriage and manner that pleased Alan. It did not occur to him to wonder why it should please him. If he had hunted that feeling down he might have been surprised to discover that it had its origin in a curious gratification over the thought that the woman who lived with Lynde had a certain refinement about her. He preferred her unsmiling dourness to vulgar garrulity.

"Are you the young minister up at Rexton?" she asked bluntly.

"Yes."

"I thought so. Lynde said she had seen you on the shore once. Well" – she cast an uncertain glance over her shoulder at the house – "I'm much obliged to you."

Alan had an idea that that was not what she had thought of saying, but as she had turned aside and was busying herself with the pails, there seemed nothing for him to do but to go.

"Wait a moment." She faced him again, and if Alan had been a vain man he might have thought that admiration looked from her piercing eyes. "What do you think of us? I suppose they've told you tales of us up there?" – with a scornful gesture of her hand in the direction of Rexton. "Do you believe them?"

"I believe no ill of anyone until I have absolute proof of it," said Alan, smiling – he was quite unconscious what a winning smile he had, which was the best of it – "and I never put faith in gossip. Of course you are gossipped about – you know that."

"Yes, I know it" – grimly – "and I don't care what they say about the Captain and me. We are a queer pair – just as queer as they make us out. You can believe what you like about us, but don't you believe a word they say against Lynde. She's sweet and good and beautiful. It's not her fault that she never went to church – it's her father's. Don't you hold that against her."

The fierce yet repressed energy of her tone prevented Alan from feeling any amusement over her simple defence of Lynde. Moreover, it sounded unreasonably sweet in his ears.

"I won't," he promised, "but I don't suppose it would matter much to Miss Oliver if I did. She did not strike me as a young lady who would worry very much about other people's opinions."

If his object were to prolong the conversation about Lynde, he was disappointed, for the old woman had turned abruptly to her work again and, though Alan lingered for a few moments longer, she took no further notice of him. But when he had gone she peered stealthily after him from the door until he was lost to sight among the pines.

"A well-looking man," she muttered. "I wish Lynde had been home. I didn't dare ask him to the house for I knew Anthony was in one of his moods. But it's time something was done. She's woman grown and this is no life for her. And there's nobody to do anything but me and I'm not able, even if I knew what to do. I wonder why she hates men so. Perhaps it's because she never knew any that were real gentlemen. This man is – but then he's a minister and that makes a wide gulf between them in another way. I've seen the love of man and woman bridge some wider gulfs though. But it can't with Lynde, I'm fearing. She's so bitter at the mere speaking of love and marriage. I can't think why. I'm sure her mother and Anthony were happy together, and that was all she's ever seen of marriage. But I thought when she told me of meeting this young man on the shore there was something in her look I'd never noticed before – as if she'd found something in herself she'd never known was there. But she'll never make friends with him and I can't. If the Captain wasn't so queer – "

She stopped abruptly, for a tall lithe figure was coming up from the shore. Lynde waved her hand as she drew near.

"Oh, Emily, I've had such a splendid sail. It was glorious.

Bad Emily, you've been carrying water. Didn't I tell you never to do that when I was away?"

"I didn't have to do it. That young minister up at Rexton met me and brought it up. He's nice, Lynde."

Lynde's brow darkened. She turned and walked away to the house without a word.

On his way home that night Alan met Isabel King on the main shore road. She carried an armful of pine boughs and said she wanted the needles for a cushion. Yet the thought came into Alan's mind that she was spying on him and, although he tried to dismiss it as unworthy, it continued to lurk there.

For a week he avoided the shore, but there came a day when its inexplicable lure drew him to it again irresistibly. It was a warm, windy evening and the air was sweet and resinous, the lake misty and blue. There was no sign of life about Four Winds and the shore seemed as lonely and virgin as if human foot had never trodden it. The Captain's yacht was gone from the little harbour where it was generally anchored and, though every flutter of wind in the scrub firs made Alan's heart beat expectantly, he saw nothing of Lynde Oliver. He was on the point of turning homeward, with an unreasoning sense of disappointment, when one of Lynde's dogs broke down through the hedge of spruces, barking loudly.

Alan looked for Lynde to follow, but she did not, and he speedily saw that there was something unusual about the dog's behaviour. The animal circled around him, still barking excitedly, then ran off for a short distance, stopped, barked again, and returned, repeating the manoeuvre. It was plain that he wanted Alan to follow him, and it occurred to the young minister that the dog's mistress must be in danger of some kind. Instantly he set off after him; and the dog, with a final sharp bark of satisfaction, sprang up the low bank into the spruces.

Alan followed him across the peninsula and then along the further shore, which rapidly grew steep and high. Half a mile down the cliffs were rocky and precipitous, while the beach beneath them was heaped with huge boulders. Alan followed the dog along one of the narrow paths with which the barrens abounded until nearly a mile from Four Winds. Then the animal halted, ran to the edge of the cliff and barked.

It was an ugly-looking place where a portion of the soil had evidently broken away recently, and Alan stepped cautiously out to the brink and looked down. He could not repress an exclamation of dismay and alarm.

A few feet below him Lynde Oliver was lying on a mass of mossy soil which was apparently on the verge of slipping over a sloping shelf of rock, below which was a sheer drop of thirty feet to the cruel boulders below. The extreme danger of her position was manifest at a glance; the soil on which she lay was stationary, yet it seemed as if the slightest motion on her part would send it over the brink.

Lynde lay movelessly; her face was white, and both fear and appeal were visible in her large dilated eyes. Yet she was quite calm and a faint smile crossed her pale lips as she saw the man and the dog.

"Good faithful Pat, so you did bring help," she said.

"But how can I help you, Miss Oliver?" said Alan hoarsely. "I cannot reach you – and it looks as if the slightest touch or jar would send that broken earth over the brink."

"I fear it would. You must go back to Four Winds and get a rope."

"And leave you here alone – in such danger?"

"Pat will stay with me. Besides, there is nothing else to do. You will find a rope in that little house where you put the water for Emily. Father and Emily are away. I think I am quite safe here if I don't move at all."

Alan's own common sense told him that, as she said, there was nothing else to do and, much as he hated to leave her alone thus, he realized that he must lose no time in doing it.

"I'll be back as quickly as possible," he said hurriedly.

Alan had been a noted runner at college and his muscles had not forgotten their old training. Yet it seemed to him an age ere he reached Four Winds, secured the rope, and returned. At every flying step he was haunted by the thought of the girl lying on the brink of the precipice and the fear that she might slip over it before he could rescue her. When he reached the scene of the accident he dreaded to look over the broken edge, but she was lying there safely and she smiled when she saw him – a brave smile that softened her tense white face into the likeness of a frightened child's.

"If I drop the rope down to you, are you strong enough to hold to it while the earth goes and then draw yourself up the slope hand over hand?" asked Alan anxiously.

"Yes," she answered fearlessly.

Alan passed down one end of the rope and then braced himself firmly to hold it, for there was no tree near enough to be of any assistance. The next moment the full weight of her body swung from it, for at her first movement the soil beneath her slipped away. Alan's heart sickened; what if she went with it? Could she cling to the rope while he drew her up?

Then he saw she was still safe on the sloping shelf. Carefully and painfully she drew herself to her knees and, clinging to the rope, crept up the rock hand over hand. When she came within his reach he grasped her arms and lifted her up into safety beside him.

"Thank God," he said, with whiter lips than her own.

For a few moments Lynde sat silent on the sod, exhausted with fright and exertion, while her dog fawned on her in an ecstasy of joy. Finally she looked up into Alan's anxious face and their eyes met. It was something more than the physical reaction that suddenly flushed the girl's cheeks. She sprang lithely to her feet.

"Can you walk back home?" Alan asked.

"Oh, yes, I am all right now. It was very foolish of me to get into such a predicament. Father and Emily went down the lake in the yacht this afternoon and I started out for a ramble. When I came here I saw some junebells growing right out on the ledge and I crept out to gather them. I should have known better. It broke away under me and the more I tried to scramble back the faster it slid down, carrying me with it. I thought it would go right over the brink" – she gave a little involuntary shudder – "but just at the very edge it stopped. I knew I must lie very still or it would go right over. It seemed like days. Pat was with me and I told him to go for help, but I knew there was no one at home – and I was horribly afraid," she concluded with another shiver. "I never was afraid in my life before – at least not with that kind of fear."

"You have had a terrible experience and a narrow escape," said Alan lamely. He could think of nothing more to say; his usual readiness of utterance seemed to have failed him.

"You saved my life," she said, "you and Pat – for doggie must have his share of credit."

"A much larger share than mine," said Alan, smiling. "If Pat had not come for me, I would not have known of your danger. What a magnificent fellow he is!"

"Isn't he?" she agreed proudly. "And so is Laddie, my other dog. He went with Father today. I love my dogs more than people." She looked at him with a little defiance in her eyes. "I suppose you think that terrible."

"I think many dogs are much more lovable – and worthy of love – than many people," said Alan, laughing.

How child-like she was in some ways! That trace of defiance – it was so like a child who expected to be scolded for some wrong attitude of mind. And yet there were moments when she looked the tall proud queen. Sometimes, when the path grew narrow, she walked before him, her hand on the dog's head. Alan liked this, since it left him free to watch admiringly the swinging grace of her step and the white curves of her neck beneath the thick braid of hair, which today was wound about her head. When she dropped back beside him in the wider spaces, he could only have stolen glances at her profile, delicately, strongly cut, virginal in its soft curves, child-like in its purity. Once she looked around and caught his glance; again she flushed, and something strange and exultant stirred in Alan's heart. It was as if that maiden blush were the involuntary, unconscious admission of some power he had over her – a power which her hitherto unfettered spirit had never before felt. The cold indifference he had seen in her face at their first meeting was gone, and something told him it was gone forever.

When they came in sight of Four Winds they saw two people walking up the road from the harbour and a few further steps brought them face to face with Captain Anthony Oliver and his old housekeeper.

The Captain's appearance was a fresh surprise to Alan. He had expected to meet a rough, burly sailor, loud of voice and forbidding of manner. Instead, Captain Anthony was a tall, well-built man of perhaps fifty. His face, beneath its shock of iron-grey hair, was handsome but wore a somewhat forbidding expression, and there was something in it, apart from line or feature, which did not please Alan. He had no time to analyze this impression, for Lynde said hurriedly, "Father, this is Mr. Douglas. He has just done me a great service."

She briefly explained her accident; when she had finished, the Captain turned to Alan and held out his hand, a frank smile replacing the rather suspicious and contemptuous scowl which had previously overshadowed it.

"I am much obliged to you, Mr. Douglas," he said cordially. "You must come up to the house and let me thank you at leisure. As a rule I'm not very partial to the cloth, as you may have heard. In this case it is the man, not the minister, I invite."

The front door of Four Winds opened directly into a wide, low-ceilinged living room, furnished with simplicity and good taste. Leaving the two men there, Lynde and the old cousin vanished, and Alan found himself talking freely with the Captain who could, as it appeared, talk well on many subjects far removed from Four Winds. He was evidently a clever, self-educated man, somewhat opinionated and given to sarcasm; he never made any references to his own past life or experiences, but Alan discovered him to be surprisingly well read in politics and science. Sometimes in the pauses of the conversation Alan found the older man looking at him in a furtive way he did not like, but the Captain was such an improvement on what he had been led to expect that he was not inclined to be over critical. At least, this was what he honestly thought. He did not suspect that it was because this man was Lynde's father that he wished to think as well as possible of him.

Presently Lynde came in. She had changed her outdoor dress, stained with moss and soil in her fall, for a soft clinging garment of some pale yellow material, and her long, thick braid of hair hung over her shoulder. She sat mutely down in a dim corner and took no part in the conversation except to answer briefly the remarks which Alan addressed to her. Emily came in and lighted the lamp on the table. She was as grim and unsmiling as ever, yet she cast a look of satisfaction on Alan as she passed out. One dog lay down at Lynde's feet, the other sat on his haunches by her side and laid his head on her lap. Rexton and its quiet round of parish duties seemed thousands of miles away from Alan, and he wondered a little if this were not all a dream.

When he went away the Captain invited him back.

"If you like to come, that is," he said brusquely, "and always as the man, not the priest, remember. I don't want you by and by to be slyly slipping in the thin end of any professional wedges. You'll waste your time if you do. Come as man to man and you'll be welcome, for I like you – and it's few men I like. But don't try to talk religion to me."

"I never talk religion," said Alan emphatically. "I try to live it. I'll not come to your house as a self-appointed missionary, sir, but I shall certainly act and speak at all times as my conscience and my reverence for my vocation demands. If I respect your beliefs, whatever they may be, I shall expect you to respect mine, Captain Oliver."

"Oh, I won't insult your God," said the Captain with a faint sneer.

Alan went home in a tumult of contending feelings. He did not altogether like Captain Anthony – that was very clear to him, and yet there was something about the man that attracted him. Intellectually he was a worthy foeman, and Alan had often longed for such since coming to Rexton. He missed the keen, stimulating debates of his college days and, now there seemed a chance of renewing them, he was eager to grasp it. And Lynde – how beautiful she was! What though she shared – as was not unlikely – in her father's lack of belief? She could not be essentially irreligious – that were impossible in a true woman. Might not this be his opportunity to help her – to lead her into clearer light? Alan Douglas was a sincere man, with himself as well as with others, yet there are some motives that lie, in their first inception, too deep even for the probe of self-analysis. He had not as yet the faintest suspicion as to the real source of his interest in Lynde Oliver – in his sudden forceful desire to be of use and service to her – to rescue her from spiritual peril as he had that day rescued her from bodily danger.

She must have a lonely, unsatisfying life, he thought. It is my duty to help her if I can.

It did not then occur to him that duty in this instance wore a much more pleasing aspect than it had sometimes worn in his experience.

ALAN DID NOT MEAN to be oversoon in going back to Four Winds, but three days later a book came to him which Captain Anthony had expressed a wish to see. It furnished an excuse for an earlier call. After that he went often. He always found the Captain courteous and affable, old Emily grimly cordial, Lynde sometimes remote and demure, sometimes frankly friendly. Occasionally, when the Captain was away in his yacht, he went for a walk with her and her dogs along the shore or through the sweet-smelling pinelands up the lake. He found that she loved books and was avid for more of them than she could obtain; he was glad to take her several and discuss them with her. She liked history and travels best. With novels she had no patience, she said disdainfully. She seldom spoke of herself or her past life and Alan fancied she avoided any personal reference. But once she said abruptly, "Why do you never ask me to go to church? I've always been afraid you would."

"Because I do not think it would do you any good to go if you didn't want to," said Alan gravely. "Souls should not be rudely handled any more than bodies."

She looked at him reflectively, her finger denting her chin in a meditative fashion she had.

"You are not at all like Mr. Strong. He always scolded me,

162

when he got a chance, for not going to church. I would have hated him if it had been worthwhile. I told him one day that I was nearer to God under these pines than I could be in any building fashioned by human hands. He was very much shocked. But I don't want you to misunderstand me. Father does not go to church because he does not believe there is a God. But I know there is. Mother taught me so. I have never gone to church because Father would not allow me, and I could not go now in Rexton where the people talk about me so. Oh, I know they do – you know it, too – but I do not care for them. I know I'm not like other girls. I would like to be but I can't be – I never can be – now."

There was some strange passion in her voice that Alan did not quite understand – a bitterness and a revolt which he took to be against the circumstances that hedged her in.

"Is not some other life possible for you if your present life does not content you?" he said gently.

"But it does content me," said Lynde imperiously. "I want no other – I wish this life to go on forever – forever, do you understand? If I were sure that it would – if I were sure that no change would ever come to me, I would be perfectly content. It is the fear that a change will come that makes me wretched. Oh!" She shuddered and put her hands over her eyes.

Alan thought she must mean that when her father died she would be alone in the world. He wanted to comfort her – reassure her – but he did not know how.

One evening when he went to Four Winds he found the door open and, seeing the Captain in the living room, he stepped in unannounced. Captain Anthony was sitting by the table, his head in his hands; at Alan's entrance he turned upon him a haggard face, blackened by a furious scowl beneath which blazed eyes full of malevolence.

"What do you want here?" he said, following up the demand with a string of vile oaths.

Before Alan could summon his scattered wits, Lynde glided in with a white, appealing face. Wordlessly she grasped Alan's arm, drew him out, and shut the door.

"Oh, I've been watching for you," she said breathlessly. "I was afraid you might come tonight – but I missed you."

"But your father?" said Alan in amazement. "How have I angered him?"

"Hush. Come into the garden. I will explain there."

He followed her into the little enclosure where the red and white roses were now in full blow.

"Father isn't angry with you," said Lynde in a low shamed voice. "It's just – he takes strange moods sometimes. Then he seems to hate us all – even me – and he is like that for days. He seems to suspect and dread everybody as if they were plotting against him. You – perhaps you think he has been drinking? No, that is not the trouble. These terrible moods come on without any cause that we know of. Even Mother could not do anything with him when he was like that. You must go away now – and do not come back until his dark mood has passed. He will be just as glad to see you as ever then, and this will not make any difference with him. Don't come back for a week at least."

"I do not like to leave you in such trouble, Miss Oliver."

"Oh, it doesn't matter about me – I have Emily. And there is nothing you could do. Please go at once. Father knows I am talking to you and that will vex him still more."

Alan, realizing that he could not help her and that his presence only made matters worse, went away perplexedly. The following week was a miserable one for him. His duties were distasteful to him and meeting his people a positive torture. Sometimes Mrs. Danby looked dubiously at him and seemed on the point of saying something – but never said it. Isabel King watched him when they met, with bold probing eyes. In his abstraction he did not notice this any more than he noticed a certain subtle change which had come over the members of his congregation – as if a breath of suspicion had blown across them and troubled their confidence and trust. Once Alan would have been keenly and instantly conscious of this slight chill; now he was not even aware of it.

When he ventured to go back to Four Winds he found the Captain on the point of starting off for a cruise in his yacht. He was urbane and friendly, utterly ignoring the incident of Alan's last visit and regretting that business compelled him to go down the lake. Alan saw him off with small regret and turned joyfully to Lynde, who was walking under the pines with her dogs. She looked pale and tired and her eyes were still troubled, but she smiled proudly and made no reference to what had happened.

"I'm going to put these flowers on Mother's grave," she said, lifting her slender hands filled with late white roses. "Mother loved flowers and I always keep them near her when I can. You may come with me if you like."

Alan had known Lynde's mother was buried under the pines but he had never visited the spot before. The grave was at the westernmost end of the pine wood, where it gave out on the lake, a beautiful spot, given over to silence and shadow.

"Mother wished to be buried here," Lynde said, kneeling to arrange her flowers. "Father would have taken her anywhere but she said she wanted to be near us and near the lake she had loved so well. Father buried her himself. He wouldn't have anyone else do anything for her. I am so glad she is here. It would have been terrible to have seen her taken far away – my sweet little mother."

"A mother is the best thing in the world – I realized that when I lost mine," said Alan gently. "How long is it since your mother died?"

"Three years. Oh, I thought I should die too when she did. She was very ill – she was never strong, you know – but I never thought she could die. There was a year then – part of the time I didn't believe in God at all and the rest I hated Him. I was very wicked but I was so unhappy. Father had so many dreadful moods and – there was something else. I used to wish to die."

She bowed her head on her hands and gazed moodily on the ground. Alan, leaning against a pine tree, looked down at her. The sunlight fell through the swaying boughs on her glory of burnished hair and lighted up the curve of cheek and chin against the dark background of wood brown. All the defiance and wildness had gone from her for the time and she seemed like a helpless, weary child. He wanted to take her in his arms and comfort her.

"You must resemble your mother," he said absently, as if thinking aloud. "You don't look at all like your father."

Lynde shook her head.

"No, I don't look like Mother either. She was tiny and dark – she had a sweet little face and velvet-brown eyes and soft curly dark hair. Oh, I remember her look so well. I wish I did resemble her. I loved her so – I would have done anything to save her suffering and trouble. At least, she died in peace."

There was a curious note of fierce self-gratulation in the girl's voice as she spoke the last sentence. Again Alan felt the unpleasant impression that there was much in her that he did not understand – might never understand – although such understanding was necessary to perfect friendship. She had never spoken so freely of her past life to him before, yet he felt somehow that something was being kept back in jealous repression. It must be something connected with her father, Alan thought. Doubtless, Captain Anthony's past would not bear inspection, and his daughter knew it and dwelt in the shadow of her knowledge. His heart filled with aching pity for her; he raged secretly because he was so powerless to help her. Her girlhood had been blighted, robbed of its meed of happiness and joy. Was she likewise to miss her womanhood? Alan's hands clenched involuntarily at the unuttered question.

On his way home that evening he again met Isabel King. She turned and walked back with him but she made no reference to Four Winds or its inhabitants. If Alan had troubled himself to look, he would have seen a malicious glow in her baleful brown yes. But the only eyes which had any meaning for him just then were the grey ones of Lynde Oliver.

DURING ALAN'S NEXT THREE VISITS to Four Winds he saw nothing of Lynde, either in the house or out of it. This surprised and worried him. There was no apparent difference in Captain Anthony, who continued to be suave and friendly. Alan always enjoyed his conversations with the Captain, who was witty, incisive, and pungent; yet he disliked the man himself more at every visit. If he had been compelled to define his impression, he would have said the Captain was a charming scoundrel.

But it occurred to him that Emily was disturbed about something. Sometimes he caught her glance, full of perplexity and – it almost seemed – distrust. She looked as if she felt hostile towards him. But Alan dismissed the idea as absurd. She had been friendly from the first and he had done nothing to excite her disapproval. Lynde's mysterious absence was a far more perplexing problem. She had not gone away, for when Alan asked the Captain concerning her, he responded indifferently that she was out walking. Alan caught a glint of amusement in the older man's eyes as he spoke. He could have sworn it was malicious amusement.

One evening he went to Four Winds around the shore. As he turned the headland of the cove, he saw Lynde and her dogs not a hundred feet away. The moment she saw him she darted up the bank and disappeared among the firs.

Alan was thunderstruck. There was no room for doubt that she meant to avoid him. He walked up to the house in a tumult of mingled feelings which he did not even then understand. He only realized that he felt bitterly hurt and grieved – puzzled as well. What did it all mean?

He met Emily in the yard of Four Winds on her way to the spring and stopped her resolutely.

"Miss Oliver," he said bluntly, "is Miss Lynde angry with me? And why?"

Emily looked at him piercingly.

"Have you no idea why?" she asked shortly.

"None in the world."

She looked at him through and through a moment longer. Then, seeming satisfied with her scrutiny, she picked up her pail.

"Come down to the spring with me," she said.

As soon as they were out of sight of the house, Emily began abruptly.

"If you don't know why Lynde is acting so, I can't tell you, for I don't know either. I don't even know if she is angry. I only thought perhaps she was – that you had done or said something to vex her – plaguing her to go to church maybe. But if you didn't, it may not be anger at all. I don't understand that girl. She's been different ever since her mother died. She used to tell me everything before that. You must go and ask her right out yourself what is wrong. But maybe I can tell you something. Did you write her a letter a fortnight ago?"

"A letter? No."

"Well, she got one then. I thought it came from you – I

didn't know who else would be writing to her. A boy brought it and gave it to her at the door. She's been acting strange ever since. She cries at night – something Lynde never did before except when her mother died. And in daytime she roams the shore and woods like one possessed. You must find out what was in that letter, Mr. Douglas."

"Have you any idea who the boy was?" Alan asked, feeling somewhat relieved. The mystery was clearing up, he thought. No doubt it was the old story of some cowardly anonymous letter. His thoughts flew involuntarily to Isabel King.

Emily shook her head.

"No. He was just a half-grown fellow with reddish hair and he limped a little."

"Oh, that is the postmaster's son," said Alan disappointedly. "That puts us further off the scent than ever. The letter was probably dropped in the box at the office and there will consequently be no way of tracing the writer."

"Well, I can't tell you anything more," said Emily. "You'll have to ask Lynde for the truth."

This Alan was determined to do whenever he should meet her. He did not go to the house with Emily but wandered about the shore, watching for Lynde and not seeing her. At length he went home, a prey to stormy emotions. He realized at last that he loved Lynde Oliver. He wondered how he could have been so long blind to it. He knew that he must have loved her ever since he had first seen her. The discovery amazed but did not shock him. There was no reason why he should not love her – should not woo and win her for his wife if she cared for him. She was good and sweet and true. Anything of doubt in her antecedents could not touch her. Probably the world would look upon Captain Anthony as a somewhat undesirable father-in-law for a minister, but that aspect of the question did not disturb Alan. As for the trouble of the letter, he felt sure he would easily be able to clear it away. Probably some malicious busybody had become aware of his frequent calls at Four Winds and chose to interfere in his private affairs thus. For the first time it occurred to him that there had been a certain lack of cordiality among his people of late. If it were really so, doubtless this was the reason. At any other time this would have been of moment to him. But now his thoughts were too wholly taken up with Lynde and the estrangement on her part to attach much importance to anything else. What she thought mattered incalculably more to Alan than what all the people in Rexton put together thought. He had the right, like any other man, to woo the woman of his choice and he would certainly brook no outside interference in the matter.

After a sleepless night he went back to Four Winds in the morning. Lynde would not expect him at that time and he would have more chance of finding her. The result justified his idea, for he met her by the spring.

Alan felt shocked at the change in her appearance. She looked as if years of suffering had passed over her. Her lips were pallid, and hollow circles under her eyes made them appear unnaturally large. He had last left the girl in the bloom of her youth; he found her again a woman on whom life had laid its heavy hand.

A burning flood of colour swept over her face as they met, then receded as quickly, leaving her whiter than before. Without any waste of words, Alan plunged abruptly into the subject.

"Miss Oliver, why have you avoided me so of late? Have I done anything to offend you?"

"No." She spoke as if the word hurt her, her eyes persistently cast down.

"Then what is the trouble?"

There was no answer. She gave an unvoluntary glance around as if seeking some way of escape. There was none, for the spring was set about with thick young firs and Alan blocked the only path.

He leaned forward and took her hands in his.

"Miss Oliver, you must tell me what the trouble is," he said firmly.

She pulled her hands away and flung them up to her face, her form shaken by stormy sobs. In distress he put his arm about her and drew her closer.

"Tell me, Lynde," he whispered tenderly.

She broke away from him, saying passionately, "You must not come to Four Winds any more. You must not have anything more to do with us – any of us. We have done you enough harm already. But I never thought it could hurt you – oh, I am sorry, sorry!"

"Miss Oliver, I want to see that letter you received the other evening. Oh" – as she started with surprise – "I know about it – Emily told me. Who wrote it?"

"There was no name signed to it," she faltered.

"Just as I thought. Well, you must let me see it."

"I cannot – I burned it."

"Then tell me what was in it. You must. This matter must be cleared up – I am not going to have our beautiful friendship spoiled by the malice of some coward. What did that letter say?"

"It said that everybody in your congregation was talking about your frequent visits here – that it had made a great scandal – that it was doing you a great deal of injury and would probably end in your having to leave Rexton."

"That would be a catastrophe indeed," said Alan drily. "Well, what else?"

"Nothing more – at least, nothing about you. The rest was about myself – I did not mind it – much. But I was so sorry to think that I had done you harm. It is not too late to undo it. You must not come here any more. Then they will forget."

"Perhaps – but I should not forget. It's a little too late for me. Lynde, you must not let this venomous letter come between us. I love you, dear – I've loved you ever since I met you and I want you for my wife."

Alan had not intended to say that just then, but the words came to his lips in spite of himself. She looked so sad and appealing and weary that he wanted to have the right to comfort and protect her.

She turned her eyes full upon him with no hint of maidenly shyness or shrinking in them. Instead, they were full of a blank, incredulous horror that swallowed up every other feeling. There was no mistaking their expression and it struck an icy chill to Alan's heart. He had certainly not expected a too ready response on her part – he knew that even if she cared for him he might find it a matter of time to win her avowal of it – but he certainly had not expected to see such evident abject dismay as her blanched face betrayed. She put up her hand as if warding a blow.

"Don't – don't," she gasped. "You must not say that – you must never say it. Oh, I never dreamed of this. If I had thought it possible you could – love me, I would never have been friends with you. Oh, I've made a terrible mistake."

She wrung her hands piteously together, looking like a soul in torment. Alan could not bear to see her pain.

"Don't feel such distress," he implored. "I suppose I've spoken too abruptly – but I'll be so patient, dear, if you'll only try to care for me a little. Can't you, dear?"

"I can't marry you," said Lynde desperately. She leaned against a slim white bole of a young birch behind her and looked at him wretchedly. "Won't you please go away and forget me?"

"I can't forget you," Alan said, smiling a little in spite of his suffering. "You are the only woman I can ever love – and I can't give you up unless I have to. Won't you be frank with me, dear? Do you honestly think you can never learn to love me?"

"It is not that," said Lynde in a hard, unnatural voice. "I am married already."

Alan stared at her, not in the least comprehending the meaning of her words. Everything – pain, hope, fear, passion – had slipped away from him for a moment, as if he had been stunned by a physical blow. He could not have heard aright.

"Married?" he said dully. "Lynde, you cannot mean it?"

"Yes, I do. I was married three years ago."

"Why was I not told this?" Alan's voice was stern, although he did not mean it to be so, and she shrank and shivered. Then she began in a low monotonous tone from which all feeling of any sort seemed to have utterly faded.

"Three years ago Mother was very ill – so ill that any shock would kill her, so the doctor Father brought from the lake told us. A man – a young sea captain – came here to see Father. His name was Frank Harmon and he had known Father well in the past. They had sailed together. Father seemed to be afraid of him – I had never seen him afraid of anybody before. I could not think much about anybody except Mother then, but I knew I did not quite like Captain Harmon, although he was very polite to me and I suppose might have been called handsome. One day Father came to me and told me I must marry Captain Harmon. I laughed at the idea at first but when I looked at Father's face I did not laugh. It was all white and drawn. He implored me to marry Captain Harmon. He said if I did not it would mean shame and disgrace for us all – that Captain Harmon had some hold on him and would tell what he knew if I did not marry him. I don't know what it was but it must have been something dreadful. And he said it would kill Mother. I knew it would, and that was what drove me to consent at last. Oh, I can't tell you what I suffered. I was only seventeen and there was nobody to advise me. One day Father and Captain Harmon and I went down the lake to Crosse Harbour and we were married there. As soon as the ceremony was over, Captain Harmon had to sail in his vessel. He was going to China. Father and I came back home. Nobody knew – not even Emily. He said we must not tell Mother until she was better. But she was never better. She only lived three months more – she lived them happily and at rest. When I think of that, I am not sorry for what I did. Captain Harmon said he would be back in the fall to claim me. I waited, sick at heart. But he did not come – he has never come. We have never heard a word of or about him since. Sometimes I feel sure he cannot be still living. But never a day dawns that I don't say to myself, 'Perhaps he will come today' – and, oh – "

She broke down again, sobbing bitterly. Amid all the daze of his own pain Alan realized that, at any cost, he must not make it harder for her by showing his suffering. He tried to speak calmly, wisely, as a disinterested friend.

"Could it not be discovered whether your – this man – is or is not living? Surely your father could find out."

Lynde shook her head.

"No, he says he has no way of doing so. We do not know if Captain Harmon had any relatives or even where his home was, and it was his own ship in which he sailed. Father would be glad to think that Frank Harmon was dead, but he does not think he is. He says he was always a fickle-minded fellow, one fancy driving another out of his mind. Oh, I can bear my own misery – but to think what I have brought on you! I never dreamed that you could care for me. I was so lonely and your friendship was so pleasant – can you ever forgive me?"

"There is nothing to forgive, as far as you are concerned, Lynde," said Alan steadily. "You have done me no wrong. I have loved you sincerely and such love can be nothing but a blessing to me. I only wish that I could help you. It wrings my heart to think of your position. But I can do nothing – nothing. I must not even come here any more. You understand that?"

"Yes."

There was an unconscious revelation in the girl's mournful eyes as she turned them on Alan. It thrilled him to the core of his being. She loved him. If it were not for that empty marriage form, he could win her, but the knowledge was only an added mocking torment. Alan had not known a man could endure such misery and live. A score of wild questions rushed to his lips but he crushed them back for Lynde's sake and held out his hand.

"Good-bye, dear," he said almost steadily, daring to say no more lest he should say too much.

"Good-bye," Lynde answered faintly.

When he had gone she flung herself down on the moss by the spring and lay there in an utter abandonment of misery and desolation.

Pain and indignation struggled for mastery in Alan's stormy soul as he walked homeward. So this was Captain Anthony's doings! He had sacrificed his daughter to some crime of his dubious past. Alan never dreamed of blaming Lynde for having kept her marriage a secret; he put the blame where it belonged – on the Captain's shoulders. Captain Anthony had never warned him by so much as a hint that Lynde was not free to be won. It had all probably seemed a good joke to him. Alan thought the furtive amusement he had so often detected in the Captain's eyes was explained now.

He found Elder Trewin in his study when he got home. The good Elder's face was stern and anxious; he had called on a distasteful errand – to tell the young minister of the scandal his intimacy with the Four Winds people was making in the congregation and remonstrate with him concerning it. Alan listened absently, with none of the resentment he would have felt at the interference a day previously. A man does not mind a pin-prick when a limb is being wrenched away.

"I can promise you that my objectionable calls at Four Winds will cease," he said sarcastically, when the Elder had finished. Elder Trewin got himself away, feeling snubbed but relieved.

"Took it purty quiet," he reflected. "Don't believe there was much in the yarns after all. Isabel King started them and probably she exaggerated a lot. I suppose he's had some notion like as not of bringing the Captain over to the church. But that's foolish, for he'd never manage it, and meanwhile was giving occasion for gossip. It's just as well to stop it. He's a good pastor and he works hard – too hard, mebbe. He looked real careworn and worried today."

The Rexton gossip soon ceased with the cessation of the young minister's visits to Four Winds. A month later it suffered a brief revival when a tall grim-faced old woman, whom a few recognized as Captain Anthony's house-keeper, was seen to walk down the Rexton road and enter the manse. She did not stay there long – watchers from a dozen different windows were agreed upon that – and nobody, not even Mrs. Danby, who did her best to find out, ever knew why she had called.

Emily looked at Alan with grim reproach when she was shown into his study, and as soon as they were alone she began with her usual abruptness, "Mr. Douglas, why have you given up coming to Four Winds?"

Alan flinched.

"You must ask Lynde that, Miss Oliver," he said quietly.

"I have asked her – and she says nothing."

"Then I cannot tell you."

Anger glowed in Emily's eyes.

"I thought you were a gentleman," she said bitterly. "You are not. You are breaking Lynde's heart. She's gone to a shadow of herself and she's fretting night and day. You went there and made her like you – oh, I've eyes – and then you left her."

Alan bent over his desk and looked the old woman in the face unflinchingly.

"You are mistaken, Miss Oliver," he said earnestly. "I love Lynde and would be only too happy if it were possible that I could marry her. I am not to blame for what has come about – she will tell you that herself if you ask her."

His look and tone convinced Emily.

"Who is to blame then? Lynde herself?"

"No, no."

"The Captain then?"

"Not in the sense you mean. I can tell you nothing more."

A baffled expression crossed the old woman's face. "There's a mystery here – there always has been – and I'm shut out of it. Lynde won't confide in me – in me who'd give my life's blood to help her. Perhaps I can help her – I could tell you something. Have you stopped coming to Four Winds – has she made you stop coming – because she's got such a wicked old scamp for a father? Is that the reason?"

Alan shook his head.

"No, that has nothing to do with it."

"And you won't come back?"

"It is not a question of will. I cannot – must not go."

"Lynde will break her heart then," said Emily in a tone of despair.

"I think not. She is too strong and fine for that. Help her all you can with sympathy but don't torment her with any questions. You may tell her if you like that I advise her to confide the whole story to you, but if she cannot don't tease her to. Be very gentle with her."

"You don't need to tell me that. I'd rather die than hurt her. I came here full of anger against you – but I see now you are not to blame. You are suffering too – your face tells that. All the same, I wish you'd never set foot in Four Winds. She wasn't happy before but she wasn't so miserable as she is now. Oh, I know Anthony is at the bottom of it all in some way but I won't ask you any more questions since you don't feel free to answer them. But are you sure that nothing can be done to clear up the trouble?"

"Too sure," said Alan's white lips.

THE AUTUMN DRAGGED AWAY. Alan found out how much a man may suffer and yet go on living and working. As for that, his work was all that made life possible for him now and he flung himself into it with feverish energy, growing so thin and hollow-eyed over it that even Elder Trewin remonstrated and suggested a vacation – a suggestion at which Alan merely smiled. A vacation which would take him away from Lynde's neighbourhood – the thought was not to be entertained.

He never saw Lynde, for he never went to any part of the shore now; yet he hungered constantly for the sight of her, the sound of her voice, the glance of her luminous eyes. When he pictured her eating her heart out in the solitude of Four Winds, he clenched his hands in despair. As for the possibility of Harmon's return, Alan could never face it for a moment. When it thrust its ugly presence into his thoughts, he put it away desperately. The man was dead – or his fickle fancy had veered elsewhere. Nothing else could explain his absence. But they could never know, and the uncertainty would forever stand between him and Lynde like a spectre. But he thought more of Lynde's pain than his own. He would have elected to bear any suffering if by so doing he could have freed her from the nightmare dread of Harmon's returning to claim her. That dread had always hung over her and now it must be intensified to agony by her love for another man. And he could do nothing – nothing. He groaned aloud in his helplessness.

One evening in late November Alan flung aside his pen and yielded to the impulse that urged him to the lake shore. He did not mean to seek Lynde – he would go to a part of the shore where there would be no likelihood of meeting her. But get away by himself he must. A November storm was raging and there would be a certain satisfaction in breasting its buffets and fighting his way through it. Besides, he knew that Isabel King was in the house and he dreaded meeting her. Since his conviction that she had written that letter to Lynde, he could not tolerate the girl and it tasked his self-control to keep from showing his contempt openly. Perhaps Isabel felt it beneath all his outward courtesy. At least she did not seek his society as she had formerly done.

It was the second day of the storm; a wild northeast gale was blowing and cold rain and freezing sleet fell in frequent showers. Alan shivered as he came out into its full fury on the lake shore. At first he could not see the water through the driving mist. Then it cleared away for a moment and he stopped short, aghast at the sight which met his eyes.

Opposite him was a long low island known as Philip's Point, dwindling down at its northeastern side to two long narrow bars of quicksand. Alan's horrified eyes saw a small schooner sunk between the bars; her hull was entirely under water and in the rigging clung one solitary figure. So much he saw before the Point was blotted out in a renewed downpour of sleet.

Without a moment's hesitation Alan turned and ran for Four Winds, which was only about a quarter of a mile away around a headland. With the Captain's assistance, something might be done. Other help could not be obtained before darkness would fall and then it would be impossible to do anything. He dashed up the steps of Four Winds and met Emily, who had flung the door open. Behind her was Lynde's pale face with its alarmed questioning eyes.

"Where is the Captain?" gasped Alan. "There's a vessel on Philip's Point and one man at least on her."

"The Captain's away on a cruise," said Emily blankly. "He went three days ago."

"Then nothing can be done," said Alan despairingly. "It will be dark long before I can get to the village."

Lynde stepped out, tying a shawl around her head.

"Let us go around to the Point," she said. "Have you matches? No? Emily, get some. We must light a bonfire at least. And bring Father's glass."

"It is not a fit night for you to be out," said Alan anxiously. "You are sheltered here – you don't feel it – but it's a fearful storm down there."

"I am not afraid of the storm. It will not hurt me. Let us hurry. It is growing dark already."

In silence they breasted their way to the shore and around the headland. Arriving opposite Philip's Point, a lull in the sleet permitted them to see the sunken schooner and the clinging figure. Lynde waved her hand to him and they saw him wave back.

"It won't be necessary to light a fire now that he has seen us," said Lynde. "Nothing can be done with village help till morning and that man can never cling there so long. He will freeze to death, for it is growing colder every minute. His only chance is to swim ashore if he can swim. The danger will be when he comes near shore; the under-tow of the backwater on the quicksand will sweep him away and in his probably exhausted condition he may not be able to make head against it."

"He knows that, doubtless, and that is why he hasn't attempted to swim ashore before this," said Alan. "But I'll meet him in the backwater and drag him in."

"You – you'll risk your own life," cried Lynde.

"There is a little risk certainly, but I don't think there is a great one. Anyhow, the attempt must be made," said Alan quietly.

Suddenly Lynde's composure forsook her. She wrung her hands.

"I can't let you do it," she cried wildly. "You might be drowned – there's every risk. You don't know the force of that backwater. Alan, Alan, don't think of it."

She caught his arm in her white wet hands and looked into his face with passionate pleading.

Emily, who had said nothing, now spoke harshly.

"Lynde is right, Mr. Douglas. You have no right to risk your life for a stranger. My advice is to go to the village for help, and Lynde and I will make a fire and watch here. That is all that can be expected of you or us."

Alan paid no heed to Emily. Very tenderly he loosened Lynde's hold on his arm and looked into her quivering face.

"You know it is my duty, Lynde," he said gently. "If anything can be done for that poor man, I am the only one who can do it. I will come back safe, please God. Be brave, dear."

Lynde, with a little moan of resignation, turned away. Old Emily looked on with a face of grim disapproval as Alan waded out into the surf that boiled and swirled around him in a mad whirl of foam. The shower of sleet had again slackened, and the wreck half a mile away, with its solitary figure, was clearly visible. Alan beckoned to the man to jump overboard and swim ashore, enforcing his appeal by gestures that commanded haste before the next shower should come. For a few moments it seemed as if the seaman did not understand or lacked the courage or power to obey. The next minute he had dropped from the rigging on the crest of a mighty wave and was being borne onward to the shore.

Speedily the backwater was reached and the man, sucked down by the swirl of the wave, threw up his arms and disappeared. Alan dashed in, groping, swimming; it seemed an eternity before his hand clutched the drowning man and wrenched him from the undertow. And, with the seaman in his arms, he staggered back through the foam and dropped his burden on the sand at Lynde's feet. Alan was reeling from exhaustion and chilled to the marrow, but he thought only of the man he had rescued. The latter was unconscious and, as Alan bent over him, he heard Lynde give a choking little cry.

"He is living still," said Alan. "We must get him up to the house as soon as possible. How shall we manage it?"

"Lynde and I can go and bring the Captain's mattress down," said Emily. Now that Alan was safe she was eager to do all she could. "Then you and I can carry him up to the house."

"That will be best," said Alan. "Go quickly."

He did not look at Lynde or he would have been shocked by the agony on her face. She cast one glance at the prostrate man and followed Emily. In a short time they returned with the mattress, and Alan and Emily carried the sailor on it to Four Winds. Lynde walked behind them, seemingly unconscious of both. She watched the stranger's face as one fascinated.

At Four Winds they carried the man to a room where

Emily and Alan worked over him, while Lynde heated water and hunted out stimulants in a mechanical fashion. When Alan came down she asked no questions but looked at him with the same strained horror on her face which it had borne ever since Alan had dropped his burden at her feet.

"Is he – conscious?" asked Lynde, as if she forced herself to ask the question.

"Yes, he has come back to life. But he is delirious and doesn't realize his surroundings at all. He thinks he is still on board the vessel. He'll probably come round all right. Emily is going to watch him and I'll go up to Rexton and send Dr. Ames down."

"Do you know who that man you have saved is?" asked Lynde.

"No. I asked him his name but could not get any sensible answer."

"I can tell you who he is – he is Frank Harmon."

Alan stared at her. "Frank Harmon. Your – your – the man you married? Impossible!"

"It is he. Do you think I could be mistaken?"

DR. AMES CAME TO FOUR WINDS that night and again the next day. He found Harmon delirious in a high fever.

"It will be several days before he comes to his senses," he said. "Shall I send you help to nurse him?"

"It isn't necessary," said Emily stiffly. "I can look after him – and the Captain ought to be back tomorrow."

"You've no idea who he is, I suppose?" asked the doctor.

"No." Emily was quite sincere. Lynde had not told her, and Emily did not recognize him.

"Well, Mr. Douglas did a brave thing in rescuing him," said Dr. Ames. "I'll be back tomorrow."

Harmon remained delirious for a week. Alan went every day to Four Winds, his interest in a man he had rescued

explaining his visits to the Rexton people. The Captain
had returned and, though not absolutely uncivil, was
taciturn and moody. Alan reflected grimly that Captain
Anthony probably owed him a grudge for saving Harmon's
life. He never saw Lynde alone, but her strained, tortured
face made his heart ache. Old Emily only seemed her
natural self. She waited on Harmon and Dr. Ames considered her a paragon of a nurse. Alan thought it was well
that Emily knew nothing more of Harmon than that he
was an old friend of Captain Anthony's. He felt sure that
she would have walked out of the sick room and never re-
entered it had she guessed that the patient was the man
whom, above all others, Lynde dreaded and feared.

One afternoon when Alan went to Four Winds Emily
met him at the door.

"He's better," she announced. "He had a good sleep this
afternoon and when he woke he was quite himself. You'd
better go up and see him. I told him all I could but he
wants to see you. Anthony and Lynde are away to Crosse
Harbour. Go up and talk to him."

Harmon turned his head as the minister approached
and held out his hand with a smile.

"You're the preacher, I reckon. They tell me you were the
man who pulled me out of that hurly-burly. I wasn't
hardly worth saving but I'm as grateful to you as if I was."

"I only – did – what any man would have done," said
Alan, taking the offered hand.

"I don't know about that. Anyhow, it's not every man
could have done it. I'd been hanging in that rigging all day
and most of the night before. There were five more of us
but they dropped off. I knew it was no use to try to swim
ashore alone – the backwater would be too much for me. I
must have been a lot of trouble. That old woman says I've
been raving for a week. And, by the way I feel, I fancy I'll be
stretched out here another week before I'll be able to use

my pins. Who are these Olivers anyhow? The old woman wouldn't talk about the family."

"Don't you know them?" asked Alan in astonishment. "Isn't your name Harmon?"

"That's right – Harmon – Alfred Harmon, first mate of the schooner, *Annie M.*"

"Alfred! I thought your name was Frank!"

"Frank was my twin brother. We were so much alike our own mammy couldn't tell us apart. Did you know Frank?"

"No. This family did. Miss Oliver thought you were Frank when she saw you."

"I don't feel much like myself but I'm not Frank anyway. He's dead, poor chap – got shot in a spat with Chinese pirates three years ago."

"Dead! Man, are you speaking the truth? Are you certain?"

"Pop sure. His mate told me the whole story. Say, preacher, what's the matter? You look as if you were going to keel over."

Alan hastily drank a glass of water.

"I – I am all right now. I haven't been feeling well of late."

"Guess you didn't do yourself any good going out into that freezing water and dragging me in."

"I shall thank God every day of my life that I did do it," said Alan gravely, new light in his eyes, as Emily entered the room. "Miss Oliver, when will the Captain and Lynde be back?"

"They said they would be home by four."

She looked at Alan curiously.

"I will go and meet her," he said quickly.

He came upon Lynde, sitting on a grey boulder under the shadow of an overhanging fir coppice, with her dogs beside her.

She turned her head indifferently as Alan's footsteps

sounded on the pebbles, and then stood slowly up.

"Are you looking for me?" she asked.

"I have some news for you, Lynde," Alan said.

"Has he – has he come to himself?" she whispered.

"Yes, he has come to himself. Lynde, he is not Frank Harmon – he is his twin brother. He says Frank Harmon was killed three years ago in the China seas."

For a moment Lynde's great grey eyes stared into Alan's, questioning. Then, as the truth seized on her comprehension, she sat down on the boulder and put her hands over her face without a word. Alan walked down to the water's edge to give her time to recover herself. When he came back he took her hands and said quietly, "Lynde, do you realize what this means for us – for us? You are free – free to love me – to be my wife."

Lynde shook her head.

"Oh, that can't be. I am not fit to be your wife."

"Don't talk nonsense, dear," he smiled.

"It isn't nonsense. You are a minister and it would ruin you to marry a girl like me. Think what the Rexton people would say of it."

"Rexton isn't the world, dearest. Last week I had a letter from home asking me to go to a church there. I did not think of accepting then – now I will go – we will both go – and a new life will begin for you, clear of the shadows of the old."

"That isn't possible. No, Alan, listen – I love you too well to do you the wrong of marrying you. It would injure you. There is Father. I love him and he has always been very kind to me. But – but – there's something wrong – you know it – some crime in his past – "

"The only man who knew that is dead."

"We do not know that he was the only man. I am the daughter of a criminal and I am no fit wife for Alan

Douglas. No, Alan, don't plead, please. I won't think differently – I never can."

There was a ring of finality in her tone that struck dismay to Alan's heart. He prepared to entreat and argue, but before he could utter a word, the boughs behind them parted and Captain Anthony stepped down from the bank.

"I've been listening," he announced coolly, "and I think it high time I took a share in the conversation. You seem to have run up against a snag, Mr. Douglas. You say Frank Harmon is dead. That's good riddance if it's true. Is it true?"

"His brother declares it is."

"Well, then, I'll help you all I can. I like you, Mr. Douglas, and I happen to be fond of Lynde, too – though you mayn't believe it. I'm fond of her for her mother's sake and I'd like to see her happy. I didn't want to give her to Harmon that time three years ago but I couldn't help myself. He had the upper hand, curse him. It wasn't for my own sake, though – it was for my wife's. However, that's all over and done with and I'll do the best I can to atone for it. So you won't marry your minister because your father was not a good man, Lynde? Well, I don't suppose he was a very good man – a man who makes his wife's life a hell, even in a refined way, isn't exactly a saint, to my way of thinking. But that's the worst that could be said of him and it doesn't entail any indelible disgrace on his family, I suppose. I am not your father, Lynde."

"Not my father?" Lynde echoed the words blankly.

"No. Your father was your mother's first husband. She never told you of him. When I said he made her life a hell, I said the truth, no more, no less. I had loved your mother ever since I was a boy, Lynde. But she was far above me in station and I never dreamed it was possible to win her love. She married James Ashley. He was a gentleman, so called – and he didn't kick or beat her. Oh no, he just tormented her refined womanhood to the verge of frenzy, that was all. He died when you were a baby. And a year later I found out your mother could love me, rough sailor and all as I was. I married her and brought her here. We had fifteen years of happiness together. I'm not a good man – but I made your mother happy in spite of her wrecked health and her dark memories. It was her wish that you should be known as my daughter, but under the present circumstances I know she would wish that you should be told the truth. Marry your man, Lynde, and go away with him. Emily will go with you if you like. I'm going back to the sea. I've been hankering for it ever since your mother died. I'll go out of your life. There, don't cry – I hate to see a woman cry. Mr. Douglas, I'll leave you to dry her tears and I'll go up to the house and have a talk with Harmon."

When Captain Anthony had disappeared behind the Point, Alan turned to Lynde. She was sobbing softly and her face was wet with tears. Alan drew her head down on his shoulder.

"Sweetheart, the dark past is all put by. Our future begins with promise. All is well with us, dear Lynde."

Like a child, she put her arms about his neck and their lips met.

A Sandshore Wooing

"Mr. Shelmardine Frowned and Switched the Unoffending Daisies Viciously with His Cane"

Fir Cottage, Plover Sands.
July Sixth.

E ARRIVED here late last night, and all day Aunt Martha has kept her room to rest. So I had to keep mine also, although I felt as fresh as a morning lark, and just in the mood for enjoyment.

My name is Marguerite Forrester – an absurdly long name for so small a girl. Aunt Martha always calls me Marguer*ite*, with an accent of strong disapproval. She does not like my name, but she gives me the full benefit of it. Connie Shelmardine used to call me Rita. Connie was my roommate last year at the Seminary. We correspond occasionally, but Aunt Martha frowns on it.

I have always lived with Aunt Martha – my parents died when I was a baby. Aunt Martha says I am to be her heiress if I please her – which means – but, oh, you do not know what "pleasing" Aunt Martha means.

Aunt is a determined and inveterate man-hater. She has no particular love for women, indeed, and trusts nobody but Mrs. Saxby, her maid. I rather like Mrs. Saxby. She is not quite so far gone in petrifaction as Aunt, although she gets a little stonier every year. I expect the process will soon begin on me, but it hasn't yet. My flesh and blood are still unreasonably warm and pulsing and rebellious.

Aunt Martha would be in danger of taking a fit if she ever saw me talking to a man. She watches me jealously, firmly determined to guard me from any possible attack of a roaring and ravening lion in the disguise of nineteenth-century masculine attire. So I have to walk demurely and assume a virtue, if I have it not, while I pine after the untasted flesh-pots of Egypt in secret.

We have come down to spend a few weeks at Fir Cottage. Our good landlady is a capacious, kindly-souled creature, and I think she has rather a liking for me. I have been chattering to her all day, for there are times when I absolutely must talk to someone or go mad.

July Tenth.

This sort of life is decidedly dull. The program of every day is the same. I go to the sandshore with Aunt Martha and Mrs. Saxby in the morning, read to Aunt in the afternoons, and mope around by my disconsolate self in the evenings. Mrs. Blake has lent me, for shore use, a very fine spyglass which she owns. She says her "man" brought it home from "furrin' parts" before he died. While Aunt and Mrs. Saxby meander up and down the shore, leaving me free to a certain extent, I amuse myself by examining distant seas and coasts through it, thus getting a few peeps into a forbidden world. We see few people, although there is a large summer hotel about a mile up the beach. Our shore haunts do not seem to be popular with its guests. They prefer the rocks. This suits Aunt Martha admirably. I may also add that it doesn't suit her niece – but that is a matter of small importance.

The first morning I noticed a white object on the rocks, about half a mile away, and turned my glass on it. There – apparently within a stone's throw of me – was a young man. He was lounging on a rock, looking dreamily out to sea. There was something about his face that reminded me of someone I know, but I cannot remember whom.

Every morning he has reappeared on the same spot. He seems to be a solitary individual, given to prowling by himself. I wonder what Aunt would say if she knew what I am so earnestly watching through my glass at times.

July Eleventh.

I shall have to cease looking at the Unknown, I am afraid.

This morning I turned my glass, as usual, on his pet haunt. I nearly fell over in my astonishment, for he was also looking through a spyglass straight at me, too, it seemed. How foolish I felt! And yet my curiosity was so strong that a few minutes afterward I peeped back again, just to see what he was doing. Then he coolly laid down his glass, rose, lifted his cap and bowed politely to me – or, at least, in my direction. I dropped my glass and smiled in a mixture of dismay and amusement. Then I remembered that he was probably watching me again, and might imagine my smile was meant for him. I banished it immediately, shut my glass up and did not touch it again. Soon after we came home.

July Twelfth.
Something has happened at last. Today I went to the shore as usual, fully resolved not even to glance in the forbidden direction. But in the end I had to take a peep, and saw him on the rocks with his glass levelled at me. When he saw that I was looking he laid down the glass, held up his hands, and began to spell out something in the deaf-mute alphabet. Now, I know that same alphabet. Connie taught it to me last year, so that we might hold communication across the schoolroom. I gave one frantic glance at Aunt Martha's rigid back, and then watched him while he deftly spelled: "I am Francis Shelmardine. Are you not Miss Forrester, my sister's friend?"

Francis Shelmardine! Now I knew whom he resembled. And have I not heard endless dissertations from Connie on this wonderful brother of hers, Francis the clever, the handsome, the charming, until he has become the only hero of dreams I have ever had? It was too wonderful. I could only stare dazedly back through my glass.

"May we know each other?" he went on. "May I come over and introduce myself? Right hand, yes; left, no."

I gasped! Suppose he were to come? *What* would happen? I waved my left hand sorrowfully. He looked quite crestfallen and disappointed as he spelled out: "Why not? Would your friends disapprove?"

I signalled: "Yes."

"Are you displeased at my boldness?" was his next question.

Where had all Aunt Martha's precepts flown to then? I blush to record that I lifted my left hand shyly and had just time to catch his pleased expression when Aunt Martha came up and said it was time to go home. So I picked myself meekly up, shook the sand from my dress, and followed my good aunt dutifully home.

July Thirteenth.

When we went to the shore this morning I had to wait in spasms of remorse and anxiety until Aunt got tired of reading and set off along the shore with Mrs. Saxby. Then I reached for my glass.

Mr. Shelmardine and I had quite a conversation. Under the circumstances there could be no useless circumlocution in our exchange of ideas. It was religiously "boiled down," and ran something like this:

"You are not displeased with me?"

"No – but I should be."

"Why?"

"It is wrong to deceive Aunt."

"I am quite respectable."

"That is not the question."

"Cannot her prejudices be overcome?"

"Absolutely no."

"Mrs. Allardyce, who is staying at the hotel, knows her well. Shall I bring her over to vouch for my character?"

"It would not do a bit of good."

"Then it is hopeless."

"Yes."

"Would you object to knowing me on your own account?"

"No."

"Do you ever come to the shore alone?"

"No. Aunt would not permit me."

"Must she know?"

"Yes. I would not come without her permission."

"You will not refuse to chat with me thus now and then?"

"I don't know. Perhaps not."

I had to go home then. As we went Mrs. Saxby complimented me on my good colour. Aunt Martha looked her disapproval. If I were really ill Aunt would spend her last cent in my behalf, but she would be just as well pleased to see me properly pale and subdued at all times, and not looking as if I were too well contented in this vale of tears.

July Seventeenth.

I have "talked" a good deal with Mr. Shelmardine these past four days. He is to be at the beach for some weeks longer. This morning he signalled across from the rocks: "I mean to see you at last. Tomorrow I will walk over and pass you."

"You must not. Aunt will suspect."

"No danger. Don't be alarmed. I will do nothing rash."

I suppose he will. He seems to be very determined. Of course, I cannot prevent him from promenading on our beach all day if he chooses. But then if he did, Aunt would speedily leave him in sole possession of it.

I wonder what I had better wear tomorrow.

July Nineteenth.

Yesterday morning Aunt Martha was serene and unsuspicious. It is dreadful of me to be deceiving her and I do feel guilty. I sat down on the sand and pretended to read the "Memoirs of a Missionary" – Aunt likes cheerful books like that – in an agony of anticipation. Presently Aunt said, majestically: "Marguer*ite*, there is a man coming this way. We will move further down."

And we moved. Poor Aunt!

Mr. Shelmardine came bravely on. I felt my heart beating to my very finger tips. He halted by the fragment of an old stranded boat. Aunt had turned her back on him.

I ventured on a look. He lifted his hat with a twinkle in his eye. Just then Aunt said, icily: "We will go home, Marguer*ite*. That creature evidently intends to persist in his intrusion."

Home we came accordingly.

This morning he signalled across: "Letter from Connie. Message for you. I mean to deliver it personally. Do you ever go to church?"

Now, I *do* go regularly to church at home. But Aunt Martha and Mrs. Saxby are both such rigid church people that they would not darken the doors of the Methodist church at Plover Sands for any consideration. Needless to say, I am not allowed to go either. But it was impossible to make this long explanation, so I merely replied: "Not here."

"Will you not go tomorrow morning?"

"Aunt will not let me."

"Coax her."

"Coaxing never has any effect on her."

"Would she relent if Mrs. Allardyce were to call for you?"

Now, I have been cautiously sounding Aunt about Mrs. Allardyce, and I have discovered that she disapproves of her. So I said: "It would be useless. I will ask Aunt if I may go, but I feel almost sure that she will not consent."

This evening, when Aunt was in an unusually genial mood, I plucked up heart of grace and asked her.

"Marguer*ite*," she said impressively, "you know that I do not attend church here."

"But, Aunt," I persisted, quakingly, "couldn't I go alone? It is not very far – and I will be very careful."

Aunt merely gave me a look that said about forty distinct and separate things, and I was turning away in despair when Mrs. Saxby – bless her heart – said: "I really think it would be no harm to let the child go."

As Aunt attaches great importance to Mrs. Saxby's opinion, she looked at me relentingly and said: "Well, I will think it over and let you know in the morning, Marguer*ite*."

Now, everything depends on the sort of humour Aunt is in in the morning.

July Twentieth.

This morning was perfect, and after breakfast Aunt said, condescendingly: "I think you may attend church if you wish, Marguer*ite*. Remember that I expect you to conduct yourself with becoming prudence and modesty."

I flew upstairs and pulled my prettiest dress out of my trunk. It is a delicate, shimmering grey stuff with pearly tints about it. Every time I get anything new, Aunt Martha and I have a battle royal over it. I verily believe that Aunt would like me to dress in the fashions in vogue in her youth. There is always a certain flavour of old-fashionedness about my gowns and hats. Connie used to say that it was delicious and gave me a piquant uniqueness – a certain unlikeness to other people that possessed a positive charm. That is only Connie's view of it, however.

But I had had my own way about this dress and it is really very becoming. I wore a little silvery-grey chip hat, trimmed with pale pink flowers, and I pinned at my belt the sweetest cluster of old-fashioned blush rosebuds from the garden. Then I borrowed a hymn book from Mrs. Blake and ran down to undergo Aunt Martha's scrutiny.

"Dear me, child," she said discontentedly, "you have gotten yourself up very frivolously, it seems to me."

"Why, Aunty," I protested, "I'm all in grey – every bit."

Aunt Martha sniffed. You don't know how much Aunt can express in a sniff. But I tripped to church like a bird.

The first person I saw there was Mr. Shelmardine. He was sitting right across from me and a smile glimmered in his eyes. I did not look at him again. Through the service I was subdued enough to have satisfied even Aunt Martha.

When church came out, he waited for me at the entrance to his pew. I pretended not to see him until he said "Good morning," in a voice vibrating and deep, which sounded as though it might become infinitely tender if its owner chose. When we went down the steps he took my hymnal, and we walked up the long, bowery country road.

"Thank you so much for coming today," he said – as if I went to oblige him.

"I had a hard time to get Aunt Martha's consent," I declared frankly. "I wouldn't have succeeded if Mrs. Saxby hadn't taken my part."

"Heaven bless Mrs. Saxby," he remarked fervently. "But is there any known way of overcoming your aunt's scruples? If so, I am ready to risk it."

"There is none. Aunt Martha is very good and kind to me, but she will never stop trying to bring me up. The process will be going on when I am fifty. And she hates men! I don't know what she would do if she saw me now."

Mr. Shelmardine frowned and switched the unoffending daisies viciously with his cane.

"Then there is no hope of my seeing you openly and above-board?"

"Not at present," I said faintly.

After a brief silence we began to talk of other things. He told me how he happened to see me first.

"I was curious to know who the people were who were always in the same place at the same time, so one day I took my telescope. I could see you plainly. You were reading and had your hat off. When I went back to the hotel I asked Mrs. Allardyce if she knew who the boarders at Fir Cottage were and she told me. I had heard Connie speak of you, and I determined to make your acquaintance."

When we reached the lane I held out my hand for the hymnal.

"You mustn't come any further, Mr. Shelmardine," I said hurriedly. "Aunt – Aunt might see you."

He took my hand and held it, looking at me seriously.

"Suppose I were to walk up to the cottage tomorrow and ask for you?"

I gasped. He looked so capable of doing anything he took it into his head to do.

"Oh, you wouldn't," I said piteously. "Aunt Martha would – you are not in earnest."

"I suppose not," he said regretfully. "Of course I would not do anything that would cause you unpleasantness. But this must not – shall not be our last meeting."

"Aunt will not let me come to church again," I said.

"Does she ever take a nap in the afternoon?" he queried.

I wriggled my parasol about in the dust uneasily.

"Sometimes."

"I shall be at the old boat tomorrow afternoon at two-thirty," he said.

I pulled my hand away.

"I couldn't – you know I couldn't," I cried – and then I blushed to my ears.

"Are you sure you couldn't?" bending a little nearer.

"Quite sure," I murmured.

He surrendered my hymnal at last.

"Will you give me a rose?"

I unpinned the whole cluster and handed it to him. He lifted it until it touched his lips. As for me, I scuttled up the lane in the most undignified fashion. At the turn I looked back. He was still standing there with his hat off.

July Twenty-fourth.

On Monday afternoon I slipped away to the shore while Aunt Martha and Mrs. Saxby were taking their regular nap and I was supposed to be reading sermons in my room.

Mr. Shelmardine was leaning against the old boat, but he came swiftly across the sand to meet me.

"This is very kind of you," he said.

"I ought not to have come," I said repentantly. "But it is so lonely there – and one can't be interested in sermons and memoirs *all* the time."

Mr. Shelmardine laughed.

"Mr. and Mrs. Allardyce are on the other side of the boat. Will you come and meet them?"

How nice of him to bring them! I knew I should like Mrs. Allardyce, just because Aunt Martha didn't. We had a delightful stroll. I never thought of the time until Mr. Shelmardine said it was four o'clock.

"Oh, is it so late as that?" I cried. "I must go at once."

"I'm sorry we have kept you so long," remarked Mr. Shelmardine in a tone of concern. "If she should be awake, what will the consequences be?"

"Too terrible to think of," I answered seriously. "I'm sorry, Mr. Shelmardine, but you mustn't come any further."

"*We* will be here tomorrow afternoon," he said.

"Mr. Shelmardine!" I protested. "I wish you wouldn't put such ideas into my head. They won't come out – no, not if I read a whole volume of sermons right through."

We looked at each other for a second. Then he began to smile, and we both went off into a peal of laughter.

"At least let me know if Miss Fiske rampages," he called after me as I fled.

But Aunt Martha was not awake – and I have been to the shore three afternoons since then. I was there today, and I'm going tomorrow for a boat sail with Mr. Shelmardine and the Allardyces. But I am afraid the former will do something rash soon. This afternoon he said: "I don't think I can stand this much longer."

"Stand what?" I asked.

"You know very well," he answered recklessly. "Meeting you in this clandestine manner, and thereby causing that poor little conscience of yours such misery. If your aunt were not so – unreasonable, I should never have stooped to it."

"It is all my fault," I said contritely.

"Well, I hardly meant that," he said grimly. "But hadn't I better go frankly to your aunt and lay the whole case before her?"

"You would never see me again if you did that," I said hastily – and then wished I hadn't.

"That is the worst threat you could make," he said.

July Twenty-fifth.

It is all over, and I am the most miserable girl in the world. Of course this means that Aunt Martha has discovered everything and the deserved punishment of my sins has overtaken me.

I slipped away again this afternoon and went for that boat sail. We had a lovely time but were rather late getting in, and I hurried home with many misgivings. Aunt Martha met me at the door.

My dress was draggled, my hat had slipped back, and the kinks and curls of my obstreperous hair were something awful. I know I looked very disreputable and also, no doubt, very guilty and conscience-stricken. Aunt gave me an unutterable look and then followed me up to my room in grim silence.

"Marguer*ite*, what does this mean?"

I have lots of faults, but untruthfulness isn't one of them. I confessed everything – at least, almost everything. I didn't tell about the telescopes and deaf-mute alphabet, and Aunt was too horror-stricken to think of asking how I first made Mr. Shelmardine's acquaintance. She listened in stony silence. I had expected a terrible scolding, but I suppose my crimes simply seemed to her too enormous for words.

When I had sobbed out my last word she rose, swept me one glance of withering contempt, and left the room. Presently Mrs. Saxby came up, looking concerned.

"My dear child, what have you been doing? Your aunt says that we are to go home on the afternoon train tomorrow. She is terribly upset."

I just curled up on the bed and cried, while Mrs. Saxby packed my trunk. I will have no chance to explain matters to Mr. Shelmardine. And I will never see him again, for Aunt is quite capable of whisking me off to Africa. He will just think me a feather-brained flirt. Oh, I am so unhappy!

July Twenty-sixth.

I am the happiest girl in the world! That is quite a different strain from yesterday. We leave Fir Cottage in an hour, but that doesn't matter now.

I did not sleep a wink last night and crawled miserably down to breakfast. Aunt took not the slightest notice of me, but to my surprise she told Mrs. Saxby that she intended taking a farewell walk to the shore. I knew I would be taken, too, to be kept out of mischief, and my heart gave a great bound of hope. Perhaps I would have a chance to send word to Francis, since Aunt did not know of the part my spyglass had played in my bad behaviour.

I meekly followed my grim guardians to the shore and sat dejectedly on my rug while they paced the sand. Francis was on the rocks. As soon as Aunt Martha and Mrs. Saxby were at a safe distance, I began my message: "All discovered. Aunt is very angry. We go home today."

Then I snatched my glass. His face expressed the direst consternation and dismay. He signalled: "I must see you before you go."

"Impossible. Aunt will never forgive me. Good-bye."

I saw a look of desperate determination cross his face. If forty Aunt Marthas had swooped down upon me, I could not have torn my eyes from that glass.

"I love you. You know it. Do you care for me? I must have my answer now."

What a situation! No time or chance for any maidenly hesitation or softening aureole of words. Aunt and Mrs. Saxby had almost reached the point where they invariably turned. I had barely time to spell out a plain, blunt "yes" and read his answer.

"I shall go home at once, get Mother and Connie, follow you, and demand possession of my property. I shall win the day. Have no fear. Till then, good-bye, my darling."

"Marguerite," said Mrs. Saxby at my elbow, "it is time to go."

I got up obediently. Aunt Martha was as grim and uncompromising as ever, and Mrs. Saxby looked like a chief mourner, but do you suppose I cared? I dropped behind them just once before we left the shore. I knew he was watching me and I waved my hand.

I suppose I am really engaged to Francis Shelmardine. But was there ever such a funny wooing? And *what* will Aunt Martha say?

The Unhappiness
of Miss Farquhar

RANCES FARQUHAR was a beauty and was sometimes called a society butterfly by people who didn't know very much about it. Her father was wealthy and her mother came of an extremely blue-blooded family. Frances had been out for three years, and was a social favourite. Consequently, it may be wondered why she was unhappy.

In plain English, Frances Farquhar had been jilted – just a commonplace, everyday jilting! She had been engaged to Paul Holcomb; he was a very handsome fellow, somewhat too evidently aware of the fact, and Frances was very deeply in love with him – or thought herself so, which at the time comes to pretty much the same thing. Everybody in her set knew of her engagement, and all her girl friends envied her, for Holcomb was a matrimonial catch.

Then the crash came. Nobody outside the family knew exactly what did happen, but everybody knew that the Holcomb – Farquhar match was off, and everybody had a different story to account for it.

The simple truth was that Holcomb was fickle and had fallen in love with another girl. There was nothing of the man about him, and it did not matter to his sublimely selfish caddishness whether he broke Frances Farquhar's heart or not. He got his freedom and he married Maud Carroll in six months' time.

The Farquhars, especially Ned, who was Frances' older brother and seldom concerned himself about her except when the family honour was involved, were furious at the whole affair. Mr. Farquhar stormed, and Ned swore, and Della lamented her vanished role of bridemaid. As for Mrs. Farquhar, she cried and said it would ruin Frances' future prospects.

The girl herself took no part in the family indignation

meetings. But she believed that her heart was broken. Her love and her pride had suffered equally, and the effect seemed disastrous.

After a while the Farquhars calmed down and devoted themselves to the task of cheering Frances up. This they did not accomplish. She got through the rest of the season somehow and showed a proud front to the world, not even flinching when Holcomb himself crossed her path. To be sure, she was pale and thin, and had about as much animation as a mask, but the same might be said of a score of other girls who were not suspected of having broken hearts.

When the summer came Frances asserted herself. The Farquhars went to Green Harbour every summer. But this time Frances said she would not go, and stuck to it. The whole family took turns coaxing her and had nothing to show for their pains.

"I'm going up to Windy Meadows to stay with Aunt Eleanor while you are at the Harbour," she declared. "She has invited me often enough."

Ned whistled. "Jolly time you'll have of it, Sis. Windy Meadows is about as festive as a funeral. And Aunt Eleanor isn't lively, to put it in the mildest possible way."

"I don't care if she isn't. I want to get somewhere where people won't look at me and talk about – that," said Frances, looking ready to cry.

Ned went out and swore at Holcomb again, and then advised his mother to humour Frances. Accordingly, Frances went to Windy Meadows.

Windy Meadows was, as Ned had said, the reverse of lively. It was a pretty country place, with a sort of fag-end by way of a little fishing village, huddled on a wind-swept bit of beach, locally known as the "Cove." Aunt Eleanor was one of those delightful people, so few and far between in this world, who have perfectly mastered the art of minding their own business exclusively. She left Frances in peace.

She knew that her niece had had "some love trouble or other," and hadn't gotten over it rightly.

"It's always best to let those things take their course," said this philosophical lady to her "help" and confidant, Margaret Ann Peabody. "She'll get over it in time – though she doesn't think so now, bless you."

For the first fortnight Frances revelled in a luxury of unhindered sorrow. She could cry all night – and all day too, if she wished – without having to stop because people might notice that her eyes were red. She could mope in her room all she liked. And there were no men who demanded civility.

When the fortnight was over, Aunt Eleanor took crafty counsel with herself. The letting-alone policy was all very well, but it would not do to have the girl die on her hands. Frances was getting paler and thinner every day – and she was spoiling her eyelashes by crying.

"I wish," said Aunt Eleanor one morning at breakfast, while Frances pretended to eat, "that I could go and take Corona Sherwood out for a drive today. I promised her last week that I would, but I've never had time yet. And today is baking and churning day. It's a shame. Poor Corona!"

"Who is she?" asked Frances, trying to realize that there was actually someone in the world besides herself who was to be pitied.

"She is our minister's sister. She has been ill with rheumatic fever. She is better now, but doesn't seem to get strong very fast. She ought to go out more, but she isn't able to walk. I really must try and get around tomorrow. She keeps house for her brother at the manse. He isn't married, you know."

Frances didn't know, nor did she in the least degree care. But even the luxury of unlimited grief palls, and

Frances was beginning to feel this vaguely. She offered to go and take Miss Sherwood out driving.

"I've never seen her," she said, "but I suppose that doesn't matter. I can drive Grey Tom in the phaeton, if you like."

It was just what Aunt Eleanor intended, and she saw Frances drive off that afternoon with a great deal of satisfaction.

"Give my love to Corona," she told her, "and say for me that she isn't to go messing about among those shore people until she's perfectly well. The manse is the fourth house after you turn the third corner."

Frances kept count of the corners and the houses and found the manse. Corona Sherwood herself came to the door. Frances had been expecting an elderly personage with spectacles and grey crimps; she was surprised to find that the minister's sister was a girl of about her own age and possessed of a distinct worldly prettiness. Corona was dark, with a different darkness from that of Frances, who had ivory outlines and blue-black hair, while Corona was dusky and piquant.

Her eyes brightened with delight when Frances told her errand.

"How good of you and Miss Eleanor! I am not strong enough to walk far yet – or do anything useful, in fact, and Elliott so seldom has time to take me out."

"Where shall we go?" asked Frances when they started. "I don't know much about this locality."

"Can we drive to the Cove first? I want to see poor little Jacky Hart. He has been so sick – "

"Aunt Eleanor positively forbade that," said Frances dubiously. "Will it be safe to disobey her?"

Corona laughed.

"Miss Eleanor blames my poor shore people for making me sick at first, but it was really not that at all. And I want to see Jacky Hart so much. He has been ill for some time with some disease of the spine and he is worse lately. I'm sure Miss Eleanor won't mind my calling just to see him."

Frances turned Grey Tom down the shore road that ran to the Cove and past it to silvery, wind-swept sands, rimming sea expanses crystal clear. Jacky Hart's home proved to be a tiny little place overflowing with children. Mrs. Hart was a pale, tired-looking woman with the patient, far-seeing eyes so often found among the women who watch sea and shore every day and night of their lives for those who sometimes never return.

She spoke of Jacky with the apathy of hopelessness. The doctor said he would not last much longer. She told all her troubles unreservedly to Corona in her monotonous voice. Her "man" was drinking again and the mackerel catch was poor.

When Mrs. Hart asked Corona to go in and see Jacky, Frances went too. The sick boy, a child with a delicate, wasted face and large, bright eyes, lay in a tiny bedroom off the kitchen. The air was hot and heavy. Mrs. Hart stood at the foot of the bed with her tragic face.

"We have to set up nights with him now," she said. "It's awful hard on me and my man. The neighbours are kind enough and come sometimes, but most of them have enough to do. His medicine has to be given every half hour. I've been up for three nights running now. Jabez was off to the tavern for two. I'm just about played out."

She suddenly broke down and began to cry, or rather whimper, in a heart-broken way.

Corona looked troubled. "I wish I could come tonight, Mrs. Hart, but I'm afraid I'm really not strong enough yet."

"I don't know much about sickness," spoke up Frances firmly, "but if to sit by the child and give him his medicine regularly is all that is necessary, I am sure I can do that. I'll come and sit up with Jacky tonight if you care to have me."

Afterwards, when she and Corona were driving away, she wondered a good deal at herself. But Corona was so evidently pleased with her offer, and took it all so much as a matter of course, that Frances had not the courage to display her wonder. They had their drive through the great green bowl of the country valley, brimming over with sunshine, and afterwards Corona made Frances go home with her to tea.

Rev. Elliott Sherwood had got back from his pastoral visitations, and was training his sweet peas in the way they should go against the garden fence. He was in his shirt sleeves and wore a big straw hat, and seemed in nowise disconcerted thereby. Corona introduced him, and he took Grey Tom away and put him in the barn. Then he went back to his sweet peas. He had had his tea, he said, so that Frances did not see him again until she went home. She thought he was a very indifferent young man, and not half so nice as his sister.

But she went and sat up with Jacky Hart that night, getting to the Cove at dark, when the sea was a shimmer of fairy tints and the boats were coming in from the fishing grounds. Jacky greeted her with a wonderful smile, and later on she found herself watching alone by his bed. The tiny lamp on the table burned dim, and outside, on the rocks, there was loud laughing and talking until a late hour.

Afterwards a silence fell, through which the lap of the waves on the sands and the far-off moan of the Atlantic surges came sonorously. Jacky was restless and wakeful, but did not suffer, and liked to talk. Frances listened to him with a new-born power of sympathy, which she thought she must have caught from Corona. He told her all the tragedy of his short life, and how bad he felt, about Dad's taking to drink and Mammy's having to work so hard.

The pitiful little sentences made Frances' heart ache. The maternal instinct of the true woman awoke in her. She took a sudden liking to the child. He was a spiritual little creature, and his sufferings had made him old and wise. Once in the night he told Frances that he thought the angels must look like her.

"You are so sweet pretty," he said gravely. "I never saw anyone so pretty, not even Miss C'rona. You look like a picture I once saw on Mr. Sherwood's table when I was up at the manse one day 'fore I got so bad I couldn't walk. It was a woman with a li'l baby in her arms and a kind of rim round her head. I would like something most awful much."

"What is it, dear?" said Frances gently. "If I can get or do it for you, I will."

"You could," he said wistfully, "but maybe you won't want to. But I do wish you'd come here just once every day and sit here five minutes and let me look at you – just that. Will it be too much trouble?"

Frances stooped and kissed him. "I will come every day, Jacky," she said; and a look of ineffable content came over the thin little face. He put up his hand and touched her cheek.

"I knew you were good – as good as Miss C'rona, and she is an angel. I love you."

When morning came Frances went home. It was raining, and the sea was hidden in mist. As she walked along the wet road, Elliott Sherwood came splashing along in a little two-wheeled gig and picked her up. He wore a raincoat and a small cap, and did not look at all like a minister – or, at least, like Frances' conception of one.

Not that she knew much about ministers. Her own minister at home – that is to say, the minister of the fashionable uptown church which she attended – was a portly, dignified old man with silvery hair and gold-

rimmed glasses, who preached scholarly, cultured sermons and was as far removed from Frances' personal life
as a star in the Milky Way.

But a minister who wore rubber coats and little caps
and drove about in a two-wheeled gig, very much mud-
bespattered, and who talked about the shore people as if
they were household intimates of his, was absolutely new
to Frances.

She could not help seeing, however, that the crisp
brown hair under the edges of the unclerical-looking cap
curled around a remarkably well-shaped forehead,
beneath which flashed out a pair of very fine dark-grey
eyes; he had likewise a good mouth, which was resolute
and looked as if it might be stubborn on occasion; and,
although he was not exactly handsome, Frances decided
that she liked his face.

He tucked the wet, slippery rubber apron of his convey-
ance about her and then proceeded to ask questions.
Jacky Hart's case had to be reported on, and then Mr.
Sherwood took out a notebook and looked over its entries
intently.

"Do you want any more work of that sort to do?" he
asked her abruptly.

Frances felt faintly amused. He talked to her as he might
have done to Corona, and seemed utterly oblivious of the
fact that her profile was classic and her eyes delicious. His
indifference piqued Frances a little in spite of her mur-
dered heart. Well, if there was anything she could do she
might as well do it, she told him briefly, and he, with equal
brevity, gave her directions for finding some old lady who
lived on the Elm Creek road and to whom Corona had
read tracts.

"Tracts are a mild dissipation of Aunt Clorinda's," he
said. "She fairly revels in them. She is half blind and has
missed Corona very much."

There were other matters also – a dozen or so of factory girls who needed to be looked after and a family of ragged children to be clothed. Frances, in some dismay, found herself pledged to help in all directions, and then ways and means had to be discussed. The long, wet road, sprinkled with houses, from whose windows people were peering to see "what girl the minister was driving," seemed very short. Frances did not know it, but Elliott Sherwood drove a full mile out of his way that morning to take her home, and risked being late for a very important appointment – from which it may be inferred that he was not quite so blind to the beautiful as he had seemed.

Frances went through the rain that afternoon and read tracts to Aunt Clorinda. She was so dreadfully tired that night that she forgot to cry, and slept well and soundly.

In the morning she went to church for the first time since coming to Windy Meadows. It did not seem civil not to go to hear a man preach when she had gone slumming with his sister and expected to assist him with his difficulties over factory girls. She was surprised at Elliott Sherwood's sermon, and mentally wondered why such a man had been allowed to remain for four years in a little country pulpit. Later on Aunt Eleanor told her it was for his health.

"He was not strong when he left college, so he came here. But he is as well as ever now, and I expect he will soon be gobbled up by some of your city churches. He preached in Castle Street church last winter, and I believe they were delighted with him."

This was all of a month later. During that time Frances thought that she must have been re-created, so far was her old self left behind. She seldom had an idle moment; when she had, she spent it with Corona. The two girls had become close friends, loving each other with the intensity of exceptional and somewhat exclusive natures.

Corona grew strong slowly, and could do little for her brother's people, but Frances was an excellent proxy, and Elliott Sherwood kept her employed. Incidentally, Frances had come to know the young minister, with his lofty ideals and earnest efforts, very well. He had got into a ridiculous habit of going to her – her, Frances Farquhar! – for advice in many perplexities.

Frances had nursed Jacky Hart and talked temperance to his father and read tracts to Aunt Clorinda and started a reading circle among the factory girls and fitted out all the little Jarboes with dresses and coaxed the shore children to go to school and patched up a feud between two 'longshore families and done a hundred other things of a similar nature.

Aunt Eleanor said nothing, as was her wise wont, but she talked it over with Margaret Ann Peabody, and agreed with that model domestic when she said: "Work'll keep folks out of trouble and help 'em out of it when they are in. Just as long as that girl brooded over her own worries and didn't think of anyone but herself she was miserable. But as soon as she found other folks were unhappy, too, and tried to help 'em out a bit, she helped herself most of all. She's getting fat and rosy, and it is plain to be seen that the minister thinks there isn't the like of her on this planet."

One night Frances told Corona all about Holcomb. Elliott Sherwood was away, and Frances had gone up to stay all night with Corona at the manse. They were sitting in the moonlit gloom of Corona's room, and Frances felt confidential. She had expected to feel badly and cry a little while she told it. But she did not, and before she was half through, it did not seem as if it were worth telling after all. Corona was deeply sympathetic. She did not say a great deal, but what she did say put Frances on better terms with herself.

"Oh, I shall get over it," the latter declared finally. "Once

I thought I never would – but the truth is, I'm getting over it now. I'm very glad – but I'm horribly ashamed, too, to find myself so fickle."

"I don't think you are fickle, Frances," said Corona gravely, "because I don't think you ever really loved that man at all. You only imagined you did. And he was not worthy of you. You are so good, dear; those shore people just worship you. Elliott says you can do anything you like with them."

Frances laughed and said she was not at all good. Yet she was pleased. Later on, when she was brushing her hair before the mirror and smiling absently at her reflection, Corona said: "Frances, what is it like to be as pretty as you are?"

"Nonsense!" said Frances by way of answer.

"It is not nonsense at all. You must know you are very lovely, Frances. Elliott says you are the most beautiful girl he has ever seen."

For a girl who has told herself a dozen times that she would never care again for masculine admiration, Frances experienced a very odd thrill of delight on hearing that the minister of Windy Meadows thought her beautiful. She knew he admired her intellect and had immense respect for what he called her "genius for influencing people," but she had really believed all along that, if Elliott Sherwood had been asked, he could not have told whether she was a whit better looking than Kitty Martin of the Cove, who taught a class in Sunday school and had round rosy cheeks and a snub nose.

The summer went very quickly. One day Jacky Hart died – drifted out with the ebb tide, holding Frances' hand. She had loved the patient, sweet-souled little creature and missed him greatly.

When the time to go home came Frances felt dull. She hated to leave Windy Meadows and Corona and her dear shore people and Aunt Eleanor and – and – well, Margaret Ann Peabody.

Elliott Sherwood came up the night before she went away. When Margaret Ann showed him reverentially in, Frances was sitting in a halo of sunset light, and the pale, golden chrysanthemums in her hair shone like stars in the blue-black coils.

Elliott Sherwood had been absent from Windy Meadows for several days. There was a subdued jubilance in his manner.

"You think I have come to say good-bye, but I haven't," he told her. "I shall see you again very soon, I hope. I have just received a call to Castle Street church, and it is my intention to accept. So Corona and I will be in town this winter."

Frances tried to tell him how glad she was, but only stammered. Elliott Sherwood came close up to her as she stood by the window in the fading light, and said –

But on second thoughts I shall not record what he said – or what she said either. Some things should be left to the imagination.

*A Strayed
Allegiance*

"WILL YOU GO to the Cove with me this afternoon?"

It was Marian Lesley who asked the question.

Esterbrook Elliott unpinned with a masterful touch the delicate cluster of Noisette rosebuds she wore at her throat and transferred them to his buttonhole as he answered courteously: "Certainly. My time, as you know, is entirely at your disposal."

They were standing in the garden under the creamy bloom of drooping acacia trees. One long plume of blossoms touched lightly the soft, golden-brown coils of the girl's hair and cast a wavering shadow over the beautiful, flower-like face beneath it.

Esterbrook Elliott, standing before her, thought proudly that he had never seen a woman who might compare with her. In every detail she satisfied his critical, fastidious taste. There was not a discordant touch about her

Esterbrook Elliott had always loved Marian Lesley – or thought he had. They had grown up together from childhood. He was an only son and she an only daughter. It had always been an understood thing between the two families that the boy and girl should marry. But Marian's father had decreed that no positive pledge should pass between them until Marian was twenty-one.

Esterbrook accepted his mapped-out destiny and selected bride with the conviction that he was an exceptionally lucky fellow. Out of all the women in the world Marian was the very one whom he would have chosen as mistress of his fine, old home. She had been his boyhood's ideal. He believed that he loved her sincerely, but he was not too much in love to be blind to the worldly advantages of his marriage with his cousin.

His father had died two years previously, leaving him wealthy and independent. Marian had lost her mother in childhood; her father died when she was eighteen. Since then she had lived alone with her aunt. Her life was quiet and lonely. Esterbrook's companionship was all that brightened it, but it was enough. Marian lavished on him all the rich, womanly love of her heart. On her twenty-first birthday they were formally betrothed. They were to be married in the following autumn.

No shadow had drifted across the heaven of her happiness. She believed herself secure in her lover's unfaltering devotion. True, at times she thought his manner lacked a lover's passionate ardour. He was always attentive and courteous. She had only to utter a wish to find that it had been anticipated; he spent every spare minute at her side.

Yet sometimes she half wished he would betray more lover-like impatience and intensity. Were all lovers as calm and undemonstrative?

She reproached herself for this incipient disloyalty as often as it vexingly intruded its unwelcome presence across her inner consciousness. Surely Esterbrook was fond and devoted enough to satisfy the most exacting demands of affection. Marian herself was somewhat undemonstrative and reserved. Passing acquaintances called her cold and proud. Only the privileged few knew the rich depths of womanly tenderness in her nature.

Esterbrook thought that he fully appreciated her. As he had walked homeward the night of their betrothal, he had reviewed with unconscious criticism his mental catalogue of Marian's graces and good qualities, admitting, with supreme satisfaction, that there was not one thing about her that he could wish changed.

This afternoon, under the acacias, they had been planning about their wedding. There was no one to consult but themselves.

They were to be married early in September and then

go abroad. Esterbrook mapped out the details of their bridal tour with careful thoughtfulness. They would visit all the old-world places that Marian wished to see. Afterwards they would come back home. He discussed certain changes he wished to make in the old Elliott mansion to fit it for a young and beautiful mistress.

He did most of the planning. Marian was content to listen in happy silence. Afterwards she had proposed this walk to the Cove.

"What particular object of charity have you found at the Cove now?" asked Esterbrook, with lazy interest, as they walked along.

"Mrs. Barrett's little Bessie is very ill with fever," answered Marian. Then, catching his anxious look, she hastened to add, "It is nothing infectious – some kind of a slow, sapping variety. There is no danger, Esterbrook."

"I was not afraid for myself," he replied quietly. "My alarm was for you. You are too precious to me, Marian, for me to permit you to risk health and life, if it were dangerous. What a Lady Bountiful you are to those people at the Cove. When we are married you must take me in hand and teach me your creed of charity. I'm afraid I've lived a rather selfish life. You will change all that, dear. You will make a good man of me."

"You are that now, Esterbrook," she said softly. "If you were not, I could not love you."

"It is a negative sort of goodness, I fear. I have never been tried or tempted severely. Perhaps I should fail under the test."

"I am sure you would not," answered Marian proudly.

Esterbrook laughed; her faith in him was pleasant. He had no thought but that he would prove worthy of it.

The Cove, so-called, was a little fishing hamlet situated on the low, sandy shore of a small bay. The houses, clus-

tered in one spot, seemed like nothing so much as larger
shells washed up by the sea, so grey and bleached were
they from long exposure to sea winds and spray.

Dozens of ragged children were playing about them,
mingled with several disreputable yellow curs that
yapped noisily at the strangers.

Down on the sandy strip of beach below the houses
groups of men were lounging about. The mackerel season
had not yet set in; the spring herring netting was past. It
was holiday time among the sea folks. They were enjoying
it to the full, a happy, ragged colony, careless of what the
morrows might bring forth.

Out beyond, the boats were at anchor, floating as grace-
fully on the twinkling water as sea birds, their tall masts
bowing landward on the swell. A lazy, dreamful calm had
fallen over the distant seas; the horizon blues were pale
and dim; faint purple hazes blurred the outlines of far-off
headlands and cliffs; the yellow sands sparkled in the
sunshine as if powdered with jewels.

A murmurous babble of life buzzed about the hamlet,
pierced through by the shrill undertones of the wrangling
children, most of whom had paused in their play to scan
the visitors with covert curiosity.

Marian led the way to a house apart from the others at
the very edge of the shelving rock. The dooryard was
scrupulously clean and unlittered; the little footpath
through it was neatly bordered by white clam shells;
several thrifty geraniums in bloom looked out from the
muslin-curtained windows.

A weary-faced woman came forward to meet them.

"Bessie's much the same, Miss Lesley," she said, in
answer to Marian's inquiry. "The doctor you sent was here
today and did all he could for her. He seemed quite
hopeful. She don't complain or nothing – just lies there
and moans. Sometimes she gets restless. It's very kind of

you to come so often, Miss Lesley. Here, Magdalen, will you put this basket the lady's brought up there on the shelf?"

A girl, who had been sitting unnoticed with her back to the visitors, at the head of the child's cot in one corner of the room, stood up and slowly turned around. Marian and Esterbrook Elliott both started with involuntary surprise. Esterbrook caught his breath like a man suddenly awakened from sleep. In the name of all that was wonderful, who or what could this girl be, so little in harmony with her surroundings?

Standing in the crepuscular light of the corner, her marvellous beauty shone out with the vivid richness of some rare painting. She was tall, and the magnificent proportions of her figure were enhanced rather than marred by the severely plain dress of dark print that she wore. The heavy masses of her hair, a shining auburn dashed with golden foam, were coiled in a rich, glossy knot at the back of the classically modelled head and rippled back from a low brow whose waxen fairness even the breezes of the ocean had spared.

The girl's face was a full, perfect oval, with features of faultless regularity, and the large, full eyes were of tawny hazel, darkened into inscrutable gloom in the dimness of the corner.

Not even Marian Lesley's face was more delicately tinted, but not a trace of colour appeared in the smooth, marble-like cheeks; yet the waxen pallor bore no trace of disease or weakness, and the large, curving mouth was of an intense crimson.

She stood quite motionless. There was no trace of embarrassment or self-consciousness in her pose. When Mrs. Barrett said, "This is my niece, Magdalen Crawford," she merely inclined her head in grave, silent acknowledgement. As she moved forward to take Marian's basket, she seemed oddly out of place in the low, crowded room. Her presence seemed to throw a strange restraint over the group.

Marian rose and went over to the cot, laying her slender hand on the hot forehead of the little sufferer. The child opened its brown eyes questioningly.

"How are you today, Bessie?"

"Mad'len – I want Mad'len," moaned the little plaintive voice.

Magdalen came over and stood beside Marian Lesley.

"She wants me," she said in a low, thrilling voice, free from all harsh accent or intonation. "I am the only one she seems to know always. Yes, darling, Mad'len is here – right beside you. She will not leave you."

She knelt by the little cot and passed her arm under the child's neck, drawing the curly head close to her throat with a tender, soothing motion.

Esterbrook Elliott watched the two women intently – the one standing by the cot, arrayed in simple yet costly apparel, with her beautiful, high-bred face, and the other, kneeling on the bare, sanded floor in her print dress, with her splendid head bent low over the child and the long fringe of burnished lashes sweeping the cold pallor of the oval cheek.

From the moment that Magdalen Crawford's haunting eyes had looked straight into his for one fleeting second, an unnamable thrill of pain and pleasure stirred his heart, a thrill so strong and sudden and passionate that his face paled with emotion; the room seemed to swim before his eyes in a mist out of which gleamed that wonderful face with its mesmeric, darkly radiant eyes, burning their way into deeps and abysses of his soul hitherto unknown to him.

When the mist cleared away and his head grew steadier, he wondered at himself. Yet he trembled in every limb and the only clear idea that struggled out of his confused thoughts was an overmastering desire to take that cold face between his hands and kiss it until its passionless marble glowed into warm and throbbing life.

"Who is that girl?" he said abruptly, when they had left the cottage. "She is the most beautiful woman I have ever seen – present company always excepted," he concluded, with a depreciatory laugh.

The delicate bloom on Marian's face deepened slightly.

"You had much better to have omitted that last sentence," she said quietly, "it was so palpably an after-thought. Yes, she is wonderfully lovely – a strange beauty, I fancied. There seemed something odd and uncanny about it to me. She must be Mrs. Barrett's niece. I remember that when I was down here about a month ago Mrs. Barrett told me she expected a niece of hers to live with her – for a time at least. Her parents were both dead, the father having died recently. Mrs. Barrett seemed troubled about her. She said that the girl had been well brought up and used to better things than the Cove could give her, and she feared that she would be very discontented and unhappy. I had forgotten all about it until I saw the girl today. She certainly seems to be a very superior person; she will find the Cove very lonely, I am sure. It is not probable she will stay there long. I must see what I can do for her, but her manner seemed rather repellent, don't you think?"

"Hardly," responded Esterbrook curtly. "She seemed surprisingly dignified and self-possessed, I fancied, for a girl in her position. A princess could not have looked and bowed more royally. There was not a shadow of embarrassment in her manner, in spite of the incongruity of her surroundings. You had much better leave her alone, Marian. In all probability she would resent any condescension on your part. What wonderful, deep, lovely eyes she has."

Again the sensitive colour flushed Marian's cheek as his voice lapsed unconsciously into a dreamy, retrospective tone, and a slight restraint came over her manner, which did not depart. Esterbrook went away at sunset. Marian asked him to remain for the evening, but he pleaded some excuse.

"I shall come tomorrow afternoon," he said, as he stooped to drop a careless good-bye kiss on her face.

Marian watched him wistfully as he rode away, with an unaccountable pain in her heart. She felt more acutely than ever that there were depths in her lover's nature that she was powerless to stir into responsive life.

Had any other that power? She thought of the girl at the Cove, with her deep eyes and wonderful face. A chill of premonitory fear seized upon her.

"I feel exactly as if Esterbrook had gone away from me forever," she said slowly to herself, stooping to brush her cheek against a dew-cold, milk-white acacia bloom, "and would never come back to me again. If that could happen, I wonder what there would be left to live for?"

ESTERBROOK ELLIOTT MEANT, or honestly thought he meant, to go home when he left Marian. Nevertheless, when he reached the road branching off to the Cove he turned his horse down it with a flush on his dark cheek. He realized that the motive of the action was disloyal to Marian and he felt ashamed of his weakness.

But the desire to see Magdalen Crawford once more and to look into the depths of her eyes was stronger than all else, and overpowered every throb of duty and resistance.

He saw nothing of her when he reached the Cove. He could think of no excuse for calling at the Barrett cottage, so he rode slowly past the hamlet and along the shore.

The sun, red as a smouldering ember, was half buried

in the silken violet rim of the sea; the west was a vast lake of saffron and rose and ethereal green, through which floated the curved shallop of a thin new moon, slowly deepening from lustreless white, though gleaming silver, into burnished gold, and attended by one solitary, pearl-white star. The vast concave of sky above was of violet, infinite and flawless. Far out dusky amethystine islets clustered like gems on the shining breast of the bay. The little pools of water along the low shores glowed like mirrors of polished jacinth. The small, pine-fringed headlands ran out into the water, cutting its lustrous blue expanse like purple wedges.

As Esterbrook turned one of them he saw Magdalen standing out on the point of the next, a short distance away. Her back was towards him, and her splendid figure was outlined darkly against the vivid sky.

Esterbrook sprang from his horse and left the animal standing by itself while he walked swiftly out to her. His heart throbbed suffocatingly. He was conscious of no direct purpose save merely to see her.

She turned when he reached her with a slight start of surprise. His footsteps had made no sound on the tide-rippled sand.

For a few moments they faced each other so, eyes burning into eyes with mute soul-probing and questioning. The sun had disappeared, leaving a stain of fiery red to mark his grave; the weird, radiant light was startlingly vivid and clear. Little crisp puffs and flakes of foam scurried over the point like elfin things. The fresh wind, blowing up the bay, tossed the lustrous rings of hair about Magdalen's pale face; all the routed shadows of the hour had found refuge in her eyes.

Not a trace of colour appeared in her face under Ester-brook Elliott's burning gaze. But when he said "Magdalen!" a single, hot scorch of crimson flamed up into her cheeks protestingly. She lifted her hand with a splendid gesture, but no word passed her lips.

"Magdalen, have you nothing to say to me?" he asked, coming closer to her with an imploring passion in his face never seen by Marian Lesley's eyes. He reached out his hand, but she stepped back from his touch.

"What should I have to say to you?"

"Say that you are glad to see me."

"I am not glad to see you. You have no right to come here. But I knew you would come."

"You knew it? How?"

"Your eyes told me so today. I am not blind – I can see further than those dull fisher folks. Yes, I knew you would come. That is why I came here tonight – so that you would find me alone and I could tell you that you were not to come again."

"Why must you tell me that, Magdalen?"

"Because, as I have told you, you have no right to come."

"But if I will not obey you? If I will come in defiance of your prohibition?"

She turned her steady luminous eyes on his pale, set face.

"You would stamp yourself as a madman, then," she said coldly. "I know that you are Miss Lesley's promised husband. Therefore, you are either false to her or insulting to me. In either case the companionship of Magdalen Crawford is not what you must seek. Go!"

She turned away from him with an imperious gesture of dismissal. Esterbrook Elliott stepped forward and caught one firm, white wrist.

"I shall not obey you," he said in a low, intense tone; his fine eyes burned into hers. "You may send me away, but I will come back, again and yet again until you have learned to welcome me. Why should you meet me like an enemy? Why can we not be friends?"

The girl faced him once more.

"Because," she said proudly, "I am not your equal. There can be no friendship between us. There ought not to be. Magdalen Crawford, the fisherman's niece, is no companion for you. You will be foolish, as well as disloyal, if you ever try to see me again. Go back to the beautiful, high-bred woman you love and forget me. Perhaps you think I am talking strangely. Perhaps you think me bold and unwomanly to speak so plainly to you, a stranger. But there are some circumstances in life when plain-speaking is best. I do not want to see you again. Now, go back to your own world."

Esterbrook Elliott slowly turned from her and walked in silence back to the shore. In the shadows of the point he stopped to look back at her, standing out like some inspired prophetess against the fiery background of the sunset sky and silver-blue water. The sky overhead was thick-sown with stars; the night breeze was blowing up from its lair in distant, echoing sea caves. On his right the lights of the Cove twinkled out through the dusk.

"I feel like a coward and a traitor," he said slowly. "Good God, what is this madness that has come over me? Is this my boasted strength of manhood?"

A moment later the hoofbeats of his horse died away up the shore.

Magdalen Crawford lingered on the point until the last dull red faded out into the violet gloom of the June sea dusk, than which nothing can be rarer or diviner, and listened to the moan and murmur of the sea far out over the bay with sorrowful eyes and sternly set lips.

The next day, when the afternoon sun hung hot and heavy over the water, Esterbrook Elliott came again to the Cove. He found it deserted. A rumour of mackerel had come, and every boat had sailed out in the rose-red dawn to the fishing grounds. But down on a strip of sparkling yellow sand he saw Magdalen Crawford standing, her hand on the rope that fastened a small white dory to the fragment of a half-embedded wreck.

She was watching a huddle of gulls clustered on the tip of a narrow, sandy spit running out to the left. She turned at the sound of his hurried foot-fall behind her. Her face paled slightly, and into the depths of her eyes leapt a passionate, mesmeric glow that faded as quickly as it came.

"You see I have come back in spite of your command, Magdalen."

"I do see it," she answered in a gravely troubled voice. "You are a madman who refuses to be warned."

"Where are you going, Magdalen?" She had loosened the rope from the wreck.

"I am going to row over to Chapel Point for salt. They think the boats will come in tonight loaded with mackerel – look at them away out there by the score – and salt will be needed."

"Can you row so far alone?"

"Easily. I learned to row long ago – for a pastime then. Since coming here I find it of great service to me."

She stepped lightly into the tiny shallop and picked up an oar. The brilliant sunshine streamed about her, burnishing the rich tints of her hair into ruddy gold. She balanced herself to the swaying of the dory with the grace of a sea bird. The man looking at her felt his brain reel.

"Good-bye, Mr. Elliott."

For answer he sprang into the dory and, snatching an oar, pushed against the old wreck with such energy that the dory shot out from the shore like a foam bell. His sudden spring had set it rocking violently. Magdalen almost lost her footing and caught blindly at his arm. As her fingers closed on his wrist a thrill as of fire shot through his every vein.

"Why have you done this, Mr. Elliott? You must go back."

"But I will not," he said masterfully, looking straight into her eyes with an imperiousness that sat well upon him. "I am going to row you over to Chapel Point. I have the oars – I will be master this once, at least."

For an instant her eyes flashed defiant protest, then drooped before his. A sudden, hot blush crimsoned her pale face. His will had mastered hers; the girl trembled from head to foot, and the proud, sensitive mouth quivered.

Into the face of the man watching her breathlessly flashed a triumphant, passionate joy. He put out his hand and gently pushed her down into the seat. Sitting opposite, he took up the oars and pulled out over the sheet of sparkling blue water, through which at first the bottom of white sand glimmered wavily but afterwards deepened to translucent, dim depths of greenness.

His heart throbbed tumultuously. Once the thought of Marian drifted across his mind like a chill breath of wind, but it was forgotten when his eyes met Magdalen's.

"Tell me about yourself, Magdalen," he said at last, breaking the tremulous, charmed, sparkling silence.

"There is nothing to tell," she answered with characteristic straightforwardness. "My life has been a very uneventful one. I have never been rich, or very well educated, but – it used to be different from now. I had some chance before – before Father died."

"You must have found it very lonely and strange when you came here first."

"Yes. At first I thought I should die – but I do not mind it now. I have made friends with the sea; it has taught me a great deal. There is a kind of inspiration in the sea. When one listens to its never-ceasing murmur afar out there, always sounding at midnight and mid-day, one's soul goes out to meet Eternity. Sometimes it gives me so much pleasure that it is almost pain."

She stopped abruptly.

"I don't know why I am talking to you like this."

"You are a strange girl, Magdalen. Have you no other companion than the sea?"

"No. Why should I wish to have? I shall not be here long."

Elliott's face contracted with a spasm of pain.

"You are not going away, Magdalen?"

"Yes – in the fall. I have my own living to earn, you know. I am very poor. Uncle and Aunt are very kind, but I cannot consent to burden them any longer than I can help."

A sigh that was almost a moan broke from Esterbrook Elliott's lips.

"You must not go away, Magdalen. You must stay here – with me!"

"You forget yourself," she said proudly. "How dare you speak to me so? Have you forgotten Miss Lesley? Or are you a traitor to us both?"

Esterbrook made no answer. He bowed his pale, miserable face before her, self-condemned.

The breast of the bay sparkled with its countless gems like the breast of a fair woman. The shores were purple and amethystine in the distance. Far out, bluish, phantom-like sails clustered against the pallid horizon. The dory danced like a feather over the ripples. They were close under the shadow of Chapel Point.

MARIAN LESLEY WAITED in vain for her lover that afternoon. When he came at last in the odorous dusk of the June night she met him on the acacia-shadowed verandah with cold sweetness. Perhaps some subtle woman-instinct whispered to her where and how he had spent the afternoon, for she offered him no kiss, nor did she ask him why he had failed to come sooner.

His eyes lingered on her in the dim light, taking in every detail of her sweet womanly refinement and loveliness, and with difficulty he choked back a groan. Again he asked himself what madness had come over him, and again for an answer rose up the vision of Magdalen Crawford's face as he had seen it that day, crimsoning beneath his gaze.

It was late when he left. Marian watched him out of sight, standing under the acacias. She shivered as with a sudden chill. "I feel as I think Vashti must have felt," she murmured aloud, "when, discrowned and unqueened, she crept out of the gates of Shushan to hide her broken heart. I wonder if Esther has already usurped my sceptre. Has that girl at the Cove, with her pale, priestess-like face and mysterious eyes, stolen his heart from me? Perhaps not, for it may never have been mine. I know that Esterbrook Elliott will be true to the letter of his vows to me, no matter what it may cost him. But I want no pallid shadow of the love that belongs to another. The hour of abdication is at hand, I fear. And what will be left for throneless Vashti then?"

Esterbrook Elliott, walking home through the mocking calm of the night, fought a hard battle with himself.

He was face to face with the truth at last – the bitter knowledge that he had never loved Marian Lesley, save with a fond, brotherly affection, and that he did love Magdalen Crawford with a passion that threatened to sweep before it every vestige of his honour and loyalty.

He had seen her but three times – and his throbbing heart lay in the hollow of her cold white hand.

He shut his eyes and groaned. What madness. What unutterable folly! He was not free – he was bound to another by every cord of honour and self-respect. And, even were he free, Magdalen Crawford would be no fit wife for him – in the eyes of the world, at least. A girl from the Cove – a girl with little education and no social standing – aye! but he loved her.

He groaned again and again in his misery. Afar down the slope the bay waters lay like an inky strip and the distant, murmurous plaint of the sea came out of the stillness of the night; the lights at the Cove glimmered faintly.

In the week that followed he went to the Cove every day. Sometimes he did not see Magdalen; at other times he did. But at the end of the week he had conquered in the bitter, heart-crushing struggle with himself. If he had weakly given way to the first mad sweep of a new passion, the strength of his manhood reasserted itself at last. Faltering and wavering were over, though there was passionate pain in his voice when he said at last, "I am not coming back again, Magdalen."

They were standing in the shadow of the pine-fringed point that ran out to the left of the Cove. They had been walking together along the shore, watching the splendour of the sea sunset that flamed and glowed in the west, where there was a sea of mackerel clouds, crimson and amber tinted, with long, ribbon-like strips of apple-green sky between. They had walked in silence, hand in hand, as children might have done, yet with the stir and throb of a mighty passion seething in their hearts.

Magdalen turned as Esterbrook spoke, and looked at him in a long silence. The bay stretched out before them, tranced and shimmering; a few stars shone down through the gloom of dusk. Right across the translucent greens and roses and blues of the west hung a dark, unsightly cloud, like the blurred outline of a monstrous bat. In the dim, reflected light the girl's mournful face took on a weird, unearthly beauty. She turned her eyes from Esterbrook Elliott's set white face to the radiant gloom of the sea.

A Strayed Allegiance

"That is best," she answered at last, slowly.

"Best – yes! Better that we had never met! I love you – you know it – words are idle between us. I never loved before – I thought I did. I made a mistake and I must pay the penalty of that mistake. You understand me?"

"I understand," she answered simply.

"I do not excuse myself – I have been weak and cowardly and disloyal. But I have conquered myself – I will be true to the woman to whom I am pledged. You and I must not meet again. I will crush this madness to death. I think I have been delirious ever since that day I saw you first, Magdalen. My brain is clearer now. I see my duty and I mean to do it at any cost. I dare not trust myself to say more. Magdalen, I have much for which to ask your forgiveness."

"There is nothing to forgive," she said steadily. "I have been as much to blame as you. If I had been as resolute as I ought to have been – if I had sent you away the second time as I did the first – this would not have come to pass. I have been weak too, and I deserve to atone for my weakness by suffering. There is only one path open to us. Esterbrook, good-bye." Her voice quivered with an uncontrollable spasm of pain, but the misty, mournful eyes did not swerve from his. The man stepped forward and caught her in his arms.

"Magdalen, good-bye, my darling. Kiss me once – only once – before I go."

She loosened his arms and stepped back proudly.

"No! No man kisses my lips unless he is to be my husband. Good-bye, dear."

He bowed his head silently and went away, looking back not once, else he might have seen her kneeling on the damp sand weeping noiselessly and passionately.

MARIAN LESLEY LOOKED at his pale, determined face the next evening and read it like an open book.

She had grown paler herself; there were purple shadows under the sweet violet eyes that might have hinted of her own sleepless nights.

She greeted him calmly, holding out a steady, white hand of welcome. She saw the traces of the struggle through which he had passed and knew that he had come off victor.

The knowledge made her task a little harder. It would have been easier to let slip the straining cable than to cast it from her when it lay unresistingly in her hand.

For an instant her heart thrilled with an unutterably sweet hope. Might he not forget in time? Need she snap in twain the weakened bond between them after all? Perhaps she might win back her lost sceptre, yet if –

Womanly pride throttled the struggling hope. No divided allegiance, no hollow semblance of queenship for her!

Her opportunity came when Esterbrook asked with grave earnestness if their marriage might not be hastened a little – could he not have his bride in August? For a fleeting second Marian closed her eyes and the slender hands, lying among the laces in her lap, clasped each other convulsively.

Then she said quietly, "Sometimes I have thought, Esterbrook, that it might be better – if we were never married at all."

Esterbrook turned a startled face upon her.

"Not married at all! Marian, what do you mean?"

"Just what I say. I do not think we are as well suited to each other after all as we have fancied. We have loved each other as brother and sister might – that is all. I think it will be best to be brother and sister forever – nothing more."

Esterbrook sprang to his feet.

"Marian, do you know what you are saying? You surely cannot have heard – no one could have told you –"

"I have heard nothing," she interrupted hurriedly. "No one has told me anything. I have only said what I have been thinking of late. I am sure we have made a mistake. It is not too late to remedy it. You will not refuse my request, Esterbrook? You will set me free?"

"Good heavens, Marian!" he said hoarsely. "I cannot realize that you are in earnest. Have you ceased to care for me?" The rigidly locked hands were clasped a little tighter.

"No – I shall always care for you as my friend if you will let me. But I know we could not make each other happy – the time for that has gone by. I would never be satisfied, nor would you. Esterbrook, will you release me from a promise which has become an irksome fetter?"

He looked down on her upturned face mistily. A great joy was surging up in his heart – yet it was mingled with great regret.

He knew – none better – what was passing out of his life, what he was losing when he lost that pure, womanly nature.

"If you really mean this, Marian," he said slowly, "if you really have come to feel that your truest love is not and never can be mine – that I cannot make you happy – then there is nothing for me to do but to grant your request. You are free."

"Thank you, dear," she said gently, as she stood up.

She slipped his ring from her finger and held it out to him. He took it mechanically. He still felt dazed and unreal.

Marian held out her hand.

"Good-night, Esterbrook," she said, a little wearily. "I feel tired. I am glad you see it all in the same light as I do."

"Marian," he said earnestly, clasping the outstretched hand, "are you sure that you will be happy – are you sure that you are doing a wise thing?"

"Quite sure," she answered, with a faint smile. "I am not

acting rashly. I have thought it all over carefully. Things are much better so, dear. We will always be friends. Your joys and sorrows will be to me as my own. When another love comes to bless your life, Esterbrook, I will be glad. And now, good-night. I want to be alone now."

At the doorway he turned to look back at her, standing in all her sweet stateliness in the twilight duskness, and the keen realization of all he had lost made him bow his head with a quick pang of regret.

Then he went out into the darkness of the summer night.

An hour later he stood alone on the little point where he had parted with Magdalen the night before. A restless night wind was moaning through the pines that fringed the bank behind him; the moon shone down radiantly, turning the calm expanse of the bay into a milk-white sheen.

He took Marian's ring from his pocket and kissed it reverently. Then he threw it from him far out over the water. For a second the diamond flashed in the moonlight; then, with a tiny splash, it fell among the ripples.

Esterbrook turned his face to the Cove, lying dark and silent in the curve between the crescent headlands. A solitary light glimmered from the low eaves of the Barrett cottage.

Tomorrow, was his unspoken thought, I will be free to go back to Magdalen.

The
Waking of Helen

ROBERT REEVES looked somewhat curiously at the girl who was waiting on him at his solitary breakfast. He had not seen her before, arriving at his summer boarding house only the preceding night.

It was a shabby farmhouse on the inland shore of a large bay that was noted for its tides, and had wonderful possibilities of light and shade for an impressionist. Reeves was an enthusiastic artist. It mattered little to him that the boarding accommodations were most primitive, the people uncultured and dull, the place itself utterly isolated, as long as he could revel in those transcendent sunsets and sunrises, those marvellous moonlights, those wonderful purple shores and sweeps of shimmering blue water.

The owner of the farm was Angus Fraser, and he and his wife seemed to be a reserved, uncouth pair, with no apparent interest in life save to scratch a bare living out of their few stony acres. He had an impression that they were childless and was at a loss to place this girl who poured his tea and brought in his toast. She did not resemble either Fraser or his wife. She was certainly not beautiful, being very tall and rather awkward, and dressed in a particularly unbecoming dark print wrapper. Her luxuriant hair was thick and black, and was coiled in a heavy knot at the nape of her neck. Her features were delicate but irregular, and her skin was very brown. Her eyes attracted Reeves' notice especially; they were large and dark and full of a half-unconscious, wistful longing, as if a prisoned soul behind them were vainly trying to reveal itself.

Reeves could find out nothing of her from herself, for she responded to his tentative questions about the place in the briefest fashion. Afterwards he interviewed Mrs.

Fraser cautiously, and ascertained that the girl's name was Helen Fraser, and that she was Angus' niece.

"Her father and mother are dead and we've brought her up. Helen's a good girl in most ways – a little obstinate and sulky now and then – but generally she's steady enough, and as for work, there ain't a girl in Bay Beach can come up to her in house or field. Angus calculates she saves him a man's wages clear. No, I ain't got nothing to say against Helen."

Nevertheless, Reeves felt somehow that Mrs. Fraser did not like her husband's niece. He often heard her scolding or nagging Helen at her work, and noticed that the latter never answered back. But once, after Mrs. Angus' tongue had been especially bitter, he met the girl hurrying along the hall from the kitchen with her eyes full of tears. Reeves felt as if someone had struck him a blow. He went to Angus and his wife that afternoon. He wished to paint a shore picture, he said, and wanted a model. Would they allow Miss Fraser to pose for him? He would pay liberally for her time.

Angus and his wife had no objection. They would pocket the money, and Helen could be spared a spell every day as well as not. Reeves told Helen of his plan himself, meeting her in the evening as she was bringing the cows home from the low shore pastures beyond the marsh. He was surprised at the sudden illumination of her face. It almost transfigured her from a plain, sulky-looking girl into a beautiful woman.

But the glow passed quickly. She assented to his plan quietly, almost lifelessly. He walked home with her behind the cows and talked of the sunset and the mysterious beauty of the bay and the purple splendour of the distant coasts. She listened in silence. Only once, when he spoke of the distant murmur of the open sea, she lifted her head and looked at him.

"What does it say to you?" she asked.

"It speaks of eternity. And to you?"

"It calls me," she answered simply, "and then I want to go out and meet it – and it hurts me too. I can't tell how or why. Sometimes it makes me feel as if I were asleep and wanted to wake and didn't know how."

She turned and looked out over the bay. A dying gleam of sunset broke through a cloud and fell across her hair. For a moment she seemed the spirit of the shore personified – all its mystery, all its uncertainty, all its elusive charm.

She has possibilities, thought Reeves.

Next day he began his picture. At first he had thought of painting her as the incarnation of a sea spirit, but decided that her moods were too fitful. So he began to sketch her as "Waiting" – a woman looking out across the bay with a world of hopeless longing in her eyes. The subject suited her well, and the picture grew apace.

When he was tired of work he made her walk around the shore with him, or row up the head of the bay in her own boat. He tried to draw her out, at first with indifferent success. She seemed to be frightened of him. He talked to her of many things – the far outer world whose echoes never reached her, foreign lands where he had travelled, famous men and women whom he had met, music, art and books. When he spoke of books he touched the right chord. One of those transfiguring flashes he delighted to evoke now passed over her plain face.

"That is what I've always wanted," she said hungrily, "and I never get them. Aunt hates to see me reading. She says it is a waste of time. And I love it so. I read every scrap of paper I can get hold of, but I hardly ever see a book."

The next day Reeves took his Tennyson to the shore and began to read the *Idylls of the King* to her.

"It is beautiful," was her sole verbal comment, but her rapt eyes said everything.

After that he never went out with her without a book –
now one of the poets, now some prose classic. He was
surprised by her quick appreciation of and sympathy
with the finest passages. Gradually, too, she forgot her
shyness and began to talk. She knew nothing of his world,
but her own world she knew and knew well. She was a
mine of traditional history about the bay. She knew the
rocky coast by heart, and every old legend that clung to it.
They drifted into making excursions along the shore and
explored its wildest retreats. The girl had an artist's eye
for scenery and colour effect.

"You should have been an artist," Reeves told her one
day when she had pointed out to him the exquisite loveliness of a shaft of light falling through a cleft in the rocks
across a dark-green pool at their base.

"I would rather be a writer," she said slowly, "if I could
only write something like those books you have read to
me. What a glorious destiny it must be to have something
to say that the whole world is listening for, and to be able
to say it in words that will live forever! It must be the
noblest human lot."

"Yet some of those men and women were neither good
nor noble," said Reeves gently, "and many of them were
unhappy."

Helen dismissed the subject as abruptly as she always
did when the conversation touched too nearly on the
sensitive edge of her soul dreams.

"Do you know where I am taking you today?" she said.

"No – where?"

"To what the people here call the Kelpy's Cave. I hate to
go there. I believe there is something uncanny about it,
but I think you will like to see it. It is a dark little cave in the
curve of a small cove, and on each side the headlands of
rock run far out. At low tide we can walk right around, but
when the tide comes in it fills the Kelpy's Cave. If you were

there and let the tide come past the points, you would be drowned unless you could swim, for the rocks are so steep and high it is impossible to climb them."

Reeves was interested.

"Was anyone ever caught by the tide?"

"Yes," returned Helen, with a shudder. "Once, long ago, before I was born, a girl went around the shore to the cave and fell asleep there – and the tide came in and she was drowned. She was young and very pretty, and was to have been married the next week. I've been afraid of the place ever since."

The treacherous cave proved to be a picturesque and innocent-looking spot, with the beach of glittering sand before it and the high gloomy walls of rock on either hand.

"I must come here some day and sketch it," said Reeves enthusiastically, "and you must be the Kelpy, Helen, and sit in the cave with your hair wrapped about you and seaweed clinging to it."

"Do you think a kelpy would look like that?" said the girl dreamily. "I don't. I think it is a wild, wicked little sea imp, malicious and mocking and cruel, and it sits here and watches for victims."

"Well, never mind your sea kelpies," Reeves said, fishing out his Longfellow. "They are a tricky folk, if all tales be true, and it is supposed to be a very rash thing to talk about them in their own haunts. I want to read you 'The Building of the Ship.' You will like it, I'm sure."

When the tide turned they went home.

"We haven't seen the kelpy, after all," said Reeves.

"I think I shall see him some day," said Helen gravely. "I think he is waiting for me there in that gloomy cave of his, and some time or other he will get me."

Reeves smiled at the gloomy fancy, and Helen smiled back at him with one of her sudden radiances. The tide was creeping swiftly up over the white sands. The sun was low and the bay was swimming in a pale blue glory. They parted at Clam Point, Helen to go for the cows and Reeves to wander on up the shore. He thought of Helen at first, and the wonderful change that had come over her of late; then he began to think of another face – a marvellously lovely one with blue eyes as tender as the waters before him. Then Helen was forgotten.

The summer waned swiftly. One afternoon Reeves took a fancy to revisit the Kelpy's Cave. Helen could not go. It was harvest time, and she was needed in the field.

"Don't let the kelpy catch you," she said to him half seriously. "The tide will turn early this afternoon, and you are given to day-dreaming."

"I'll be careful," he promised laughingly, and he meant to be careful. But somehow when he reached the cave its unwholesome charm overcame him, and he sat down on the boulder at its mouth.

"An hour yet before tide time," he said. "Just enough time to read that article on impressionists in my review and then stroll home by the sand shore."

From reading he passed to day-dreaming, and day-dreaming drifted into sleep, with his head pillowed on the rocky walls of the cave.

How long he had slept he did not know, but he woke with a start of horror. He sprang to his feet, realizing his position instantly. The tide was in – far in past the headlands already. Above and beyond him towered the pitiless unscalable rocks. There was no way of escape.

Reeves was no coward, but life was sweet to him, and to die like that – like a drowned rat in a hole – to be able to do nothing but wait for that swift and sure oncoming death! He reeled against the damp rock wall, and for a moment sea and sky and prisoning headlands and white-lined tide whirled before his eyes.

Then his head grew clearer. He tried to think. How long had he? Not more than twenty minutes at the outside. Well, death was sure and he would meet it bravely. But to wait – to wait helplessly! He should go mad with the horror of it before those endless minutes would have passed!

He took something from his pocket and bent his head over it, pressing his lips to it repeatedly. And then, when he raised his face again, a dory was coming around the headland on his right, and Helen Fraser was in it.

Reeves was dizzy again with the shock of joy and thankfulness. He ran down over the little stretch of sand still uncovered by the tide and around to the rocks of the headlands against which the dory was already grating. He sprang forward impulsively and caught the girl's cold hands in his as she dropped the oars and stood up.

"Helen, you have saved me! How can I ever thank you? I – "

He broke off abruptly, for she was looking up at him, breathlessly and voicelessly, with her whole soul in her eyes. He saw in them a revelation that amazed him; he dropped her hands and stepped back as if she had struck him in the face.

Helen did not notice the change in him. She clasped her hands together and her voice trembled.

"Oh, I was afraid I should be too late! When I came in from the field Aunt Hannah said you had not come back – and I knew it was tide time – and I felt somehow that it had caught you in the cave. I ran down over the marsh and took Joe Simmon's dory. If I had not got here in time – "

She broke off shiveringly. Reeves stepped into the dory and took up the oars.

"The kelpy would have been sure of its victim then," he said, trying to speak lightly. "It would have almost served me right for neglecting your warning. I was very careless. You must let me row back. I am afraid you have overtasked your strength trying to cheat the kelpy."

Reeves rowed homeward in an absolute silence. Helen did not speak and he could not. When they reached the dory anchorage he helped her out.

"I think I'll go out to the Point for a walk," he said. "I want to steady my nerves. You must go right home and rest. Don't be anxious – I won't take any more chances with sea kelpies."

Helen went away without a word, and Reeves walked slowly out to the Point. He was grieved beyond measure at the discovery he believed he had made. He had never dreamed of such a thing. He was not a vain man, and was utterly free from all tendency to flirtation. It had never occurred to him that the waking of the girl's deep nature might be attended with disastrous consequences. He had honestly meant to help her, and what had he done?

He felt very uncomfortable; he could not conscientiously blame himself, but he saw that he had acted foolishly. And of course he must go away at once. And he must also tell her something she ought to know. He wished he had told her long ago.

The following afternoon was a perfect one. Reeves was sketching on the sand shore when Helen came. She sat down on a camp stool a little to one side and did not speak. After a few moments Reeves pushed away his paraphernalia impatiently.

"I don't feel in a mood for work," he said. "It is too dreamy a day – one ought to do nothing to be in keeping. Besides, I'm getting lazy now that my vacation is nearly over. I must go in a few days."

He avoided looking at her, so he did not see the sudden pallor of her face.

"So soon?" she said in a voice expressive of no particular feeling.

"Yes. I ought not to have lingered so long. My world will be forgetting me and that will not do. It has been a very pleasant summer and I shall be sorry to leave Bay Beach."

"But you will come back next summer?" asked Helen quickly. "You said you would."

Reeves nerved himself for his very distasteful task.

"Perhaps," he said, with an attempt at carelessness, "but if I do so, I shall not come alone. Somebody who is very dear to me will come with me – as my wife. I have never told you about her, Helen, but you and I are such good friends that I do not mind doing so now. I am engaged to a very sweet girl, and we expect to be married next spring."

There was a brief silence. Reeves had been vaguely afraid of a scene and was immensely relieved to find his fear unrealized. Helen sat very still. He could not see her face. Did she care, after all? Was he mistaken?

When she spoke her voice was perfectly calm.

"Thank you, it is very kind of you to tell me about her. I suppose she is very beautiful."

"Yes, here is her picture. You can judge for yourself."

Helen took the portrait from his hand and looked at it steadily. It was a miniature painted on ivory, and the face looking out from it was certainly lovely.

"It is no wonder you love her," said the girl in a low tone as she handed it back. "It must be strange to be so beautiful as that."

Reeves picked up his Tennyson.

"Shall I read you something? What will you have?"

"Read 'Elaine,' please. I want to hear that once more."

Reeves felt a sudden dislike to her choice.

"Wouldn't you prefer something else?" he asked, hurriedly turning over the leaves. " 'Elaine' is rather sad. Shan't I read 'Guinevere' instead?"

"No," said Helen in the same lifeless tone. "I have no sympathy for Guinevere. She suffered and her love was unlawful, but she was loved in return – she did not waste her love on someone who did not want or care for it. Elaine did, and her life went with it. Read me the story."

Reeves obeyed. When he had finished he held the book out to her.

"Helen, will you take this Tennyson from me in remembrance of our friendship and of the Kelpy's Cave? I shall never forget that I owe my life to you."

"Thank you."

She took the book and placed a little thread of crimson seaweed that had been caught in the sand between the pages of "Elaine." Then she rose.

"I must go back now. Aunt will need me. Thank you again for the book, Mr. Reeves, and for all your kindness to me."

Reeves was relieved when the interview was over. Her calmness had reassured him. She did not care very much, after all; it was only a passing fancy, and when he was gone she would soon forget him.

He went away a few days later, and Helen bade him an impassive good-bye. When the afternoon was far spent she stole away from the house to the shore, with her Tennyson in her hand, and took her way to the Kelpy's Cave.

The tide was just beginning to come in. She sat down on the big boulder where Reeves had fallen asleep. Beyond stretched the gleaming blue waters, mellowing into a hundred fairy shades horizonward. The shadows of the rocks were around her. In front was the white line of the incoming tide; it had almost reached the headlands. A few minutes more and escape would be cut off – yet she did not move.

When the dark green water reached her, and the lapping wavelets swished up over the hem of her dress, she lifted her head and a sudden strange smile flashed over her face.

Perhaps the kelpy understood it.

Young Si

R. BENTLEY had just driven into the yard with the new summer boarder. Mrs. Bentley and Agnes were peeping at her from behind the parlour curtains with the keen interest that they – shut in by their restricted farm life – always felt in any visitor from the outside world lying beyond their boundary of purple misted hills.

Mrs. Bentley was a plump, rosy-cheeked woman with a motherly smile. Agnes was a fair, slim schoolgirl, as tall as her mother, with a sweet face and a promise of peach blossom prettiness in the years to come. The arrival of a summer boarder was a great event in her quiet life.

"Ain't she pretty?" whispered Mrs. Bentley admiringly, as the girl came slowly up the green slope before the house. "I do hope she's nice. You can generally calculate on men boarders, but girls are doubtful. Preserve me from a cranky boarder! I've had enough of them. I kinder like her looks, though."

Ethel Lennox had paused at the front door as Mrs. Bentley and Agnes came into the hall. Agnes gazed at the stranger with shy, unenvious admiration; the latter stood on the stone step just where the big chestnut by the door cast flickering gleams and shadows over her dress and shining hair.

She was tall, and gowned in some simple white material that fell about her in graceful folds. She wore a cluster of pale pink roses at her belt, and a big, picturesque white hat shaded her face and the glossy, clinging masses of her red hair – hair that was neither auburn nor chestnut but simply red. Nor would anyone have wished it otherwise, having once seen that glorious mass, with all its wonderful possibilities of rippling luxuriance.

Her complexion was of that perfect, waxen whiteness that goes with burnished red hair and the darkest of dilated violet eyes. Her delicately chiselled features wore what might have been a somewhat too decided impress of spirit and independence, had it not been for the sweet mouth, red and dimpled and curving, that parted in a slow, charming smile as Mrs. Bentley came forward with her kindly welcome.

"You must be real tired, Miss Lennox. It's a long drive from the train down here. Agnes, show Miss Lennox up to her room, and tea will be ready when you come down."

Agnes came forward with the shy grace that always won friends for her, and the two girls went slowly up the broad, old-fashioned staircase, while Mrs. Bentley bustled away to bring in the tea and put a goblet of damask roses on the table.

"She looks like a picture, doesn't she, John?" she said to her husband. "I never saw such a face – and that hair too. Would you have believed red hair could be so handsome? She seems real friendly – none of your stuck-up fine ladies! I've had all I want of them, I can tell you!"

"Sh – sh – sh!" said Mr. Bentley warningly, as Ethel Lennox came in with her arm about Agnes.

She looked even more lovely without her hat, with the soft red tendrils of hair lying on her forehead. Mrs. Bentley sent a telegraphic message of admiration across the table to her husband, who was helping the cold tongue and feeling his way to a conversation.

"You'll find it pretty quiet here, Miss Lennox. We're plain folks and there ain't much going and coming. Maybe you don't mind that, though?"

"I like it. When one has been teaching school all the year in a noisy city, quiet seems the one thing to be desired. Besides, I like to fancy myself something of an artist. I paint and sketch a little when I have time, and Miss Courtland, who was here last summer, said I could not find a more suitable spot. So I came because I knew that mackerel fishing was carried on along the shore, and I would have a chance to study character among the fishermen."

"Well, the shore ain't far away, and it's pretty – though maybe us folks here don't appreciate it rightly, being as we're so used to it. Strangers are always going crazy over its 'picturesqueness,' as they call it. As for 'character,' I reckon you'll find all you want of that among the Pointers; anyway, I never seed such critters as they be. When you get tired of painting, maybe you can amuse yourself trying to get to the bottom of our mystery."

"Oh, have you a mystery? How interesting!"

"Yes, a mystery – a mystery," repeated Mr. Bentley solemnly, "that nobody hain't been able to solve so far. I've give it up – so has everyone else. Maybe you'll have better luck."

"But what is it?"

"The mystery," said Mr. Bentley dramatically, "is – Young Si. He's the mystery. Last spring, just when the herring struck in, a young chap suddenly appeared at the Point. He appeared – from what corner of the globe nobody hain't ever been able to make out. He bought a boat and a shanty down at my shore and went into a sort of mackerel partnership with Snuffy Curtis – Snuffy supplying the experience and this young fellow the cash, I reckon. Snuffy's as poor as Job's turkey; it was a windfall for him. And there he's fished all summer."

"But his name – Young Si?"

"Well, of course, that isn't it. He did give himself out as Brown, but nobody believes that's his handle – sounds unnatteral here. He bought his establishment from 'old Si,' who used to fish down there and was a mysterious old critter in a way too. So when this young fellow stepped in from goodness knows where, some of the Pointers christened him Young Si for a joke, and he never gets anything else. Doesn't seem to mind it. He's a moody, keep-to-himself sort of chap. Yet he ain't unpopular along shore, I believe. Snuffy was telling me they like him real well, considering his unsociableness. Anyways, he's as handsome a chap as I ever seed, and well eddicated too. He ain't none of your ordinary fishermen. Some of us kind of think he's a runaway – got into some scrape or another, maybe, and is skulking around here to keep out of jail. But wife here won't give in to that."

"No, I never will," said Mrs. Bentley firmly. "Young Si comes here often for milk and butter, and he's a perfect gentleman. Nobody'll ever convince me that he has done anything to be ashamed of, whatever's his reason for wasting his life down there at that shore."

"He ain't wasting his life," chuckled Mr. Bentley. "He's making money, Young Si is, though he don't seem to care about that a mite. This has been a big year for mackerel, and he's smart. If he didn't know much when be begun, he's ahead of Snuffy now. And as for work, I never saw his beat. He seems possessed. Up afore sunrise every blessed morning and never in bed till midnight, and just slaving away all between time. I said to him t'other day, says I: 'Young Si, you'll have to let up on this sort of thing and take a rest. You can't stand it. You're not a Pointer. Pointers can stand anything, but it'll kill you.'

"He give one of them bitter laughs of his. Says he: 'It's no difference if it does. Nobody'll care,' and off he walks, sulky like. There's something about Young Si I can't understand," concluded Mr. Bentley.

Ethel Lennox was interested. A melancholy, mysterious hero in a setting of silver-rimmed sand hills and wide blue sweeps of ocean was something that ought to lend piquancy to her vacation.

"I should like to see this prince in disguise," she said. "It all sounds very romantic."

"I'll take you to the shore after tea if you'd like," said Agnes eagerly. "Si's just splendid," she continued in a confidential aside as they rose from the table. "Pa doesn't half like him because he thinks there's something queer about him. But I do. He's a gentleman, as Ma says. I don't believe he's done anything wrong."

ETHEL LENNOX SAUNTERED out into the orchard to wait for Agnes. She sat down under an apple tree and began to read, but soon the book slipped from her hands and the beautiful head leaned back against the grey, lichened trunk of the old tree. The sweet mouth drooped wistfully. There was a sad, far-away look in the violet eyes. The face was not that of a happy girl, so thought Agnes as she came down the apple tree avenue.

But how pretty she is! she thought. Won't the folks around here stare at her! They always do at our boarders, but we've never had one like her.

Ethel sprang up. "I had no idea you would be here so soon," she said brightly. "Just wait till I get my hat."

When she came out they started off, and presently found themselves walking down a grassy, deep-rutted lane that ran through mown hay fields, green with their rich aftergrowth, and sheets of pale ripening oats and golden-green wheat, until it lost itself in the rolling sand hills at the foot of the slope.

Beyond the sand hills stretched the shining expanse of the ocean, of the faint, bleached blue of hot August seas, and reaching out into a horizon laced with long trails of pinkish cloud. Numberless fishing boats dotted the shimmering reaches.

"That furthest-off boat is Young Si's," said Agnes. "He always goes to that particular spot."

"Is he really all your father says?" asked Miss Lennox curiously.

"Indeed, he is. He isn't any more like the rest of the shore men than you are. He's queer, of course. I don't believe he's happy. It seems to me he's worrying over something, but I'm sure it is nothing wrong. Here we are," she added, as they passed the sand hills and came out on the long, level beach.

To their left the shore curved around in a semi-circle of dazzling whiteness; at their right stood a small grey fish-house.

"That's Young Si's place," said Agnes. "He lives there night and day. Wouldn't it make anyone melancholy? No wonder he's mysterious. I'm going to get his spyglass. He told me I might always use it."

She pushed open the door and entered, followed by Ethel. The interior was rough but clean. It was a small room, lighted by one tiny window looking out on the water. In one corner a rough ladder led up to the loft above. The bare lathed walls were hung with fishing jackets, nets, mackerel lines and other shore appurtenances. A little stove bore a kettle and a frying pan. A low board table was strewn with dishes and the cold remnants of a hasty repast; benches were placed along the walls. A fat, bewhiskered kitten, looking as if it were cut out of black velvet, was dozing on the window sill.

"This is Young Si's cat," explained Agnes, patting the creature, which purred joyously and opened its sleepy green eyes. "It's the only thing he cares for, I believe. Witch! Witch! How are you, Witch? Well, here's the spyglass. Let's go out and have a look. Si's catching mackerel," announced Agnes a few minutes later, after she had scrutinized each boat in turn, "and he won't be in for an hour yet. If you like, we have time for a walk up the shore."

The sun slipped lower and lower in the creamy sky, leaving a trail of sparkles that ran across the water and lost itself in the west. Sea gulls soared and dipped, and tiny "sand peeps" flitted along the beach. Just as the red rim of the sun dipped in the purpling sea, the boats began to come in.

"Most of them will go around to the Point," explained Agnes, with a contemptuous sweep of her hand towards a long headland running out before them. "They belong there and they're a rough crowd. You don't catch Young Si associating with the Pointers. There, he's getting up sail. We'll just have time to get back before he comes in."

They hurried back across the dampening sand as the sun disappeared, leaving a fiery spot behind him. The shore was no longer quiet and deserted. The little spot where the fishing house stood had suddenly started into life. Roughly clad boys were running hither and thither, carrying fish or water. The boats were hauled up on the skids. A couple of shaggy old tars, who had strolled over from the Point to hear about Young Si's catch, were smoking their pipes at the corner of his shanty. A mellow afterlight was shining over sea and shore. The whole scene delighted Ethel's artist eyes.

Agnes nudged her companion.

"There! If you want to see Young Si," she whispered, pointing to the skids, where a busy figure was discernible in a large boat, "that's him, with his back to us, in the cream-coloured boat. He's counting out mackerel. If you go over to that platform behind him, you'll get a good look when he turns around. I'm going to coax a mackerel out of that stingy old Snuffy, if I can."

She tripped off, and Ethel walked slowly over to the boats. The men stared at her in open-mouthed admiration as she passed them and walked out on the platform behind Young Si. There was no one near the two. The others were all assembled around Snuffy's boat. Young Si was throwing out the mackerel with marvellous rapidity, but at the sound of a footstep behind him he turned and straightened up his tall form. They stood face to face.

"Miles!"

"Ethel!"

Young Si staggered back against the mast, letting two silvery bloaters slip through his hands overboard. His handsome, sunburned face was very white.

Ethel Lennox turned abruptly and silently and walked swiftly across the sand. Agnes felt her arm touched, and turned to see Ethel standing, pale and erect, beside her.

"Let us go home," said the latter unsteadily. "It is very damp here – I feel chilled."

"Oh, dear!" exclaimed Agnes penitently. "I ought to have told you to bring a shawl. It is always damp on the shore after sunset. Here, Snuffy, give me my mackerel. Thank you. I'm ready now, Miss Lennox."

They reached the lane before Agnes remembered to ask the question Ethel dreaded.

"Oh, did you see Young Si? And what do you think of him?"

Ethel turned her face away and answered with studied carelessness. "He seems to be quite a superior fisherman so far as I could see in the dim light. It was very dusky there, you know. Let us walk a little faster. My shoes are quite wet."

When they reached home, Miss Lennox excused herself on the plea of weariness and went straight to her room.

BACK AT THE SHORE Young Si had recovered himself and stooped again to his work. His face was set and expressionless. A dull red burned in each bronzed cheek. He threw out the mackerel mechanically, but his hands trembled.

Snuffy strolled over to the boat. "See that handsome

girl, Si?" he asked lazily. "One of the Bentleys' boarders, I hear. Looks as if she might have stepped out of a picture frame, don't she?"

"We've no time to waste, Curtis," said Young Si harshly, "with all these fish to clean before bedtime. Stop talking and get to work."

Snuffy shrugged his shoulders and obeyed in silence. Young Si was not a person to be trifled with. The catch was large and it was late before they finished. Snuffy surveyed the full barrels complacently.

"Good day's work," he muttered, "but hard – I'm dead beat out. 'Low I'll go to bed. In the name o' goodness, Si, whar be you a-goin' to?"

Young Si had got into a dory and untied it. He made no answer, but rowed out from the shore. Snuffy stared at the dory blankly until it was lost in the gloom.

"Ef that don't beat all!" he ejaculated. "I wonder if Si is in his right senses? He's been actin' quar right along, and now to start off, Lord knows whar, at this hour o' night! I really don't believe it's safe to stay here alone with him."

Snuffy shook his unkempt head dubiously.

Young Si rowed steadily out over the dark waves. An eastern breeze was bringing in a damp sea fog that blurred darkly over the outlines of horizon and shore. The young fisherman found himself alone in a world of water and grey mist. He stopped rowing and leaned forward on his oars.

"To see her here, of all places!" he muttered. "Not a word, scarcely a look, after all this long heartbreak! Well, perhaps it is better so. And yet to know she is so near! How beautiful she is! And I love her more than ever. That is where the sting lies. I thought that in this rough life, amid all these rude associations, where nothing could remind me of her, I might forget. And now – "

He clenched his hands. The mist was all around and

about him, creeping, impalpable, phantom-like. The dory rocked gently on the swell. From afar came the low persistent murmur of the ocean.

THE NEXT DAY Ethel Lennox declined to visit Si's shore. Instead she went to the Point and sketched all day. She went again the next day and the next. The Point was the most picturesque part of the shore, she averred, and the "types" among its inhabitants most interesting. Agnes Bentley ceased to suggest another visit to Si's shore. She had a vague perception that her companion did not care to discuss the subject.

At the end of a week Mrs. Bentley remarked: "What in the world can have happened to Young Si? It's a whole week since he was here for milk or butter. He ain't sick, is he?"

Mr. Bentley chuckled amusedly.

"I 'low I can tell you the reason of that. Si's getting his stuff at Walden's now. I saw him going there twice this week. 'Liza Walden's got ahead of you at last, Mary."

"Well, I never did!" said Mrs. Bentley. "Well, Young Si is the first that ever preferred 'Liza Walden's butter to mine. Everyone knows what hers is like. She never works her salt half in. Well, Young Si's welcome to it, I'm sure; I wish him joy of his exchange."

Mrs. Bentley rattled her dishes ominously. It was plain her faith in Young Si had received a severe shock.

Upstairs in her room, Ethel Lennox, with a few undried tears glistening on her cheeks, was writing a letter. Her lips were compressed and her hand trembled:

"I have discovered that it is no use to run away from fate," she wrote. "No matter how hard we try to elude it, and how sure we are that we have succeeded, it will rise and meet us where we least expect it. I came down here tired and worn out, looking for peace and rest – and lo! the most disquieting element of my life is here to confront me.

"I'm going to confess, Helen. 'Open confession is good for the soul,' you know, and I shall treat myself to a good dose while the mood is on.

"You know, of course, that I was once engaged to Miles Lesley. You also know that that engagement was broken last autumn for unexplained reasons. Well, I will tell you all about it and then mail this letter speedily, before I change my mind.

"It is over a year now since Miles and I first became engaged. As you are aware, his family is wealthy, and noted for its exclusiveness. I was a poor school teacher, and you may imagine with what horror his relatives received the news of Miles' attentions to one whom they considered his inferior. Now that I have thought the whole matter over calmly, I scarcely blame them. It must be hard for aristocratic parents who have lavished every care upon a son, and cherished for him the highest hopes, when he turns from the women of his own order to one considered beneath him in station. But I did not view the subject in this light then; and instead of declining his attentions, as I perhaps should have done, I encouraged them – I loved him so dearly, Nell! – and in spite of family opposition, Miles soon openly declared his attachment.

"When his parents found they could not change his purpose, their affection for him forced them into outward acquiescence, but their reluctant condescension was gall and wormwood to me. I saw things only from my own point of view, and was keenly sensitive to their politely concealed disapprobation, and my offended vanity found its victim in Miles. I belonged to the class who admit and resent slights, instead of ignoring them, as do the higher bred, and I thought he would not see those offered to me. I grew cold and formal to him. He was very patient, but his ways were not mine, and my manner puzzled and annoyed him. Our relations soon became strained, and the trifle necessary for an open quarrel was easily supplied.

"One evening I went to a large At Home given by his mother. I knew but few and, as Miles was necessarily busy with his social duties to her guests, I was, after the first hurried greeting, left unattended for a time. Not being accustomed to such functions, I resented this as a covert insult and, in a fit of jealous pique, I blush to own that I took the revenge of a peasant maid and entered into a marked flirtation with Fred Currie, who had paid me some attention before my engagement. When Miles was at liberty to seek me, he found me, to all appearances, quite absorbed in my companion and oblivious of his approach. He turned on his heel and went away, nor did he come near me the rest of the evening.

"I went home angry enough, but so miserable and repentant that if Miles had been his usual patient self when he called the following evening I would have begged his forgiveness. But I had gone too far; his mother was shocked by my gaucherie, and he was humiliated and justly exasperated. We had a short, bitter quarrel. I said a great many foolish, unpardonable things, and finally I threw his ring at him. He gave me a startled look then, in which there was something of contempt, and went away without another word.

"After my anger had passed, I was wretchedly unhappy. I realized how unworthily I had acted, how deeply I loved Miles, and how lonely and empty my life would be without him. But he did not come back, and soon after I learned he had gone away – whither no one knew, but it was supposed abroad. Well, I buried my hopes and tears in secret and went on with my life as people have to do – a life in which I have learned to think, and which, I hope, has made me nobler and better.

"This summer I came here. I heard much about a certain mysterious stranger known as 'Young Si' who was fishing mackerel at this shore. I was very curious. The story sounded romantic, and one evening I went down to see him. I met him face to face and, Helen, it was Miles Lesley!

"For one minute earth, sky and sea reeled around me. The next, I remembered all, and turned and walked away. He did not follow.

"You may be sure that I now religiously avoid that part of the shore. We have never met since, and he has made no effort to see me. He clearly shows that he despises me. Well, I despise myself. I am very unhappy, Nell, and not only on my own account, for I feel that if Miles had never met me, his mother would not now be breaking her heart for her absent boy. My sorrow has taught me to understand hers, and I no longer resent her pride.

"You need hardly be told after this that I leave here in another week. I cannot fabricate a decent excuse to go sooner, or I would."

In the cool twilight Ethel went with Agnes Bentley to mail her letter. As they stopped at the door of the little country store, a young man came around the corner. It was Young Si. He was in his rough fishing suit, with a big herring net trailing over his shoulder, but no disguise could effectually conceal his splendid figure. Agnes sprang forward eagerly.

"Si, where have you been? Why have you never been up to see us for so long?"

Young Si made no verbal reply. He merely lifted his cap with formal politeness and turned on his heel.

"Well, I never!" exclaimed Agnes, as soon as she recovered her powers of speech. "If that is how Young Si is going to treat his friends! He must have got offended at something. I wonder what it is," she added, her curiosity getting the better of her indignation.

When they came out they saw the solitary figure of Young Si far adown, crossing the dim, lonely shore fields. In the dusk Agnes failed to notice the pallor of her companion's face and the unshed tears in her eyes.

"I'VE JUST BEEN DOWN to the Point," said Agnes, coming in one sultry afternoon about a week later, "and Little Ev said as there was no fishing today he'd take us out for that sail tonight if you wanted to go."

Ethel Lennox put her drawing away listlessly. She looked pale and tired. She was going away the next day, and this was to be her last visit to the shore.

About an hour before sunset a boat glided out from the shadow of the Point. In it were Ethel Lennox and Agnes, together with Little Ev, the sandy-haired, undersized Pointer who owned the boat.

The evening was fine, and an off-shore breeze was freshening up rapidly. They did not notice the long, dark bank of livid cloud low in the northwest.

"Isn't this glorious!" exclaimed Ethel. Her hat was straining back from her head and the red rings of her hair were blowing about her face.

Agnes looked about her more anxiously. Wiser in matters of sea and shore than her companion, there were some indications she did not like.

Young Si, who was standing with Snuffy at their skids, lowered his spyglass with a start.

"It is Agnes Bentley and – and – that boarder of theirs," he said anxiously, "and they've gone out with Little Ev in that wretched, leaky tub of his. Where are their eyes that they can't see a squall coming up?"

"An' Little Ev don't know as much about managing a boat as a cat!" exclaimed Snuffy excitedly. "Sign 'em to come back."

Si shook his head. "They're too far out. I don't know that the squall will amount to very much. In a good boat, with someone who knew how to manage it, they'd be all right. But with Little Ev – " He began walking restlessly up and down the narrow platform.

The boat was now some distance out. The breeze had stiffened to a slow strong wind and the dull-grey level of the sea was whipped into white-caps.

Agnes bent towards Ethel. "It's getting too rough. I think we'd better go back. I'm afraid we're in for a thunder squall. Look at the clouds."

A long, sullen muttering verified her words.

"Little Ev," she shouted, "we want to go in."

Little Ev, thus recalled to things about him, looked around in alarm. The girls questioned each other with glances of dismay. The sky had grown very black, and the peals of thunder came louder and more continuously. A jagged bolt of lightning hurtled over the horizon. Over land and sea was "the green, malignant light of coming storm."

Little Ev brought the boat's head abruptly round as a few heavy drops of rain fell.

"Ev, the boat is leaking!" shrieked Agnes, above the wind. "The water's coming in!"

"Bail her out then," shouted Ev, struggling with the sail. "There's two cans under the seat. I've got to lower this sail. Bail her out."

"I'll help you," said Ethel.

She was very pale, but her manner was calm. Both girls bailed energetically.

Young Si, watching through the glass, saw them. He dropped it and ran to his boat, white and resolute.

"They've sprung a leak. Here, Curtis, launch the boat. We've got to go out or Ev will drown them."

271

They shot out from the shore just as the downpour came, blotting out sea and land in one driving sheet of white rain.

"Young Si is coming off for us," said Agnes. "We'll be all right if he gets here in time. This boat is going to sink, sure."

Little Ev was completely demoralized by fear. The girls bailed unceasingly, but the water gained every minute. Young Si was none too soon.

"Jump, Ev!" he shouted as his boat shot alongside. "Jump for your life!"

He dragged Ethel Lennox in as he spoke. Agnes sprang from one boat to the other like a cat, and Little Ev jumped just as a thunderous crash seemed to burst above them and air and sky were filled with blue flame.

The danger was past, for the squall had few difficulties for Si and Snuffy. When they reached the shore, Agnes, who had quite recovered from her fright, tucked her dripping skirts about her and announced her determination to go straight home with Snuffy.

"I can't get any wetter than I am," she said cheerfully. "I'll send Pa down in the buggy for Miss Lennox. Light the fire in your shanty, Si, and let her get dry. I'll be as quick as I can."

Si picked Ethel up in his strong arms and carried her into the fish-house. He placed her on one of the low benches and hurriedly began to kindle a fire. Ethel sat up dazedly and pushed back the dripping masses of her bright hair. Young Si turned and looked down at her with a passionate light in his eyes. She put out her cold, wet hands wistfully.

"Oh, Miles!" she whispered.

Outside, the wind shook the frail building and tore the shuddering sea to pieces. The rain poured down. It was already settling in for a night of storm. But, inside, Young

Si's fire was casting cheery flames over the rude room, and Young Si himself was kneeling by Ethel Lennox with his arm about her and her head on his broad shoulder. There were happy tears in her eyes and her voice quivered as she said, "Miles, can you forgive me? If you knew how bitterly I have repented – "

"Never speak of the past again, my sweet. In my lonely days and nights down here by the sea, I have forgotten all but my love."

"Miles, how did you come here? I thought you were in Europe."

"I did travel at first. I came down here by chance, and resolved to cut myself utterly adrift from my old life and see if I could not forget you. I was not very successful." He smiled down into her eyes. "And you were going away tomorrow. How perilously near we have been to not meeting! But how are we going to explain all this to our friends along shore?"

"I think we had better not explain it at all. I will go away tomorrow, as I intended, and you can quietly follow soon. Let 'Young Si' remain the mystery he has always been."

"That will be best – decidedly so. They would never understand if we did tell them. And I daresay they would be very much disappointed to find I was not a murderer or a forger or something of that sort. They have always credited me with an evil past. And you and I will go back to our own world, Ethel. You will be welcome there now, sweet – my family, too, have learned a lesson, and will do anything to promote my happiness."

Agnes drove Ethel Lennox to the station next day. The fierce wind that had swept over land and sea seemed to have blown away all the hazy vapours and oppressive heats in the air, and the morning dawned as clear and fresh as if the sad old earth with all her passionate tears had cleansed herself from sin and stain and come forth radiantly pure and sweet. Ethel bubbled over with joyousness. Agnes wondered at the change in her.

"Good-bye, Miss Lennox," she said wistfully. "You'll come back to see us some time again, won't you?"

"Perhaps," smiled Ethel, "and if not, Agnes, you must come and see me. Some day I may tell you a secret."

About a week later Young Si suddenly vanished, and his disappearance was a nine-day's talk along shore. His departure was as mysterious as his advent. It leaked out that he had quietly disposed of his boat and shanty to Snuffy Curtis, sent his mackerel off and, that done, slipped from the Pointers' lives, never more to re-enter them.

Little Ev was the last of the Pointers to see him tramping along the road to the station in the dusk of the autumn twilight. And the next morning Agnes Bentley, going out of doors before the others, found on the doorstep a basket containing a small, vociferous black kitten with a card attached to its neck. On it was written: "Will Agnes please befriend Witch in memory of Young Si?"

A House Divided against Itself

ALL THE OMENS had pointed to it for days. Big George . . . who was five foot one . . . wondered how he could have been blind to them. Salt had howled dismally all Monday. On Tuesday Little George . . . who was six foot two . . . had smashed the mirror he had shaved by for forty years. On Wednesday Big George had failed to pick up a pin he had seen. On Thursday Little George had walked under Tom Appleby's ladder at the lobster cannery. And on Friday . . . Friday, mind you . . . Big and Little George between them had contrived to spill the salt at supper. Was it any wonder disaster followed? Directly after that fatal meal Little George had sneaked off to the lottery at the Point and brought the thing home.

Big George was not superstitious. What did spilled salt and broken mirrors matter to a good Presbyterian? But he did believe in dreams . . . having Biblical warrant for the same. And he had had a horrible one two weeks previously, of seeing the full moon, one moment burning black, the next livid red, coming nearer and nearer to the earth . . . waking, just as it seemed near enough to be touched, with a howl of agony that shattered the stillness of the spring night at Little Spruce for yards around. Big George, who had kept a careful and copious diary of his dreams for forty years, looked them all over and concluded that none of them had been as awe-inspiring as this one.

Then there was that peculiar sound the gulf had been making of late. When the Old Lady of the Gulf moaned like that, somebody was going to sup sorrow. But Little George did not connect it with his winning the fifth prize in the lottery Captain Leon Buote had been getting up down at Chapel Point in aid of the Old Sailors' Home. Little George had bought a ticket off Young Mosey Gautier, just to

277

please the kid, and on the night when the numbers were drawn he thought he might as well saunter round to Chapel Point and see if he had any luck.

He had!

"Little" George Beelby and "Big" George Beelby were cousins. Big George was six years the older, and the adjective that had been appropriate in childhood stuck to him, as things stick in Rose River and Little Spruce Cove, all his life. The two Georges were old sailors and 'longshore fishermen and they had lived together in Little George's little house at Spruce Cove for thirty years. Big George had been born a bachelor but Little George was a widower. His marriage was so far in the dim past that Big George had almost forgiven him for it, though he occasionally cast it up to him in the frequent quarrels by which they enlivened what might otherwise have been the rather monotonous life of retired sea-folk.

They were not and never had been beautiful, though that fact worried them little. Big George had a face that was actually broader than it was long and a flaming red beard. He could not cook but he was a good washer and mender. He could also knit socks and write poetry. Big George quite fancied himself as a poet. He had written an epic which he was fond of declaiming in a surprisingly great voice for his thin body. When he was low in his mind he felt that he had missed his calling. Also, that nearly everybody in the world was going to be damned.

"I should'a been a poet," he would say mournfully to his orange-hued cat. The cat always agreed with him but Little George sometimes snorted contemptuously.

If he had a vanity it was in the elaborate anchors tattooed on the backs of his hands. He was a Liberal in politics and had Laurier's picture hanging over his bed. He thought Little Spruce Cove the most desirable spot on earth and resented any insinuation to the contrary.

"I like to have the sea, the blue lone sea, at my very doorstep like this," he boomed to the "writing man," who had asked if they never found Little Spruce lonesome.

"Just part of his poetical nature," Little George had explained aside, so that the writing man should not think Big George feeble-minded. Little George lived in secret terror and Big George in secret hope that the writing man would put them in a book.

By the side of Big George, Little George looked enormous. His freckled face was literally half forehead, and a network of large purplish-red veins over nose and cheeks looked like some monstrous spider. He wore a great drooping grey moustache, like a horseshoe, that did not seem to belong to his face at all. But he was a genial soul and enjoyed his own good cooking, especially his famous pea soups and clam chowders. His political idol was Sir John Macdonald, whose picture hung over the clock shelf, and he had been heard to say . . . not in Big George's hearing . . . that he admired women in the abstract. He had a harmless hobby of collecting skulls from the old Indian graveyard down at Big Spruce and ornamenting the fence of his potato plot with them. He and Big George quarreled about it every time he brought a new skull home. Big George declared that it was indecent and unnatural and un-Presbyterian. But the skulls remained on the poles.

IT WAS LATE AT NIGHT when Little George returned from the raffle, so the explosion was deferred till morning. Little George unwrapped something from the parcel he was carrying, looked at it dubiously, shook his head, and tried the effect of it on the clock shelf. Something in him liked it. Something else was uneasy.

"She's got a real fine figger," he muttered, with a doubtful glance at Big George sleeping soundly in his bunk with a yellow cat rolled up in a golden ball on his stomach. "But

I don't know what he'll think of her . . . I really don't. Nor the minister."

These considerations did not keep Little George awake. He fell promptly asleep and Aurora, goddess of the dawn, kept her vigil on the clock shelf through the hours of darkness and was the first thing Big George's eyes rested on when he opened them in the morning. There she stood, her lithe, lovely form poised on tiptoe, smitten by a red-gold beam from the sun that was rising across the harbour.

"What the devil is that?" said Big George, thinking this was another dream. He flung himself out of his bunk, upsetting an indignant cat, and walked across the room.

"It ain't a dream," he said incredulously. "It's a statoo . . . a naked statoo!"

The dog . . . whose name was Salt . . . that had been curled up at Little George's feet, bounded to the floor after the cat . . . whose name was Mustard. He liked the cat well enough but he wasn't going to have her sitting there on the floor grinning at him. The resultant disturbance awoke Little George, who sat up drowsily and inquired what the row was about.

"George Beelby," said Big George ominously, "what is that up there?"

"Oh, that. That's an alabaster statooette. I drew it for fifth prize at Captain Buote's lottery last night. Rather pretty, ain't it?"

Big George's voice boomed out.

"Pretty! It's indecent and obscene, that's what it is. You take it right down and fire it out in the gulf as far as you can fire it."

If Big George had not thus flown off the handle, it is probable that Little George would have done exactly that, being somewhat uneasy regarding the minister and the look of the thing generally. But he was not going to be bullied into doing it by that little runt of a Big George and he'd let him see it.

"Oh, I guess not," he retorted coolly. "I guess it's going to stay right there. Stop yelping now and let your hair curl."

Big George's scanty love-locks showed no sign of curling but his red beard fairly crackled with indignation. He began striding about the room in a fine rage, biting first his right hand and then his left. Salt fled one way and Mustard another, leaving the Georges to fight it out.

" 'Tain't right to have any kind of statoos, let alone naked ones. It's agin God's law. 'Thou shalt not make unto thee any graven immidge . . .' "

"Good gosh! I ain't made it and I ain't worshipping it . . ."

"That'll come . . . that'll come. And a French gew-gaw at that."

"No, 'tain't . . . it's made in Germany and her name's there at the bottom . . . Aurorer. Jest a gal, that's all."

"Do you think the Apostle Paul ever carried a thing like that around with him?" demanded Big George. "Or" . . . as an afterthought that might influence Little George . . . "Sir John A. Macdonald?"

"Not likely. St. Paul was kind of a woman-hater like yourself. As for Sir John, he was too busy defeating the Grits at every election to have time for the fine arts. Sir Wilfrid would have more probably. Now stop chewing your fists and pretend you're grown up even if you ain't, Georgie. See if you can dress yourself like a man."

"Thank you . . . thank you." Big George became ominously calm. "As for Sir Wilfrid, *he's* dressed. And I am entirely satisfied to be classed with the Apostle Paul. Entirely! My conscience guides my conduct, you ribald old thing."

"Been making a meal of the dictionary, it seems," retorted Little George, yanking his pants off their nail, "and it don't seem to have agreed with your stomach.

Better take a dose of sody. Your conscience, as you call it, hain't nothing to do with it . . . only your prejurdices. Look at that writing man. Hain't he got half a dozen of them statoos in his summer cottage up the river?"

"If he's a fool . . . and wuss . . . is that any reason why you should be? Think of that and your immortal soul, George Beelby."

"This ain't my day for thinking," retorted the imperturbable Little George. "Now that you've blown off your steam, just set the porridge pot on. You'll feel better when you've had your breakfast. Can't 'preciate works of art properly on a empty stomach, Georgie."

Big George glared at him. Then he grabbed the porridge pot, yanked open the door and hurled the pot through it. The pot bounded and leaped and clattered down the rocks to the sandy cove below. Salt and Mustard fled out after it.

"Some day you'll drive me too far," said Little George darkly. "You're just a narrow-minded, small-souled old maid, that's what *you* are. If you hadn't a dirty mind you wouldn't be throwing a fit 'cause you see a stone woman's legs. Your own don't look so artistic, prancing around in that shirt-tail, let me tell you that. You really ought to wear pajamas, Georgie."

"I fired your old pot out to show you I'm in earnest," roared Big George. "I tell you I won't have no naked hussy in this house, George Beelby."

"Yell louder, can't you?" said Little George. "This happens to be *my* house."

"Oh, it is, is it? Very well. Very well. I'll tell you this right here and now. It ain't big enough for me and you and your Roarer."

"You ain't the first person that idee's occurred to," said Little George. "I've had too many tastes of your jaw of late."

282

Big George stopped prancing and tried to look as dignified as a man with nothing on but a shirt can look as he
laid down the ultimatum he never doubted would bring
Little George to his senses.

"I've stood all I'm a-going to. I've stood them skulls of
yours for years but I tell you right here and now, George
Beelby, I won't stand for that atrocity. If it's to remain . . . *I*
leave."

"As for leaving or staying, suit yourself. Aurorer stays
there on that clock shelf," retorted Little George, striding
out and down the rocks to rescue his maltreated porridge
pot.

BREAKFAST WAS A GLOOMY MEAL. Big George looked very
determined, but Little George was not worried. They had
had a worse row than this last week when he had caught
Big George stealing a piece of raisin pie he had put away
for his own snack. But when the silent meal was over and
Big George ostentatiously dragged an old, battered, bulg-
ing valise out from under the bunk and began packing his
few chattels into it, Little George realized that the crisis
was serious. Well, all right . . . all right. Big George needn't
think he could bully him into giving up Aurorer. He had
won her and he was going to keep her, and Big George
could go to Hades.

Little George really thought Hades. He had picked up
the word from the minister and thought it sounded more
respectable than hell.

Little George watched Big George stealthily out of his
pale woolly eyes as he washed up the dishes and fed
Mustard, who came scratching at the window pane. The
morning's sunlit promise had been delusive and it was
now, as Little George reflected testily, one of them still
dark misty days calc'lated to dampen one's spirits. This
was what came of ladders and looking-glasses!

Big George packed his picture of Laurier and the model of a ship with crimson hull and white sails that had long adorned the caticornered shelf above his bunk. These were indisputably his. But when it came to their small library there was a difficulty.

"Which of these books am I to take?" he demanded frostily.

"Whichever you like," said Little George, getting out his baking board. There were only two books in the lot he cared a hoot about anyhow. Foxe's *Book of Martyrs* and *The Horrible Confession and Execution of John Murdock (one of the Emigrants who lately left this Country) who was hanged at Brockville, Upper Canada, on the third day of September last for the inhuman murder of his own brother.*

When Little George saw Big George pack the latter in his valise, he had much ado to suppress a grisly groan.

"I'm leaving you the Martyrs and all the dime novels," said Big George defensively. "What about the dog and cat?"

"You'd better take the cat," said Little George, measuring out flour. "It'll match your whiskers."

This suited Big George. Mustard was his favourite.

"And the weegee board?"

"Take it. I don't hold no dealings with the devil."

Big George shut and strapped his valise, put the reluctant Mustard into a bag and, with the bag over his shoulder and his Sunday hat on his head, he strode out of the house and down the rocks without even a glance at Little George, who was ostentatiously making raisin pie.

Little George watched him out of sight, still incredulously. Then he looked at the white, beautiful cause of all the mischief exulting on the clock shelf.

"Well, he didn't get you out, my beauty, and I'm jiggered if he's ever going to. No, siree! I've said it and I'll stick to it.

Anyhow, my ears won't have to ache any longer listening to that old epic of his. And now I can wear my earrings again."

LITTLE GEORGE REALLY THOUGHT Big George would come back when he had cooled down. But he underrated the strength of Big George's principles or stubbornness.

The first thing he heard was that Big George had rented Tom Wilkins' old shanty at Upper Spruce and was living there. But not with Mustard. If Big George did not come back, Mustard did. Mustard was scratching at the window three days after her ignominious departure in a bag. Little George let her in and fed her. It wasn't his fault if Big George couldn't keep his cat. He, Little George, wasn't going to see no dumb animal starve. Mustard stayed home until Sunday when Big George, knowing Little George was safely in church, came down to Little Spruce and got her. All to no purpose. Again Mustard came back . . . and yet again. After the third attempt Big George gave it up in bitterness of soul.

"Do I want his old yeller flannel cat?" he demanded of the writing man. "God knows I don't. What hurts my feelings is that he knew the critter would go back. That's why he offered her so free. The depth of that man! I hear he's going round circulating mean false things about me and saying I'll soon be sick of living on salt codfish and glad to sneak back for a smell of good cooking. He'll see . . . he'll see. I ain't never made a god of my stomach as he does. You should 'a' heard the riot he raised one day last month 'cause I et a piece of mouldy old raisin pie he'd cached for himself, the greedy pig. And saying it'll be too lonesome here for one of my gabby propensities. Yessir, he said them words! Me, lonesome! This place just suits me down to the ground. See the scenery. I'm a lover of nature, sir, my favourite being the moon. And them contented cows up on the Point pasture. I could gaze at 'em by the hour. They're all the society I want, sir . . . present company always excepted. Not," added Big George feelingly, "but what Little George had his p'ints. The blueberry puddings that man could make! And them clam chowders of his stuck to the ribs better'n most things. But I had my soul to think of, hadn't I? And my morals?"

THE QUARREL AND SEPARATION of the Georges caused quite a sensation in Rose River and along the coves. Few thought it would last. But the spring and summer passed without a reconciliation and people gave up expecting it. The Beelbys had always been a stubborn gang. Neither of the old men preserved any dignified reserve regarding their mutual wrongs. When they met, as they occasionally did, they glared at each other and passed on in silence. But each was forever waylaying neighbours and passers-by to tell his side of the story.

"I hear he's going about telling I kicked the dog in the abdomen," Little George would snort. "What's abdomen, mister?"

"Belly," said his victim bluntly.

"Look at that now. I knew he was lying. I never kicked no dog in the belly. Touched his ribs with the toe of my boot once, that's all . . . for good and sufficient cause. Says I lured his cat back. What do I want of his cat? Always bringing dead rats in and leaving them around. And determined to sleep on *my* abdomen at night. If he'd fed his cat right she wouldn't 'a' left him. But I ain't going to turn no broken-hearted, ill-used beast out of my door. I hear he's raving round about moons and contented cows. The only use that man has for moons is to predict the weather and as for contented cows or discontented cows, it's all one to him. But I'm glad he's happy. So am I. I can sing all I want to now without having someone sarcastically saying, 'A good voice for chawing turnips,' or 'Hark from the tombs a doleful sound,' or maddening things like that. I had to endure that for years. But did I make a fuss about it? Or about his yelping that old epic of his half the night . . . cackling and chortling and guffawing and gurgling and yapping and yarring till I felt as if I'd been run through a meat chopper? Did I mind his always conterdicting me? No, it kept life from being too tejus. Did I mind his being a fundamentalist? No, I respected his principles and I give up wearing these earrings because he didn't think they was Presbyterian ornaments. Did I mind his getting up at unearthly hours Sunday mornings to pray? Very devowt! I did not. Some people might 'a' said his method of praying was irreverent . . . talking to God same as he would to me or you. I didn't mind the irreverence but what I didn't like was his habit of swinging right round in the middle of a prayer and giving the devil a licking. Still, did I make a fuss over it? No, I overlooked all them things and yet when I bring home a beautiful statooette like Aurorer there, Big George up and throws three different kinds. Well, I'd rather have Aurorer than him any day and you can tell him so. She's easier to look at for one thing and for another she don't sneak into the pantry unbeknownst to me and eat up my private snacks. I ain't said much about this affair . . . I've let Big George do the talking . . . but some day when I get time I'm going to talk an awful lot, mister."

"I'm told that poor ass of a Little George spends most of his spare time imagining he's strewing flowers on my grave," Big George told the minister. "And I hear he's been making fun of my prayers. Will you believe it, he had the impidence to tell me once that I had to make my prayers shorter 'cause they interfered with his morning nap? Did I shorten them? Not by a jugful. Spun 'em out twice as long. What I put up with from that man! His dog nigh about chewed up my Victory bond but did I complain? God knows I didn't. But when my cat had kittens on his shirt he tore up the turf. Talking of cats, I hear my cat has kittens again. You'd think Little George might 'a' sent me one. I hear there's three. And I haven't got a thing except a couple of ducks. They're company . . . but knowing you have to eat 'em up some day spoils things. Look a'here, minister. Why did Jacob let out a howl and weep when he kissed Rachel?"

The minister didn't know, or if he did he kept it to himself. Some Rose Riverites thought the minister was too fond of drawing the Georges out.

"Because he found out it wasn't what it was cracked up to be," chuckled Big George. He was happy all day because he had put one over on the minister.

But Big George was soon in no mood for joking about kisses ancient or modern. He nearly had an apoplectic fit when he heard that some of the summer boarders up the river had gone to Little George, under the impression that *he* was the poet, and asked him to recite his epic. The awful thing was that Little George did. Went through it from start to finish and never let on he wasn't the true author.

"From worshipping immidges to stealing poetry is only what you'd expect. You can see how that man's character's degen'rating."

"Mebbe the Widow Terlizzick'll reform him," chuckled his auditor.

"What's that?"

"Didn't you know Little George is going to see her Sunday nights? Folks think it will be a match."

Big George was literally struck dumb for a time, but after that he turned himself loose on the subject to the delighted Riverites and Covites.

"Wants to work another wife to death, I s'pose. I really thought Little George had more sense. But you can't trust a man who's been married once . . . though you'd think he'd be the very one to know better. And him the ugliest man on the north shore! Not that the fair Terlizzick is any beauty with that big hairy mole on her chin and her sloppy ankles. I'd say she looked like a dog fight. And fat! It's well he's not buying her by the pound. She's been married twice already. Some folks never seem to know when to stop. Her father got drunk once and walked up the church aisle in his nightshirt. Nice thing to have in the family. I'm sorry for Little George but it's certainly coming to him. I hear he sits in church and looks at her like an intoxicated dog. Next thing he'll be serenading her. Did I ever tell you Little George thinks he can sing? Once I says to him, 'D'ye call that yowling music?' But the Terlizzicks never had any ear. Well, she'll have her troubles. I could tell a few things if I wanted to."

Big George took Little George's matrimonial designs very much to heart. When he was observed standing on a rock waving his short arms wildly in the air, it was a safe bet that he was not, as heretofore, shouting his epic out to waves and stars, but abusing the Widow Terlizzick. She was, he told the world, a hooded cobra, a big fat slob, a rapacious female animal and a tigress. He professed profound pity for Little George. The poor fellow little dreamed what he was in for. Taking two men's leavings! But them widders did bamboozle people so. And the Terlizzick had so much experience. Two husbands done in. A lady really orter be more economical with husbands.

All these compliments, being duly reported to Little George and Mrs. Terlizzick, may or may not have pleased them. Little George kept his own counsel and brought up Mustard's three kittens ostentatiously.

The white goddess of the morning still stood tiptoe on the clock shelf but the dust had gathered on her shapely legs. When Captain Leon started up another lottery at

Chapel Point, Little George said it orter be stopped by law
and Mosey Gautier had to run for his life when he tried to
sell a ticket to him.

SPRING AND SUMMER PASSED; autumn wore away. The Rose
River folks banked their houses with seaweed and the
summer boarders departed . . . all but the writing man,
who always hung on to his shanty till the gulf froze over.

One evening Big George set out to walk around the
shore to Lighthouse Point. It was a long walk and he had
various rheumatic spots about his anatomy, but there
would be some cronies at the lighthouse and Big George
thought an evening of social intercourse would be better
for his nerves than playing tit-tat-x, right hand against left,
at home. These short days and long, early-falling evenings
were depressing, he admitted. And the Wilkins' shanty
was draughty. The lighthouse keeper's wife might even
give them a bite of lunch. Big George's cooking had not
improved much. He had an uneasy suspicion that he was
too old to learn. But he would not let his thoughts dwell
on Little George's suet puddings and clam chowders and
hot biscuits. That way madness lay.

There had been a skim of snow that morning, melting
into dampness as the sun rose for an hour or two of
watery brightness before shrouding himself in clouds.
The brief day had grown cold and raw as it wore on, and
now land and sea lay wrapped in a grey brooding stillness. Far away Big George heard a train whistle blow
distinctly. The Old Lady of the Gulf moaned now and
then. A storm was coming up but Big George was not
afraid of storms. He would come home by the river road;
the tide would be too high on his return to come by the
Hole in the Wall.

As a matter of fact, when he reached the long red
headland known as the Hole in the Wall, he blankly

realized that the tide was already ahead of him. There was no getting around it. He could not climb its steep rugged sides, and to go back to where a road led down to the shore meant a lot of extra walking.

A daring inspiration came to Big George. Since he could not get around the Hole in the Wall, could he go through it? Nobody ever had gone through it. But there had to be a first time for anything. It was certainly bigger than last year. Nothing venture, nothing win.

The Hole in the Wall had begun with a tiny opening through the relatively thin side of the headland. Every year it grew a little larger as the yielding sandstone crumbled under wave and frost. It was a fair size now. Big George was small and thin. He reckoned if he could get his head through, the rest of him could follow.

He lay down and cautiously began squirming through. It was tighter than he had thought. The sides seemed suddenly very thick. All at once Big George decided that he was not cut out for a pioneer. He would go back to the road. He tried to. He could not move. Somehow his coat had got ruckled up around his shoulders and jammed him tight. Vainly he twisted and writhed and tugged. The big rock seemed to hold him as in a grip of iron. The more he struggled the tighter he seemed to get wedged in. Finally he lay still with a cold sweat of horror breaking out over him. His head was through the Hole in the Wall. His shoulders were tight in it. His legs . . . where were his legs? There was no sensation in them but they were probably hanging down the rock wall on the hinder side.

What a position to be in! On a lonely shore on a fast-darkening November night with a storm coming up! He would never live through it. He would die of heart failure before morning, like old Captain Jobby, who tried to climb through a gate when he was drunk and stuck there.

Nobody could see him and it was no use to yell. Before

him as behind him was nothing but a curving shadowy cove bounded by another headland. No house, no human being in sight. Nevertheless, Big George yelled with what little breath he had at command.

"Wouldn't you just as soon sing as make that noise?" queried Little George, sticking his head around the huge boulder that screened him.

Big George stared at the familiar spidery nose and huge moustache. Of all the men in River and Cove to catch him in this predicament, that it should be Little George! What the devil was he doing squatted here a mile away from home on such a night?

"I wasn't aiming to sing, not being afflicted as some folks are," said Big George sarcastically. "I was just trying to fill my lungs with air."

"Why don't you come all the way through?" jeered Little George, coming around the boulder.

" 'Cause I can't and you know it," said Big George savagely. "Look here, George Beelby, you and I ain't friends but I'm a human being, ain't I?"

"There are times when I can see a distant resemblance to one in you," acknowledged Little George, sitting calmly down on a jut of the boulder.

"Well then, in the name of humanity, help me out of this."

"I dunno's I can," said Little George dubiously. "Seems to me the only way would be to yank you back by the legs and I can't get around the Point to do that."

"If you can get a good grip on my shoulder or on my coat, you can yank me out this way. It only wants a good pull. I can't get my arms free to help myself."

"And I dunno's I will," went on Little George, as if he had not been interrupted.

"You . . . dunno's . . . you will! D'ye mean to say you'll leave me here to die a night like this? Well, George Beelby . . ."

"No, I ain't aiming to do that. It'll be your own fault if you're left here. You've got to show you've some sense if I'm going to pull you out. Will you come home and behave yourself if I do?"

"If you want me to come home you know all you've got to do," snapped Big George. "Shoot out your Roarer."

"Aurorer stays," said Little George briefly.

"Then I stay too." Big George imitated Little George's brevity . . . partly because he had very little breath to use for talking at all. Little George took out his pipe and proceeded to light it.

"I'll give you a few minutes to reflect 'fore I go. I don't aim to stay long here in the damp. I dunno how a little wizened creature like you will stand it here all night. Anyhow, you'll have some feeling after this for the poor camel trying to get through the needle's eye."

"Call yourself a Christian!" sneered Big George.

"Don't be peevish now. This ain't a question of religion . . . this is a question of common sense," retorted Little George.

Big George made a terrific effort to free himself, but not even a tremor of the grim headland was produced thereby.

Little George jeered, "You'd orter see yourself with your red whiskers sticking out of that hole. And I s'pose the rest of you is sticking out on the other side. Beautiful rear view if anyone comes along. Not that anyone likely will this time of night. But if you're still alive in the morning I'm going to get the writing man to take a snap of your hind legs. Be sensible, Georgie. I've got pea soup for supper . . . hot pea soup."

"Take your pea soup to hell," said Big George.

Followed a lot of silence. Big George was thinking hard. He knew where his extremities were now, for the cold was nipping them like a weasel. The rock around him was

293

hard as iron. It was beginning to rain and the wind was rising. Already the showers of spray were spuming up from the rocks when the waves struck them. By morning he would be dead or gibbering.

But it was bitter to knuckle under to Little George and that white-limbed hussy on the clock shelf. Big George tried to pluck a little honour from the jaws of defeat.

"If I do come back, will you promise not to marry that fat widow?"

"I ain't promising nothing . . . but I never had any intention of marrying any widow, fat or lean."

Big George could not repress a jeer.

"I s'pose that means she wouldn't have you."

"She didn't get the chance to have me or not have me. I ain't contracting any alliance with the house of Terlizzick. Well, I'm for home and pea soup. Coming, Georgie?"

Big George emitted a sigh, partly of exhaustion, partly of surrender. Life was too complicated. He was beaten.

"Pull me out of this damn hole," he said sourly, "and I don't care how many naked women you have round."

"One's enough," said Little George.

He got a grip somehow of Big George's coat over his shoulders and tugged manfully. Big George howled. He was sure his legs were being torn off at the hips. Then he found they were still attached to his body, standing on the rock beside Little George.

"Wring your whiskers out and hurry," said Little George. "I'm afraid that pea soup'll be scorched. It's sitting on the back of the stove."

This was comfort now . . . with the cold rain beating down outside and the gulf beginning to bellow. The stove was purring a lyric of beech and maple and Mustard was licking her beautiful family under it. The pea soup was sublime. After all, them earrings rather became Little George . . . balanced the moustache, so to speak.

And Aurorer . . . but what was the matter with Aurorer?

"What you been doing with that old heathen graven immidge of yours?" demanded Big George, setting down half drunk his cup of militant tea with a thud.

"Give her a coat of bronze paint," said Little George proudly. "Looks real tasty, don't it? Knew you'd be sneaking home some of these long-come-shorts and thought I'd show you I could be considerate of your principles."

"Then you can scrape it off again," said Big George firmly. "Think I'm going to have an unclothed nigger sitting up there? If I've gotter be looking at a naked woman day in and day out, I want a white one for decency's sake!"

Editorial Note

These stories were originally published in the following magazines and newspapers, and are listed in the order of appearance in this collection. Where the original illustrations accompanying the stories are available, they have been included. Obvious typographical errors have been corrected, spelling and punctuation normalized.

1. The Magical Bond of the Sea, *Springfield Republican*, 20 September 1903.
2. The Life-Book of Uncle Jesse, *Housekeeper*, August 1909.
3. Mackereling out in the Gulf, *Springfield Republican*, 8 October 1905.
4. Fair Exchange and No Robbery, *Springfield Republican*, 15 September 1907.
5. Natty of Blue Point, *Forward*, 13 August 1904.
6. The Light on the Big Dipper, *Churchman*, 17 March 1906.
7. An Adventure on Island Rock, *Boys' World*, 1 December 1906.
8. How Don Was Saved, *Boys' World*, 18 June 1904.
9. A Soul That Was Not at Home, *Springfield Republican*, 21 March 1909.
10. Four Winds, *Housewife*, October and November 1908.
11. A Sandshore Wooing, *Designer*, August 1903.

12. The Unhappiness of Miss Farquhar, *Springfield Republican*, 12 July 1903.
13. A Strayed Allegiance, *Arthur's Home Magazine*, July 1897.
14. The Waking of Helen, *Waverley Magazine*, 31 August 1901.
15. Young Si, *Waverley Magazine*, 3 August 1901.
16. A House Divided against Itself, *Canadian Home Journal*, March 1930.

Acknowledgements

The late Dr. Stuart Macdonald gave me permission to begin the research that culminated in my collection of Montgomery's stories; Professors Mary Rubio and Elizabeth Waterston encouraged and advised me; Professor C. Anderson Silber gave his always constant support. Librarians were unfailingly helpful.

L. M. Montgomery

For the most complete listing, see Russell, Russell, and Wilmshurst, *Lucy Maud Montgomery: A Preliminary Bibliography*, University of Waterloo Library Bibliography Series, No. 13 (Waterloo: University of Waterloo Library, 1986).

THE "ANNE" BOOKS (in order of Anne's life)

Anne of Green Gables, 1908
Anne of Avonlea, 1909
Anne of the Island, 1915
Anne of Windy Poplars, 1936
Anne's House of Dreams, 1917
Anne of Ingleside, 1939
Rainbow Valley, 1919
Rilla of Ingleside, 1920

THE "EMILY" BOOKS

Emily of New Moon, 1923
Emily Climbs, 1925
Emily's Quest, 1927

OTHER NOVELS (in chronological order)

Kilmeny of the Orchard, 1910

The Story Girl, 1911
The Golden Road, 1913
The Blue Castle, 1926
Magic for Marigold, 1929
A Tangled Web, 1931
Pat of Silver Bush, 1933
Mistress Pat, 1935
Jane of Lantern Hill, 1937

COLLECTIONS OF SHORT STORIES

Chronicles of Avonlea, 1912
Further Chronicles of Avonlea, 1920
The Road to Yesterday, 1974
The Doctor's Sweetheart, and Other Stories, 1979
Akin to Anne: Tales of Other Orphans, 1988

POETRY

The Watchman, and Other Poems, 1916
Poetry of Lucy Maud Montgomery, 1987